COLD CANVAS

When life doesn't imitate art...

Adacus May

Copyright © 2024 Adacus May

All rights reserved

The characters and events portrayed in this book are fictitious. Any similarity to real persons, living or dead, is coincidental and not intended by the author.

No part of this book may be reproduced, or stored in a retrieval system, or transmitted in any form or by any means, electronic, mechanical, photocopying, recording, or otherwise, without express written permission of the publisher.

For Mum and Dad. Thank you.

CONTENTS

Title Page
Copyright
Dedication
Beginnings
Thanks
Chapter 1	1
Chapter 2	14
Chapter 3	24
Chapter 4	36
Chapter 5	54
Chapter 6	69
Chapter 7	80
Chapter 8	95
Chapter 9	102
Chapter 10	114
Chapter 11	125

Chapter 12	130
Chapter 13	140
Chapter 14	149
Chapter 15	161
Chapter 16	175
Chapter 17	191
Chapter 18	208
Chapter 19	220
Chapter 20	228
Chapter 21	242
Chapter 22	248
Chapter 23	262
Chapter 24	279
Chapter 25	298
Chapter 26	306
Chapter 27	326
Chapter 28	337
Chapter 29	343
Chapter 30	346

BEGINNINGS

This story was inspired by a visit to the National Gallery in London to see the work of one of the great nineteenth-century American artists.

On entering the exhibition I was captured by a striking photograph of the artist whose eyes looked out with a story to tell, so I wrote it. Although this book is not about him and does not represent any of the events, relationships or facts of his life, the photograph stirred my imagination.

Whilst this is a complete work of fiction it of course includes places and people who actually existed and events that took place during this amazing golden era in America's history. All names, characters, places, events and incidents in this book are either the product of my imagination or have been used in a fictitious manner for dramatic effect.

THANKS

With huge gratitude to friends and family who encouraged and supported me in the writing of this book. Thank you for cheering me on!

Special thanks to Zarina and Diane for being brave enough to be the first to read it and for giving me your feedback and insights.

CHAPTER 1

July 1868

'Stop! Get your hands off me! Trying to steal from me are you?' The shrieking voices of two wretched Newsboys, with nothing in the world worth stealing, fighting noisily in the street assaulted all his senses. Putting his hands over his ears he stared up at the ceiling and knew that being here was a terrible mistake.

It had been this never-ending cacophony of unfamiliar noises that had prematurely dragged him from his sleep. How he longed for his own bed and waking to the gentle sounds of Spring Street where bird song had been the accompaniment to his mornings since he could first remember. Here, the clattering of carriage wheels and hooves on cobbles, and the loud discordant tune of man, threw his senses off balance.

Since dawn, a fly had transfixed him as it buzzed above his head repeatedly bumping against the plaster, held down unable to rise any higher. He felt held down too, by the inevitability of his future and the physical and mental burden of the shackles that bound him and fixed him to the bed.

His back was even more painful and stiff than usual this morning, aggravated by the soft downy mattress, but with great effort he raised himself up carefully and sat awkwardly on the edge of the bed. Staring down at his feet, tanned from barefoot days in the garden, he could not believe he had only been here for two days. Was time destined to pass this slowly now?

His uncle had extended the hospitality of his comfortable home unreservedly and was offering him the promise of a good career, he should be more grateful, but he felt trapped. Uncle William, the epitome of so much he admired and aspired to in his own life and yet, so different.

Uncle William approached everything with the same steady, unfaltering temperament and Ned was sure that his uncle's heart had never had cause to beat faster or that anything had ever taken his breath away. Except perhaps once.

He was certain that even if he were to suddenly drop down dead in front of him, Uncle William would not flap but would deal with the tragedy before him with strength and calm practicality, his sadness and grief muted, sitting quietly waiting for its turn. To some he may appear uncaring and unmoved by events but the truth was he cared deeply, always putting himself aside for others, considering their needs first.

Ned was of the opposite disposition, nervous and often unsure of himself, always just one step away from worry and disquiet. He knew any familial similarities they had were rooted in their devotion to those they loved, Ned openly tender hearted, Uncle William quietly so.

The last two long nights had been humid and the days searingly hot which only added to his feeling of being stifled. No air moved and all motion seemed slowed. Even any conversation seemed laborious and weighed down by the heat, almost too much effort. So had passed long hours with his uncle and aunt over the last two days in dense silence, the effort of speaking too great for them all.

Even any slight reprieve offered by the breath of a breeze brought with it the shifting of dust that settled heavy in his lungs, lees that no cough could expel, leaving him feeling congested all the time.

Now, as he lifted the pitcher of tepid water to fill the basin his hand trembled a little, what was he expected to do in this new way of living?

The face staring back at him from the mirror

showed that the shadow of a moustache had started to appear but nothing of any note anywhere else on his face. A thick healthy specimen was of course expected in time but he was far from sporting even a suggestion of his own burnsides and this morning he could have been an imposter; a child borrowing his father's razor play-acting at what was to come.

As he flicked the razor clumsily around the corners of his upper lip trying to define the outline of something resembling a moustache, he drew blood which dripped and grew crimson on his nightshirt, like watercolour paint cockling the paper it touched. The sight of the blood jolted him from his stupor, everything seemed so dead but here he was, a living creature with blood pumping in his veins. Now, on this his first day at W. Adams & R. J. Morris, he would wear with embarrassment, the crimson badge of a bare-faced clumsy youth.

He dressed slowly and deliberately to stop his mind wandering to what lay ahead and as he lifted the black stock from his trunk a small scrap of paper dropped from its folds. Just five words in his mother's hand *'Always find time to paint.'*

Her words were a second razor cut. Today he would step onto the treadmill of working life, selling his soul for a regular wage and the respectability and material trappings of middle-class America. He could not believe that his own mother had helped orchestrate this life sentence. Destined now to be office-bound and living by the clock, today she dangled in front of him the only thing he really wanted to spend every waking hour doing, painting!

There had been practicalities to consider of course and he knew the opportunities for him in Watertown were in every sense more limited than those the city offered but what of his soul? The peace and contentment he woke up to every day on Spring Street was surely the essence of his elan and the foundation to all his ambitions and dreams. Without it what would determine the direction of his life?

His thoughts brought him such distress that his fingers would not obey him as he struggled and contorted to fasten the stiff and unyielding stock. Finally, the noose was around his neck.

He took a step backwards for a final look at himself. It was true that his clothes convincingly portrayed him as a man but underneath he felt as rigid and lifeless as a wooden manikin and knew that others would shape his movements from now on.

He made his way down to the dining room, passing the unsmiling Adams' family portraits as he descended the stairs, eyes watching, the family resemblance striking across the generations from capotain to top hat. On entering the dining room, if his uncle and aunt had spotted his shaving cut, they were too kind to mention it.

Already seated at the table waiting for him, the china and silverware were set out with precision on a creaseless white linen tablecloth, like a communion table lovingly and reverently set for the Eucharist. They both smiled fleetingly in his direction as he pulled out a chair and joined the daily ritual of this intimate union.

He found breakfasts at No.11 an excruciating affair. Only his hunger pains were sated by the copious amounts of corn bread, hot cakes and eggs. His need for conversation and companionship were not. This was all so far from the noisy, chaotic breakfasts at home that he loved.

Passing mostly in silence, apart from an occasional word as coffee was offered or plates were replenished, it was to be endured today and every day.

In the absence of conversation, from across the table, he quietly took in his uncle and aunt.

Uncle William was a big man, not fat but broad and muscular and even though his muscles had begun to slacken and he did not stand as tall as he once did, Ned could see the echoes of the young man he would have been. An open, not quite handsome face, with no guile hiding in the crevices or cruelty lurking in his dark eyes. It was a kind face.

He had been a constant and reassuring presence in their home when he was growing up, and in the absence of a husband and father at Greenbrook, he had brought a welcome stability and ballast to all their lives. Ned knew that he would not even exist if it were not for his uncle.

Ned's mother had always adored her big brother even before he had rescued her when she was five years old. On a sunny day nearing fifty years ago they were just two boisterous children chasing up and down the shore as the waves crashed onto the beach. The story went that suddenly a wave had whipped his mother's feet from under her and she found herself carried out to sea, bobbing like a cork, although more often under than on the surface.

Every time she went under she swallowed water. One, two, three, four times she counted but no five, just blackout. Then a loud gasping sound, her own gasping sound, and she was back above water and in William's arms.

He held her so tightly that it had made her cough up the salty water. *'Do you think yourself a mermaid little one?'* William had chided before brushing the hair from her face and pressing his cheek to hers in relief. His mother had told them this story so many times over the years her eyes always shining with the memory of it and her hero.

'Did you sleep well?'

'Well enough thank you uncle.'

'Excellent, my sister would be vexed to think that we were not ensuring your every comfort.'

Ned was still too cross with his mother to answer in her favour.

'Today I hope you are at the beginning of something to which you can industriously apply yourself. It is a wonderful opportunity for you and I hope you grasp it with fervour. There are many young men who would like to be in your shoes.'

'Please rescue me uncle' was his desperate plea but the words actually came out of his mouth as 'Yes Uncle, I will do my best to apply myself fully.'

'Very good.'

And that was it before a return to the rhythmic sound of knife and fork on plate.

In the renewed silence, Ned reflected that the only words he had ever exchanged with his aunt were about food and his linen requirements. This seemed to be her only place of comfort when conversing with him.

A homely petite woman, you might pass her in the street and not even notice her, except if you cared to really look, you would be fixed by her beautiful violet eyes. She was quiet and somehow seemed a little at odds with herself and her surroundings like she was a stranger in her own home.

Childless, Ned could sense the void in her and could see that she had never had a vent for any of the maternal instincts she naturally had. He assumed that, without nourishment, these had simply withered and died over the years. She had dedicated herself to being a supportive wife and to keeping a comfortable and smart home commensurate with her husband's social standing. She did this diligently without resentment and with obvious generosity and affection towards him. Despite their limited interactions Ned had a growing affection for her and her unassuming and gentle ways.

The ritual completed, in an uncharacteristically theatrical way, Uncle William took out his pocket watch announcing that it was time they left for the office. Ned felt the dread of it in the pit of his stomach and as a wave of nausea rose he nearly re-presented his eggs and cornbread for all to see. Taking in a deep quiet breath, he followed his uncle's lead in rising from the table, slowly and ensuring no sudden movements. As he stepped away from the breakfast table he felt the treadmill begin to move under his feet.

A brisk ten-minute walk later the brass plaque told him they were at the prison door.

In contrast to the noise on the street, inside there was a hush, which made Ned feel like he should tiptoe quietly. The reception area was a sober affair of dark wood panelling and polished floors but all thankfully lifted by the sunlight streaming in through the large south-facing windows.

Walls were hung with elaborately framed architectural drawings and centre-stage were two portraits; a particularly good likeness of a much younger Uncle William and next to it, a slightly dour looking man who Ned assumed must be Robert Morris.

'Good morning Mr. Adams.' The smartly dressed young man behind the desk rose quickly from his chair.

'Good morning Mr. Lawrence. Let me introduce my nephew Edward Miller who joins us today as a student under Mr. Dawson's direction.'

'Good morning Mr. Miller and welcome to W. Adams & R. J. Morris.'

'Thank you Mr. Lawrence.' Ned thought that he

was probably no more than three years his elder but his demeanour was of a much older man. Was this what awaited him? Again, it made him want to run.

Uncle William and his partner Robert Morris had established a successful Atelier in their Boston office four years earlier. This was a shrewd business decision, both for the more inexpensive labour it afforded the practice, and for the opportunity to grow the talent they needed from within. William Adams and Robert Morris' one shared desire was to be widely recognised and respected for their contributions to architecture. They believed profits would follow and they did.

Ned was to be one of six students and would be working under the tutelage of Richard Dawson one of the practice's most prolific and respected architects. Mr. Dawson did not come to this role generously. He was selfish and ambitious but at least the authority and power he was given over the students, served to feed his ego in the absence of the status he craved as a Partner in the practice, something he unashamedly continued to petition for.

He pushed his students to do better by criticism and humiliation making them feel useless in contrast to himself, to them, he would be their god.

From his very first meeting with Dawson, Ned did not like him. As he had offered his hand in welcome, he had looked directly into Ned's eyes and the look said, *'you are only here by fortune of birth and there will be no special privileges for you.'* What he actually said with a smirk was *'Cut yourself shaving I see...'*

Dawson dully introduced him to his fellow students, masters John Barnes Simon Baker, Francis Jones, James Brady and Henry Owens. All sombre and physically shrivelled by their new and overwhelming environment, except perhaps Francis who dared to smile on their first greeting, a quick bright smile that found its way in through a crack in the bleakness Ned felt. He knew they would be allies.

The studio was bright but stark, no distractions here, the only embellishment the ornate wall clock that ticked away confidently, a face and hands that would measure the days and their productivity.

Drafting tables were lined up with precision, in two rows of three, intentionally spaced to discourage conversation and distractions. In contrast to the substance of the oak panelling, the tables were a modest construction of white pine tilting tops with simple wrought iron tripod bases. They wore the scars of their years of use, tattooed with the ink of careless past endeavours, and as Ned ran his fingers along the surface of the table that was to be his, he had the familiar feeling of the blank canvas before it is transformed by the artist. It comforted him.

Transported back momentarily he could feel the sea breeze, the gulls soaring above him, sitting on a cliff top, brush on paper. He felt free. Now perched awkwardly on his drafting stool, he was back in the reality of the studio, he did not want it. He did not want these sights and sounds to be any part of the composition of his days.

In his discomfort, Ned unfastened the two lower buttons of his vest, fixed his eyes on the wall clock, and resigned himself to beginning the journey of free man to slave.

CHAPTER 2

4th May 1851

Amelia was feeling weary, it was an unseasonably hot day and the paint was drying too quickly on the paper making it hard to work. Shifting in her chair for the hundredth time, this baby was laying heavier than any other she had carried. She was older though and had already borne seven babies. Feeling the burden of managing her family and home alone these past four months, with only the inept help of the bumbling Martha, it had all taken its toll on her.

She lamented the lack of time to paint these days feeling the loss of it acutely. She was truly herself when she painted, escaping all that was mundane and disappointing about her life and entering a place where she was the architect of her own happiness, as she tried to capture the perfect artistry of the creator.

Today Amelia had not been able to catch the beauty and complexity of the sprig of bunchberry propped up in front of her. It had sparkled so brightly with dew when she picked it from the garden this morning. Now, its bright-green elliptic leaves were beginning to wilt in the heat and its white star-like flowers no longer seemed so pure to her. The glory and intricacy of its pepper-sprinkled umbels had faded, its moment had passed, so had hers. With growing frustration, she reluctantly returned her brush to its pot.

In her restlessness her mind churned over and over like butter. This baby would be born into uncertain times and would likely never know its father. Her husband Walter was gone along with all his promises of a better life for their family. That was as empty a promise today as it was when they first met. Every get rich quick enterprise had failed him over the years and if it had not been for her small trust fund, the generosity of Walter's Aunt Adeline, and for her brother's devotion and kindness to her, Amelia knew they would have sunk years ago.

Ever since Walter had first read about the California gold rush in the newspapers it had been like an obsession to him. It was all he talked about for months and she saw the glint of gold in his eyes, as he schemed and planned, never inviting her opinion once. It was a foregone conclusion, he would go, he would leave them.

He had begun his journey on that day by taking a coach from Watertown to Boston and from there the accommodation train all the way through to New York City where he would stay with his cousin overnight in preparation for his long voyage.

Then on 13th December he had sailed from New York to San Francisco on the *Surprise,* at least she expected he had, she had heard nothing from him since he left. She assumed he was alive. It would take over three months to complete the journey and she thought he would probably get around to writing to her once he had dealt with his other, greater, priorities.

Walter always put himself first and any act of caring about the welfare of his wife and his family was generally designed to induce affection, so desperate was he to be liked. Motherless at three years old and raised by his father with the help of his Aunt Adeline, Amelia understood why he felt like such a lost soul, in fact it was something that attracted her to him in the early days of their courtship. Over time she learnt that he would use this to get what he wanted and to manipulate things in his favour. So, the sympathy had left her gradually over the years, as her eyes began to see the truth of the shallow and self-serving man she had married.

This child she was carrying was the gift she was left with, and although they had not known she was expecting a child at the time of his leaving, he would have gone anyway.

In those last few days before he left Amelia had felt his urgency and desperation to get away and begin his adventure. Despite his constant proffering of enthusiastic and affectionate gestures towards her and the children she knew he had already abandoned them. As he had packed his belongings, he seemed to her like a man about to be released from prison, savouring all the anticipation of being a free man again.

When the day of his departure had come, he had risen long before dawn and Amelia had heard him shuffling around the house talking quietly to someone, himself. There was no one else that shared his enthusiasm or cared to hear of his plans.

He made much of kissing and embracing his children, offering them fatherly advice and encouragement that would have to last them while he was away. To him, the tears of his youngest were a measure of his value and worth to them, not a sign of their distress. He was highly satisfied by this.

Charlotte and Ida were too young to fully understand what was happening and the promise from their father of his return with gold trinkets and pretty dresses had been enough to allay their tears. Being a little older Alice and Mabel had stood close to their mother, watching her face for signs of how they should behave and feel. They could not read anything in her expression at all and so they stood close together holding each other's hands behind their backs so as not to give away their worries, they would be as grown-up as their mother.

The eldest, John, had hung back observing his father's admirable performance as a loving father, but as Walter had made his way along the line of his children and finally come to John, he could not meet his eye because John recognised him for what he was.

As he shook his son's hand he said, '*You are the man of the house now John, take care of your mother and sisters while I am away*' John simply nodded. He had taken up that mantle years ago, protecting his mother and organising and managing his younger siblings. He had long been their General and they all adored him.

As Walter turned from them to leave, he had tripped and stumbled, one final, fitting discomposure for a weak and pathetic man John thought.

Angry at embarrassing himself in front of his wife and children, Walter crossed their threshold onto the street for the last time and did not look back despite Charlotte and Ida's enthusiastic waving and shouting *'goodbye papa, papa!, papa!'* Still in their sight, as he walked away from them down Spring Street, but already gone.

Over the months since then, Amelia had been perplexed by how little she felt the lack of his presence in their lives, how easy it had been to cast off the intimacy of their earlier married life. Perhaps there had never really been love at all and she had simply been a young woman in love with the idea of it.

In her heart she knew that their marriage had been like a bad play with every scene worse than the last, and as she re-committed herself to being both mother and father to her children, she realised he meant little to her now. They had reached their *final act* long ago and so she found the love and affection she craved in other places.

Back from her thoughts, Amelia picked up her fan in a futile attempt to cool herself as beads of perspiration grew and slipped from her temple. She did not feel particularly well and even the Tansy tea had done little to settle her stomach today. Then a sudden familiar pain struck and she knew it was time.

'John!' she called out.

A few seconds later John appeared at the studio door.

'Yes mamma?'

'Tell Martha to watch your sisters and then run and fetch your Great Aunt Adeline, tell her it is time. Be quick.'

John understood the significance of his mother's briefest of instructions and a few minutes later he was at his great aunt's door, heart beating loudly in his ears, breathlessly delivering his urgent message.

Two hours later Edward William Miller slipped into the world easily. Swirls of auburn hair, a mirror of her own, surrounded a tiny strawberry-shaped face that had her father's long slim nose at its centre. His delicate long fingers, those of an artist.

The moment her baby had been placed in her arms Amelia begun to cry, she knew this would be her last child and she grieved the end of that part of her life, the sacred act of bringing a child into being.

'Oh, my dear, why do you cry? This is a happy day.' Aunt Adeline leant over and kissed Amelia's cheek.

'I am happy aunt, this child will be a blessing to me, to us all.'

'He is a handsome little fellow that is for sure. More Adams than Miller I think!' and she gave

Amelia a little wink.

'*He **is** an Adams.*' Amelia said under her breath.

Aunt Adeline pretended not to hear and said nothing. It was true she loved her nephew but she was not blind to his selfishness or his failings as a husband and father. She too thought he would play little part in this child's life.

Adeline was always a calming presence at Greenbrook and as she had tidied Amelia up she had sent up a silent prayer of thanks that mother and baby were both safe and well. The doctor had not arrived in time and so it had been left it to Adeline and Martha to deliver this baby safely into the world. Martha, little more than a child herself, had been just about sufficient in helping Adeline as she prepared Amelia for the birth, boiling water, ferrying everything she needed from the kitchen to the bed, but at the point the baby appeared she had fallen down in a faint, leaving Adeline to attend to them all.

Now in the calm after the storm, with the baby swaddled and Martha up off the floor, Adeline took a deep breath for the first time as relief washed over her.

'Martha, are you recovered child?'

Slumped in a chair, Martha nodded dumbly. Transfixed by the scene before her, she thought

Mrs. Miller looked like the Madonna, a halo of light around her head.

'Then go and fetch the children to their mother. Make haste.'

Martha stood up, and never taking her eyes off Amelia and the baby, backed out of the room reverently.

As they awaited the arrival of the children, Adeline's eyes drifted to the two small, framed paintings by Amelia's bed. They were macabre and she had told Amelia many times over the years that she thought them unhealthy, too vivid a reminder of her terrible loss. Two tiny sleeping angels. One almost incomplete in outline, seeming blurred without definition, too premature for breath. The other, perfect, ready for life but not able. Her lost babies, painted, immortalised by their mother so that she would never lose them. Adeline did not hold with the growing fashion for death pictures *securing the shadow, ere the substance fades.* She did not think you should live life within the shadows of the past.

Again, Adeline gave silent thanks to God, for the safe arrival of this baby.

As Amelia's little flock gathered around her bed, 'Little Ned' was carefully passed from sister to sister, Alice and Mabel motherly and gentle in their handling of the baby, Charlotte and Ida a little bemused and overwhelmed by something so much smaller than themselves. Each child in turn kissed their brother's forehead, the younger ones copying their older siblings, Little Ned grimacing with each kiss.

Finally, John and as he held his brother and kissed his forehead the baby opened his unseeing dark eyes and looked into John's face like he saw him. Amelia caught the look in her two sons' eyes and saw the coming and going of something she could not name but which darkly stirred her heart.

CHAPTER 3

August 1862

It was a hive of activity in the Miller kitchen this morning and as Ned paused at the door he took in the frenetic scene.

Like a perfectly orchestrated quadrille, danced to the sound of a silent fiddler, his mother and sisters seemed to reel and whirl in perfect harmony within the four corners of the dance floor. Even Martha seemed to have found her feet and was keeping rhythm and pace.

With no need of a caller, each seemed to intuitively know their position and steps, as they passed each other to the left and to the right with lightness and precision. As they moved, their hooped skirts swayed to and fro like church bells ringing out a call to worship, while their aprons flashed white, pure as clergy vestments.

As he stood quietly observing his family, steam filled the air blurring and softening the scene, creating a dream-like backdrop to their dance. Peaches, plums and quinces bobbed impatiently in large pans of water awaiting their hot bath, and regimented rows of Mason jars were lined up along the pine table just like the soldiers they would carry a taste of home to.

Along with his mother, Alice and Mabel had thrown themselves wholeheartedly into doing their bit to support the brave Union soldiers. Both considered far too young and attractive to volunteer as nurses as they would have liked, instead they sent hope and sustenance to those they sought to comfort in the form of bottled fruits and preserves, and warmth in the guise of knitted gloves and socks.

Most weeks now would be punctuated by some fundraising event or door to door collecting in their neighbourhood. In fact, Ned often wondered how they had used their time before the war began.

The Miller women were much admired in the town, although it was clear to him that they were not always liked, as they industriously played their part in supporting the war effort. Their commitment and dedication to these charitable works left others lacking, that was for certain, and so resentment towards them grew.

He knew his mother and sisters would rather be holding bake sales or bottling fruit for the soldiers than sitting with the ladies of the town busying their fingers as part of a quilting bee. They would never seek opportunities to sip tea from china cups and benignly discuss how terrible the war was, how tragic the plight of the soldiers, before passing each other yet another piece of cake. Plainly put, he knew his mother and sisters did not care beans for what others thought, or for the snide remarks that were made as soon as their backs were turned. They were finer than that.

Just today alone the Miller women would bottle upwards of five dozen jars of fruit. They would do far more than their share and still not consider it enough.

Alice was most definitely in charge today. Not long married, she and her beau Jim Short had wed on a Thursday and he had left for the war on the Friday which seemed odd to Ned, why get married if you are going to leave?

He did not dislike Jim - it had been nice to have a man to go fishing with and to talk to about men's things - but Ned did think him a bit dumb with nothing interesting to say.

Alice seemed different to Ned since she had married. No more making silly faces at him over the breakfast table, no more chasing him and Ida around the garden until they were breathless and fell down laughing, no more fun. This change in her was a mystery to him and he wondered if he had done something wrong.

He had also seen the change in Mabel since her sister had married. They had been as close as two sisters could be, two peas in a pod his mother had always said, but something had immeasurably shifted between them. When they stood close to each other, they seemed apart, as if Jim stood between them even though he was not there.

Suddenly stopping mid-dance Alice turned to face him *'Ned Miller, what time do you call this? Much of the work is done and you are still idling with sleep in your eyes.'*

Ned was affronted, it was a Saturday with no school and it was only just past eight o'clock. His mother gave him a quick understanding smile but one which also conveyed that he needed to shape up. He could never bear to disappoint her or cause her worry and it upset him deeply if she were ever angry with him. Everyone said he was too tender-hearted but he did not know what that meant, this was the only heart he had and he did not know how to turn it from tender to hard if that was what was required.

Alice continued heckling him *'You have missed breakfast but there is still fresh cornbread and some honey on the side, be quick though we need pears and apples enough to fill at least two dozen jars and no shaking the trees, we do not want them bruised and damaged. Make haste, Lottie will help you.'*

As the dance re-commenced, Ned wove his way through the spins and turns, perching himself on a stool at the end of the heavily laden kitchen table. He ate his breakfast quickly, swallowing almost without chewing, not allowing himself the luxury of time to enjoy the warm cornbread. He did not want to linger too long under his mother and sisters' watchful eyes.

As he looked across at Lottie, she appeared as unenthusiastic as he felt because like him, she knew just how many pears and apples they had to pick. The trees were laden it was true, but it was chilly for the time of year, and there was a steady drizzle of rain. They would be soaked by the wet leaves; their feet would get muddied and their stockings would be damp for the whole day.

By the time he had finished his breakfast, Lottie had already dutifully collected the fruit baskets from the cold room. Taking one from her hand, stepping outside, they surveyed the trees for the ones that would ensure they could complete their mission as quickly as possible. Their pretty walled garden was home to at least a dozen mature fruit trees that stood today like towering verdant umbrellas in the late summer rain, so plenty to choose from, but which ones?

'Let's start with these two' Lottie said as they

approached the two apple trees nearest the stream. *'You climb, I will catch.'*

Nodding, Ned set the ladder against the trunk of the closest of the two trees.

Climbing up to its lower branches he searched for the nearest and juiciest apples he could reach to drop down to his sister. Then looking down he appraised the best dropping point through the tree's branches and foliage.

Her face framed by clusters of leaves, Lottie looked up at him eagerly, hopping from foot to foot in a vain attempt to keep her feet dry. Her steady dark brown eyes, hair a golden mass of unruly curls around her freckled face, tall and slender he thought she looked like a beautiful sunflower. As she smiled up at him he knew she was by far his favourite sister.

'Ready?'

'Ready.'

Carefully he took aim and began dropping each plucked apple into Lottie's outstretched hands.

'*One.*'

'*Two.*'

'*Three.*' Lottie called out with enthusiasm, as she placed each apple into a basket; careful not to bruise them.

'Are you going to count every piece of fruit?' Ned asked with exasperation.

'I may.' She answered stubbornly. *'Alice and mamma will be so pleased to know exactly how many we have.'*

'Fifteen.'

'Sixteen.' The apples kept dropping.

Ned had now picked clean the lower branches of its ripe fruit and he would need to climb higher for the next batch. Reaching up, he stretched to grasp a higher limb of the tree and hauled himself up, finding a safe foothold. Aligning himself now with Lottie's 'counting towards success' he was satisfied that he could get to at least fifty apples on this level.

'Thirty-eight.'

'Thirty-nine.'

They were making good progress and Ned was finding the rhythm of their labours quite enjoyable now. He was sure he would earn himself chore-free painting time this afternoon and this spurred him on.

He had painted this tree, indeed every tree in their garden, many times. Different seasons, different times of the day, but never from within its branches. The vista was so different from here as he studied the leaves up close and then looked through them re-focussing his eyes on the house and the town beyond. As the tree became the observer rather than the observed, inverting the perspective of the earthbound, he was transfixed by the view.

'Quit your daydreaming Ned' and as Lottie's words reached his ears, he was jolted from his thoughts.

Resuming the count he stretched for his next prey. As he did, a sound like the crack of rifle shot met his ears, as the branch he was standing on gave way. Falling heavily like a windfall, he hit the ground hard, landing at Lottie's muddy feet.

Everything seemed to stop for a few moments except the sound of rippling water in his ears, he had landed on the bank of the stream, thankfully not in it.

Then his mother was at his side. Kneeling close, touching his face, gently squeezing his limbs like she was testing a peach for its ripeness, her hands still wet and sticky from bottling the fruit. Ned saw the fear and worry in her face as her eyes dulled and a cloud of grey seemed to colour her skin, he knew he must not be the cause of her suffering.

'Look mamma, we collected 40 apples, are you pleased?' and as he raised the apple he was still clutching in his hand to her face, she kissed each

of his fingers one by one, so gently that her kisses felt like feathers landing fleetingly before being blown away by the wind.

'Shush my love, do not speak.'

'Alice run and fetch Doctor Wilson. Mabel bring blankets. Make haste both of you!' Her voice was shrill and harsh, not weakened by her anguish and fear, but angry, even furious perhaps that this had happened to her child.

He was very lucky the doctor had said, the soft ground had cushioned his fall and there were no broken bones, but there was some trauma to his back. For Ned this meant, sharp pain when he tried to walk, a knife in his back when he sat, no reprieve from the agony except when he slept.

Complete bed rest and Laudanum were prescribed, and for the next week his mother hardly left his side, fussing him and attending to his every need. After a long week of incarceration, gentle exercise was recommended and Amelia had held him up as he took his first cautious steps around his room. She had rubbed his back and kneaded his limbs like bread dough, and with every healing touch, he was released from his agony.

Then one morning a few days later a letter brought the worst possible news. He heard her screams from the kitchen and she did not come to his bedside again.

In a field, two weeks ago, a soldier had been shot down. Lying in the mud, his mother's face before him, kisses like feathers on his forehead. John Walter Miller, aged 23 years, loved but now lost.

As the letter had dropped from her hand she had fallen to her knees. Amelia Miller's heart had been broken twice that day in the garden but she had not known it until she read the terrible words from Samuel Dudley.

31 August 1862

Dear Mrs. Miller,

It is with the deepest regret and sorrow that I write to inform you that your son John was killed in the fighting yesterday. He died by a single rifle shot and I pray that it may be some small comfort to you to know that he died instantly and did not suffer.

He fought bravely and showed admirable courage in the face of great trials and I consider it an honour to have fought alongside him and to have called him my friend.

He spoke so fondly of you and your family and carried your photograph and your last letter with him. I hope it brings you some peace to know you were always carried close to his heart.

Conditions on the battlefield are difficult and

chaotic and much as I know you would long for it, I do not believe he would ever have been returned home to you.

Be assured that his fellow soldiers and I buried him, with all the respect and dignity he deserved on departing this life, under an oak tree on a grassy verge here at Chinn Ridge. Your photograph and letter with him in his breast pocket. A small cross made by my hand marks his grave and for as long as that remains his place will be known in this world.

Please accept my deepest condolences. Your son was the finest of men and a brave soldier and I will never forget him. May his soul rest in peace.

With sympathy,

Samuel J. Dudley

What followed was long months of darkness, every one of them subsumed by their grief, drowning in it. But there was no mercy and with each new day they were forced to dress, to eat, to do all the things of the living.

The light had dimmed in their mother's eyes and she seemed to see nothing except the pictures playing in her mind as she stared out blindly at them all. Her grief seemed to permeate the very walls of their home, and everything seemed hopeless especially during the hours from candle-lighting until dawn when her despair was at its deepest and they would hear her walking the floors back and forth endlessly.

She longed to hold her lost child, the child that would never return to her arms, but would lie buried in a field far away. They all prayed that rest would come to her mind, that she would find some peace, but in their hearts they knew she would never recover from it.

As soon as Uncle William had received the news, he had arranged to be absent from his business affairs and had travelled to be with his sister. She was drowning for a second time and he must try to save her.

CHAPTER 4

January 1883

She had goaded him constantly this morning, peck, peck, pecking like an unwelcome Northern Flicker drumming loudly on the trunk of a tree.

'It has been months since you sold a painting.'

'How can I furnish our home with fine furniture if you do not bring us any money?'

'Can you not ask your uncle for help?'

'I have had no new dress for a year. You seem happy for your wife to be seen in rags.'

She went on and on at him, never waiting for his answers, just a continuous listing of her complaints.

On days like today, Ned would find himself wondering why he had ever married Nancy, perhaps it would have been better if they had never met at all. Was he such a different man ten years ago or had he experienced a kind of madness?

At the time, it was true that Nancy had

magnified the heady intoxication he already felt at leaving the practice and in the simplest of ways, had embodied everything of the wild and free adventure he longed for. In her, he had secured the fanciful hope of a harmonious future together, all the while disregarding the discordant realities of the present. He had cast sense and reason aside, acted with urgency, for fear the vision she had inextricably become part of would fade from his sight.

It was much easier to understand why Nancy had wanted to marry him. He would save her from the meagre existence she felt she was above and give her the finer life she thought she deserved. He was sure she had felt real affection towards him too.

Her requirements had been simple enough he supposed if a little unrealistic; an impressive home, socialising with people of wealth and influence, a servant or two to wait on her. This was her plan for a happy and fulfilled life and she expected him to facilitate it. Where these lofty aspirations and sense of entitlement had come from he had never understood, he had been at pains not to promise it, and she certainly was not born to it.

Hers was an all too familiar sorry story. Alcoholic father, neglectful mother, an only child brought up in grinding poverty. He understood why she had needed to live on her wits before he met her and respected her ambition to make a better life for herself, but he struggled with the cold ruthlessness that had taken root in her; core rotted by cruelty and disappointment.

She had grown up quick and clever despite her appetite for learning being bitterly starved. An enthusiastic and happy student, without any warning, her father had pulled her out of school at ten years old. He had other plans for her and she would be put to work to ensure his liquor kept flowing by taking in laundry and dying the goose feathers and ribbons for Miss McCabe's millinery creations.

In a room not much bigger than a closet and lit only by a tiny window that was impossible to open, she worked for a paltry nickel a gross colouring, drying and packing these embellishments for fine ladies' hats, while she lived in rags and stained her fingers black with the mix of vibrant shades of aniline dyes. It paid better than the laundry and she preferred the work, enjoying the soft feel of the feathers and ribbons, grateful for the array of pretty colours to help quash the greyness of her surroundings.

She was good at arithmetic, able to let her father know if they were being short paid by Miss McCabe or asked too much in rent arrears for their measly three rooms. It also meant she was able to swindle her father out of a nickel or two each week, as she wrote down on a piece of paper for him how two and two equalled five, he was easy to fool.

She had enjoyed reading too but there had never been any time for books outside the classroom, there were no books at home at all, not even a bible. So, with feather and dye on scraps of paper, she took to writing down little poems that she made up in her head, just for the pleasure of looking at the words.

Dainty goose feather so downy and soft
Now coloured so brightly and hung aloft
One day a lady's hat to prettily adorn
On a fine and pleasant Sunday morn

When she made her deliveries to Miss McCabe's, careful to stay out of sight as she had been instructed so she would not lower the prestige of the establishment, she would see the elegant young ladies choosing their hats with no care for the cost. They might buy three at a time - *so nice to have a choice depending on how one feels do you not think?* - to go with an elegant gown of blue or pink. She had fashioned her own bonnet with a few stolen feathers and scraps of ribbon, but with never a cause for a Sunday outing, in her tiny workroom, she was left only to her imagining of a pretty dress to equal it in brightness and gaiety.

In the confines of her musty, airless world, Nancy had laboured day after day while her father drank away all their money and her mother absented herself to who knew where. She knew where.

One day, pushed too far by her feckless father and the ever-wandering hands of his drunken friends, she had wielded her laundry bat against them all for the last time. Meagre belongings quietly packed and a pouch of hard-earned nickels secreted inside her bodice, she shut the door behind her for the final time. At seventeen and on the streets, she would knock on as many doors as it took to find employment, anything rather than go home.

On sight of a raggedy-looking girl, door after door was shut in her face, or not opened at all if she was spied through a window from inside. Eventually she found herself on Pinckney Street, a respectable neighbourhood of smart houses and smart people. As she approached the midpoint in the street, turned away from every house so far, a door finally opened to her and stayed open.

A tall, rather plump, plain-looking woman looked out at her coldly, she seemed flustered and was perspiring a little.

'What do you want girl? I have nothing to give you

if you seek favours from me.' The woman's hand remained firmly on the edge of the door, blocking entry, ready to close it quickly if necessary.

'Madam, I seek nothing from you. On the contrary I have something to offer you.'

The woman looked puzzled *'What could you possibly be able to offer me?'*

Nancy thought quickly. *'You look overwrought madam, like you have too much work to do for a lady of your delicacy and breeding, it grieves me to see someone so genteel put upon so gravely.'*

Nancy could see from the woman's expression that she had struck gold.

'This is a busy house and I have boarders to attend to with no help from anyone since my maid left these three days since. I will not tolerate a thief.'

'It is a terrible business when someone you have given a home and employment to acts in such a despicable way. My father always taught me that honesty is surely one of the finest qualities a person can possess. I am sorry you have been treated so ill.'

'Thank you but no matter. How can I help you? Or how do you suggest you can help me?'

'Madam I am hard working and diligent please put me to work to ease your burden.' She went on quickly *'I can do it all, sweep the carpets, make the beds, take care of the laundry, set the fires, all of it.*

A fine lady like yourself should not be emptying the slops, let me do it.'

The woman said nothing but looked Nancy up and down from her matted unkempt hair to her blackened fingernails and dirty shoes.

'Please do not be misled by my appearance madam, I find myself in difficult circumstances currently it is true, but I keep myself clean and know what is proper.' She hid her hands behind her back. *'Cleanliness is next to Godliness they say.'*

'You have references I take it?'

'I do not madam but you will not find me lacking in any way' she was stretching the truth, *'and I only seek bed and board with perhaps a quarter a week for the necessities to live cleanly as any young woman should.'*

The woman loosened her hand on the door a little. *'You ask me to take a risk girl.'* Her words hung in the air between them and Nancy said nothing.

'Very well, I shall give you a try, but mark my words, you will be out on the street quick sharp if you cross me or bring trouble to this respectable establishment.'

Nancy had told him the stories of her childhood in great detail many times, and where Mrs. Dean was concerned, he had felt Nancy's tremendous pride that in her desperation, Mrs. Dean had been such easy prey for her.

Ned too remembered the first time he set eyes on Nancy.

He could never have known when he arrived on Pinckney Street how his life would be forever changed by this place and as he climbed the steps to the front door and knocked, he could not have foreseen that the door was opening to such a significant crossroads in his life.

A handsome brownstone three-storey town house, clean and tidy, if a little unfashionable in its decoration and furnishings, it would serve him well for the next two weeks while he waited for the summer house at Smith's Point to be made ready for him. As he stepped over Mrs. Dean's threshold, for the first time, he felt like his own man.

The year preceding that day had been difficult. Uncle William's health had deteriorated following a bad bout of influenza and he had been left weaker for it. Tiredness overcame him more easily and his limbs became stiff and rusty. His vigour seemed to leave him and with Aunt May's encouragement, and the nearest she ever got to insistence, he agreed to retire from the practice.

They would move from No.11. The city was becoming increasingly overcrowded and their neighbourhood was changing quickly and not to their liking. They would move out to Roxbury for the fresher air and a more tranquil life.

Uncle William had encouraged Ned to continue living with him and Aunt May and commute into the city but Ned decided not to go with them. The move, and his uncle's retirement, was the catalyst he needed to begin his true life as an artist and he gave notice at W. Adams & R. J. Morris to his uncle's genuine dismay. Uncle William had been like a father to him and despite his disappointment that Ned would throw away all that he had learnt and achieved over the last four years, he gave him his blessing.

At the Atelier when Pock had heard of his plans, Frank said that he had simply commented that *'Perhaps as a failed architect Mr. Miller is better suited to be an impoverished artist.'* No one paid any mind to Pock or his bitterness.

With some help, he had been able to secure a long-term lease on a summer house near Smith's Point in Manchester. Frontline to the sea, when he had first visited with the agent the house had felt familiar, like he had been there before. As he had walked through its rooms he knew he would be able to paint there.

Until the summer house was ready for him, Mrs. Dean's on Pinckney Street, would be the bridge between No. 11 and Smith's Point.

When the news had reached his mother, she had written to him by return.

20th October 1872

My darling Ned,

Your uncle has written to inform me of your decision to leave the practice. I know he has advised you against this and has pleaded with you to consider your future and financial security. I too share his concerns.

We have relied on my brother's kindness and generosity for so many years and I had hoped that he would be rewarded by seeing you become a partner in the practice. I know this is something he dearly wanted.

Your uncle is a man of great character and decency and could not be less like your father, who chased so many unsuccessful business ventures, then abandoned his family. Be careful my darling not to follow the way of such a selfish man who is lost to his family and to himself.

While I am much troubled by the insecure nature of your future, I am comforted that you will be following your heart and using your considerable talents, something that should never be wasted.

Your sisters are all well and send their love to you. We all hope that you might visit us soon when the weather improves.

You have my blessing my darling and I shall await your news.

Your loving mamma

He had been surprised by how much his mother's blessing meant to him. He had not known that he needed it and had not sought it. She was of course right about Uncle William, his constancy in their lives, he would never forget what he had done for him.

Now residing at Pinckney Street, very quickly, he would discover that Mrs. Dean ran a highly respectable establishment and took more than a little interest in the moral behaviour of her boarders. As the 'mother of the house' she was at great pains to promote clean habits and Godly living.

Meals were a formal affair and boarders were required to join the table not a minute late. After grace was said, from her position at the head of the table, Mrs. Dean would direct their discussions and ensure their conversation never drifted to inappropriate subjects or things of an indelicate nature.

The front door was locked for the night at ten o'clock sharp and earlier on a Sunday. Mrs. Dean held the only key and as no one ever wanted to risk her wrath, the house ran like clockwork.

Her current boarders were all young single men and exclusively New Englanders. No immigrant would ever secure a room in her house. Most were long term boarders who lived happily within the security and constraints of a respectable family home. No female visitors were allowed and no guests at all were to be entertained in the bedrooms, she provided a perfectly adequate parlour for her gentleman boarders and their visitors.

He was the youngest of five paying residents: a lawyer, two teachers and a printer. Arthur Drew, the lawyer, had been boarding with Mrs. Dean for over three years and understandably took on an air of seniority over the other boarders. He was dour and humourless, which Mrs. Dean seemed to like and being a lawyer, she definitely considered him a feather in her cap of respectability and good standing.

They continually endorsed each other.

'I very much agree Mrs. Dean and commend your sensible and intelligent approach to such a difficult matter.'

'Thank you Mr. Drew, as an accomplished man of the law, your favour for my views is highly prized.'

And so it went on.

Widowed and childless, the house brought Rose Dean a good income along with the company she craved, as the little social life she had enjoyed, had died with her husband seven years ago. She took immense pride in the well run home she offered her boarders, the only exception to her labours was the cleaning and laundry which her girl Nancy did, badly, in return for her room and board.

For six dollars a week, Ned had a simple but comfortable room on the top floor. The single bed had a brightly coloured counterpane and a little table stood alongside it where he placed a photograph of his family. There was a washstand and basin and a rather weathered armchair in front of the fire. On a small table by the chair was a kerosene lamp with cobalt glass fonts and finely etched glass chimneys to light his evenings.

The walls were covered in a busy but cheerful wallpaper of foliage and delicately shaded cabbage roses, and the window's cream blinds were very effective in warming the grey light they let in. His room looked out onto Louisburg Square and each morning he would stand at the window and say *'good day'* to the statue of Christopher

Columbus standing silently in the gardens there. It was a bright space with the light perfect for sketching and he decided he would take the opportunity to draw and paint as much as possible during his stay. A simple vase of flowers, the changing view from his window, all held attraction for the artist's eye.

His meals were provided and fresh linen supplied each week. His shirts and undergarments were laundered as he required although undergarments would only be accepted if they were placed inside a small drawstring linen bag for fear these intimate garments might corrupt the innocent Nancy.

The first time he had seen her, he had walked in on her changing his bed linen.

'I am sorry sir, the mistress said you were out for your walk and would not be returning until candle-lighting.' She did a strange kind of reluctant bobbing by way of a curtsy.

'Indeed, that was my plan, but the weather has turned much colder and there was no longer any pleasure in the walk.'

'Yes sir.' She stood awkwardly unsure of whether to stay or go.

'I do not mean to interfere with your work, shall I leave you to complete it? Or perhaps it would be acceptable for me to stay but leave the door open

while you complete your task?'

She looked hesitantly towards the door.

'Yes sir' she nodded.

'Very well.'

Leaving the door ajar, he hung his coat and hat on the back of it, then crossed the room to the fire the girl had already lit for him. As he sat in the chair to remove his boots, he found the intimacy of their situation distracting, and while he never looked in her direction, he could feel her looking at him. She was unsettling him in an unfamiliar but pleasant way. Warming his hands by the fire, with his back still to her, he asked her name.

'Nancy sir, Nancy Sullivan.'

'I am very pleased to meet you Miss Sullivan.' he said without turning.

In his mind's eye, she was pale-skinned and pretty and her eyes were burnt umber in colour. Her dress was chromium oxide green and drowned her small frame. It was pulled tight at the waist with a length of cord to give her some shape and he thought it was probably a hand-me-down from her more ample mistress. Her auburn hair was a mass of escaped curls that she had tried, unsuccessfully, to contain under her white cap. She was about his age, a little younger perhaps.

As he turned to look at her now, he was right, except that she was not pretty, she was exquisite.

'Finished sir. Will there be anything else?'

'No thank you.'

She looked at him directly, insolently even perhaps, and hurried out closing the door noisily behind her. In the aftermath of the whirlwind she was, from memory, he sketched her quickly to capture the storm.

Recollecting their first meeting now brought him no pleasure only pain. She had captivated him from the very first moment he saw her, but he desperately continued to search for anything of merit beyond the look of her, anything fine and sweet that he could cherish.

He would not paint today, she had got into his brain this morning like a worm constantly turning the soil over and disrupting all flow of thought or deed, so he stayed at window looking out at the sea and the falling snow.

As his eyes reached into the distance where the land met the sea, rugged grey rocks were turned to white by the snow and lay like tumbled playing cards on the sand. The bleak promontory framed the changing hues of the sea elevating its light like a mirror, while pine trees stood like watchmen near the shore. It was a living, ever changing vista, his constant enchantress.

Focussing his eyes closer now they settled on the rowan tree, its branches drooping under the weight of the snow and its red berries dusted with white icing, her voice was in his ears again.

'Come to me, don't keep me waiting, you know I don't like to be kept waiting...'

He would not go to her she could wait and stew. He would avoid her today and not look on her face or listen to her protestations until his ill temper had subsided. He would write to Lottie instead and enquire after the progress of his young nephews.

Love and family had come late to Lottie but it seemed to him that since she had met Luke, she had more than made up for all the lost years. Hers was a happy and loving home and in truth everything that he had hoped for himself. Letters from Uncle Ned delighted her boys Edward and John who Lottie said adored his little sketches and the funny stories about bobcats and raccoons. It would lift his spirits to enter a child's world for a while.

As he sat at his desk to begin the door knocked. He smiled to himself, it could only be Charles, who else would be mad enough to take on the thick snow and biting wind? He expected a visit from Laurie later this evening, but for now, a few cordial hours with his dear friend Charles would be the perfect antidote to wretched time spent with Nancy.

The letter to Lottie could wait until tomorrow.

CHAPTER 5

May 1851

It was true to say that things had not gone quite the way Walter Miller had hoped and he felt sorry for himself, but as always, he found someone or something else to blame for his misfortune.

That December morning when he had taken the early accommodation train from Albany Street, he had been full of excitement and anticipation for the adventure ahead, exhilarated by the prospect of finally making his fortune. Even though it would take him away from his dear wife and children and he would endure a difficult journey of over three months to California, he was eager to make his mark in the world.

Walter had spent weeks carefully organising his travel arrangements and purchasing the provisions bound for desperate gold-rushers all bought from reputable wholesalers in New York City. He had used up most of their savings to secure his passage and the merchandise, and although he did not discuss it with her, he knew Amelia was in agreement despite her not showing him the enthusiasm and appreciation he deserved. He was content that she would manage with what was left and would she not be so much better off in the long term when he made his fortune and she and the children could have the best of everything? He would be admired for being such a great provider and for his enterprise and business acumen.

After all his travel expenses were paid he had one hundred and forty-five dollars to invest in his wall tent, a few pieces of simple furniture, a cot, and the merchandise he needed to get him going. He would be starting with the basics; dried goods, flour, coffee and tea, whiskey, tobacco, kerosene, salt, molasses, and candy to lift the spirits of the hard-working miners. He would also provide some basic flatware and hardware and functional work clothing supplies and build up from there.

He had bought himself a gun.

Walter would work from dawn to dusk every day if that is what it was going to take, he might even provide a hearty drinking place in the evenings; there was surely extra profit to be made from intoxicated men.

He had done his calculations, if he could trade half his goods with at least a five times' mark up by the Fall, he would be able to re-order and expand his merchandise to include higher value items for the winter like coats, hats and gloves and luxury items like cigars. He would have enough to build himself a wood cabin and really establish his business, the sign above the door, *W. C. Miller, Fine Provisions*. The price of gold was at its highest since the rush had begun, his customers pockets would be laden with nuggets and bags of dust, all coming in his direction.

He had arrived in New York City at eight o'clock on the evening of the 12th and Cousin Henry had been there to meet him at the station but that was when fortune had first begun to cruelly turn against him.

He and Henry had been close as boys. Aunt Adeline had brought Walter into the heart of her family after his mother had died, treating him like a son alongside her own five boys. It was a boisterous, loving home and Walter had spent many happy days on the farm with her and Uncle John. Both encouraged Walter, alongside their own children, to respect animals and the land and fostered in them all daily gratitude for God's provision.

Their house was large and you could say grand although more practical than fine in its furnishings Walter had always thought. It had the biggest kitchen he had ever seen which would host mealtimes not just for the family but upwards of five farm labourers, a cook, and a maid. That did not include the myriad of animals that would come and go; two farm dogs, a mouser and any manner of farm animal that needed nursing. On cold damp days, the smell of the food and wet animals was an unpleasant concoction, it still made him retch just to think of it.

A long oak table dominated the space with blackened oak benches that ran its full length down each side and at each end was an incongruous ornate carver from where his aunt or uncle would stand to say grace before each meal.

They had encouraged all their eight children in their education including the girls, and never made any assumption that they would take on the farm, although three of Henry's brothers did just that. When Henry said he wanted to be a lawyer, he may just as well have said he wanted to be a blacksmith, it made no difference to his aunt and uncle.

Because of this shared boyhood, Walter had expected to find his cousin pleased to see him after such a long time, like two long separated brothers. He was wrong.

As he had stepped down onto the platform at

Canal Street and looked around it had been easy to spot Henry. At six feet two, nearly seven feet in his top hat, he towered above everyone else.

'*Cousin! It is so good to see you.*' Walter had stepped forward to embrace his cousin, but Henry had stepped back a little and extended his hand in a more formal welcome.

'*Cousin, a good journey I hope?*' Henry asked without smiling.

'*Indeed, yes.*'

A porter stood close by with Walter's bags awaiting instructions.

'*I have a carriage waiting to take us to the Upper East Side in the name of Mr. Henry Mason, please take the gentleman's bags, the driver expects you directly.*'

'*Yes sir, right away.*'

The Porter hurried on ahead of them. '*We should make easy progress at this time of day and arrive home within the half hour.*'

Aboard the coach to Henry's house, conversation was stilted and formal and never wandered into anything of substance, Henry mostly taking advantage of the journey to point out some of the landmarks of the city. Walter was aware of this diversion on his part but sure that once they reached Henry's home bonhomie would be restored.

Even by the dim light of the streetlamps, Walter could see and feel the excitement and vibrancy of this metropolis. The streets were long and straight and the snow on the ground seemed to highlight the squareness of everything. He liked its uniformity, its towering linear buildings, so different from home where everything seemed haphazard and mis-shapen.

As they drew up in front of a handsome four-storey brownstone, Walter was impressed, his cousin had done very well for himself and he took some perverse kind of personal pride in that. Inside they were warmly greeted by Lucy. She was everything Walter had imagined for his cousin, small and pretty with a gentle demeanour, the very opposite of his Amelia.

She had arranged a light supper for them but retired early so that the cousins could spend time together alone. He would be introduced to the children in the morning and she warned him they were extremely excited to meet him and hear everything about the adventures he had planned.

After a somewhat perfunctory supper and conversation about the weather and nothing that really mattered at all, they settled themselves in Henry's study, where despite the comfortable surroundings and the warmth from the fire, there was a tangible chill in the air. Henry shifted awkwardly in his chair.

'You have a fine home Henry. You have done very well for yourself I see.'

'Thank you. We are indeed fortunate.'

'I too hope I will be able to achieve such a place for my family.'

'How are Amelia and the children?'

'They are all in good health. Amelia is content with her painting and time with the children. John will be a fine young man I am sure; I have high hopes for him.'

'Will they cope sufficiently without you? Amelia is a capable woman but managing a home and five children with only the help of a maid will be hard I would expect.'

'My dear cousin, that is why I travel to California so that I can give my family everything they could ever desire and the comforts they deserve. I consider it my duty as a husband and father to put them first whatever the personal cost to me.'

Henry paused before answering.

'Could you not serve them well with some more local enterprise so that you need not be absent for so long?'

'I find there are not opportunities closer to home

for such an enterprising fellow as me. If I had the advantages of living in a great city like this as you do that may be different but some of us are called to go out and seek our fortune.' His self-congratulatory smile was not met with a smile from Henry who just did not seem to appreciate the sacrifice Walter was making for his family. When had he become so dull and humourless?

'I fear we see things from a vastly different perspective cousin. I could no more leave Lucy and the children to fend for themselves than run for President! Perhaps I just do not seek the excitement you do, rather my contentment lies with my family. As you will well remember, my mother and father always encouraged their children to count their blessings and to be grateful for all God provides. God has provided me with the most wonderful loving wife and two beautiful children, my cup is full.'

'Cousin, I hope you do not suggest that I am abandoning my family?'

'I simply proffer that you already have so much to be grateful for, and perhaps in that, a responsibility to be present.'

'Sir, I do not care for what you are suggesting. I had hoped that you would support me in this venture and encourage me in my plan. I had hoped that we could talk business, as I am sure I have a very profitable proposition for you, but I see that perhaps

what I seek to do has highlighted your own lack of ambition. Those that are brave and take risks often shame those who take the easier path in life.'

'I am sorry if that is your opinion of me and that my concern for you and your family is received in such an ungenerous way. Be assured that my mother will remain as always a good friend to Amelia and the children and will help in any way that is needed while you are away.'

Walter thought Henry was about to say more but then seemed to swallow his words. Averting his eyes from Walter and quietly tapping his fingers on the arm of his chair, eventually he spoke, softly.

'I fear there is nothing more of merit to share between us cousin and so I will bid you goodnight.'

Henry was on his feet before Walter could answer and walked briskly across the room opening the study door. It was clear that their conversation was over.

Walter complied silently and joined him by the door where the maid suddenly seemed to appear from nowhere.

'Clara, please show Mr. Miller to his room.'

'Yes sir. The Blue room is ready for you Mr. Miller if you will follow me.'

Henry turned to Walter *'I hope you sleep well.*

We will wake you at six, that will be sufficient time for you to meet the children, eat breakfast and comfortably make your sail time. Goodnight cousin.'

Walter lingered on the threshold for a few moments looking into Henry's impassive face. He was confused and angry in equal measure, but decided to bid his cousin goodnight, it would serve him well to retire early anyway.

'Goodnight cousin.'

The next morning, as Lucy had suggested, the children were enthusiastic to hear about his plans eagerly asking question after question. Walter found their excitement tiresome and was frustrated that their constant chattering overtook any opportunity for meaningful conversation with Henry or even Lucy.

'Children let Cousin Walter eat his breakfast in peace. He can only answer one question at a time.' Lucy tried her best but it was almost impossible to quell their frenzied curiosity.

Walter had wanted to revisit last evening's conversation with Henry, to clarify any misunderstanding, but it was impossible. When it came time to leave, Henry had arranged a carriage to take Walter to the ship and as Walter climbed in, for the first time, fear entered his body.

'Goodbye Walter. God's speed.'

'Goodbye Henry.' As the carriage pulled away Walter looked back over his shoulder but Henry had already disappeared from the sidewalk. He had turned his back on him.

At great expense, Walter had managed to secure passage on the clipper *Surprise* and it would set sail from Sandy Hook with the promise of the fastest sea journey to San Francisco.

She was an impressive vessel, her long slim hull was painted black and rose out of the water like a leviathan, her figurehead a gleaming gilded flying eagle that would soar above the waves. The arms of New York were proudly carved on her pointed stern and her masts pointed skywards; their virgin white sails furled awaiting their release.

Surprise would work hard. Heavy-laden with valuable cargo bound for desperate gold-rushers in California, she would then sail on to China, her mission another kind of gold, tea. He was the only passenger onboard and estimated he had paid his weight in flour with a little extra for his food. He may have paid dearly for his passage but it was the quickest route without risking the dangers of the journey through the Isthmus of Panama.

The cramped conditions onboard barely met the most basic of human needs, and he had to quickly adjust to the constant smell of bodily expulsions that filled the air and seeped into every surface, even dismally flavouring his food. He almost longed for the smell of the farm kitchen now as nostalgia and sentimentality sweetened his memory of it.

For the first part of the journey, the rough sea and freezing temperatures prevented him venturing above decks with any frequency, but once they had passed around Cape Horn, the sea settled, the days lengthened and the cutting winds began to warm a little.

On the sixty-fifth day the rumours started. A man had been struck down by Typhus. The crew were directed to butter the decks twice a day with zinc chloride which brought on a strange breathlessness to those poor fellows down on their hands and knees. Every soul on board took precautions to distance themselves from one another as far as was possible in carrying out their duties. Like all were lepers, fearful of any touch, each man abandoned to his own fate.

Eventually, Walter's nose became accustomed to the putrid smell brought on by the almost constant procession of men with buckets full of excrement and other slops that were thrown over the side.

Anyone with the merest cough was viewed with suspicion and given a wide berth. Every day

Walter counted the number of men on board, partly to pass the time, mostly to check whether anyone was missing. Perhaps he had miscounted, but was there now one less man than he originally thought? Where was the tall bald fellow with the clumsily tattooed mermaid on his arm? Walter had often thought that the inker must have been drunk when he did the deed. Could he have been quietly dropped over the side during the voyage, seen off by Captain Dumaresq with a short prayer, his white shrouded body disappearing slowly into the depths?

The crew seemed to move silently and little talk passed between them, constrained by their unspoken fears perhaps, afraid to tempt fate by being too cheerful. Only the gentle sound of creaking ropes and timbers and the flapping of sails like bedsheets on a clothesline were a constant companion, the *Surprise* almost silently dipping and rising in the water like a ghost ship.

The voyage had seemed never-ending even though the captain would go to great lengths on their arrival to ensure everyone onboard knew that the *Surprise* had indeed set a new record for the fastest passage from New York City to San Francisco. Ninety-six days and fifteen hours. The longest ninety-six days and fifteen hours of Walter's life. He was sure that substantial wagers had been at stake and wished he had been in on it.

And so it was that on 19 March 1851 as he had disembarked in San Francisco Bay, he had fallen to his knees, a combination of a prayer of thanksgiving and legs that had forgotten how to stand on solid ground. All his weariness left him in that moment, he was here, he was ready.

Walter had intended to write to Amelia and the children when he arrived in San Francisco, but with so many final arrangements to make before his journey on to Sacramento, decided it should wait until he was settled and trading. It would be much better for Amelia to hear from him once the store was set up and he was a success, so had given it no more thought.

After nearly five hard days of travel across rough terrain, Walter had found an advantageous plot on a busy route through to the Sierra Nevada. Once he had flattened the ground, he had erected his tent, inside, stringing a piece of canvas across the full width to divide it in two. The front would serve as the store where he would attend his customers. At the back he would set up his cot, a small stove, a kerosene lamp, a wash basin and jug and a bucket for his business. Here he would also store the whiskey and tobacco and stash the gold that would come his way. He would sleep with his gun in his hand and set an animal trap at the front of the tent to ward off any unwanted visitors – animal or human.

Now after nearly two months of hard work he had to admit that all was not going as planned. Business had been slow and the customers he did have were fickle and unappreciative of the quality of his goods, always haggling for a better price. The profits he needed to buy his winter merchandise were not materialising and as he lay down on his cot to sleep, gun loaded and ready, he knew he needed help.

CHAPTER 6

August 1869

Dawson was his usual cheerless self this morning. He had them doing the drudgework on the preliminary designs for a big project in Revere Street and today, like every other day, he gave no encouragement or praise, at most he might offer *'it will suffice for its purpose I suppose.'*

Despite Ned's negative feelings towards him, all would say, he was an unattractive man in every sense. A thin badly engineered face was home to small close-set eyes made even smaller by the brows that sat heavily on top. His nose was large and was accentuated by the skirt of his greying moustache. He always seemed to have the expression of someone with a bad smell under their nose, sniffing the air and lifting his nostrils at the corners like a curtain going up. By his nature he rarely smiled but by design perhaps too not wanting to show his bad teeth. He thought of his mother, she hated her teeth.

The architecture of his face was made all the worse by his pocked skin, that was their nickname for him, Pock.

If Ned had learnt anything in the last year, it was that from Dawson's perspective, Ned was only there to make him look good. He was an artist, he had a good eye, he had the ability to transform Dawson's design ideas beyond what he could have achieved himself, while Dawson ensured he took all the glory.

The days at W. Adams & R. J. Morris passed well enough, he was learning, and he enjoyed the camaraderie of his fellow students who all towed the Dawson line, except Frank. Now as Dawson stood over Frank's work stabbing the paper with his finger, Ned was sure something was about to happen.

'Why are the dormers positioned like this? Do you not see the opportunity to use these to enhance the central tower and the round-head windows below?'

'I had assumed an equal distribution of light entering into the Mansard roof Mr. Dawson.'

'This practice designs beautiful buildings for practical use but it is no good to us if we have someone on the inside of the building saying, "oh see the equal distribution of light coming into this room" if from the street the building is an eyesore, so you must achieve both.'

Ned surreptitiously glanced across at the drawing, regretfully, he knew Pock was right.

Even from where he sat he could see exactly what needed to change to make the design work.

'...and the cornicing is too plain, too brutal and adds nothing to the design, why on earth would you use something so lacking in any aesthetic virtues?'

'Yes I see your point Mr. Dawson, but I thought as you had used these yourself in your Boylston Street designs, you would consider them suitable. It was really a homage to your own fine work sir.'

Dawson was furious. He was now red Pock.

'I will not tolerate such insolence, you hang by a thin thread sir, so be mindful of your actions. It will be a miracle indeed if you are to progress to a career of any merit based on the last year of study. I am sure your family have a firm hope that you will establish a secure future for yourself and indeed for them, rather than maintaining the very modest means into which you were born. You would be wise to consider the consequences of your pride, although I concede it is indeed possible to be proud and poor, if uncomfortable.'

Now it was Frank that was angry, mouth clamped shut, temple pulsing.

Pock smiled as he knew he had landed his blow on target, he glanced across at the other students to be sure they had witnessed Frank's humiliation, satisfied they had, he left the room. Ned looked across at his friend. He knew he was wounded and would be smarting from the references to his parents who Ned knew were decent, hard-working people.

'It is just Pock. When do we ever pay heed to anything he has to say?'

'Perhaps when there is some truth in it? I would happily knock him to the floor for his comments about my family and take the consequences, but as for his assertions about my abilities, I fear he is right. I am not like you, you seem to find it so easy, you are such a natural Ned and your eyes see things differently to mine.'

'You are too hard on yourself. We are all different, and some just take a little longer to learn what comes naturally to others, please just give it time.'

'Time? I wish I believed that time would change the facts.'

Ned did not know what else to say to encourage him.

'Shall we take a walk out to The Gardens at lunch? The weather is fine and it may do you good to take in the air?'

Frank hesitated *'No thank you Ned, I think I should work on my corrections. You will gain greater benefit from it if you go alone.'* Then he took a deep breath and returned to his work.

Ned knew he should leave him to himself so did

not push him further.

He would take the walk to clear his head and when lunch came, he headed towards N. D. Cotton artists' suppliers on Tremont Street.

As he walked, the streets seemed quiet today with just the sound of the occasional carriage rattling by and the wind flapping the colourful bunting left over from the National Peace Jubilee. What a wonderful time they had all had, even mamma had ventured with his sisters to the city to experience the musical extravaganza of the five-hundred-piece orchestra and the dozens of choral groups. Every man, woman and child had been happily caught up in it all and Boston had felt alive with song and celebration long after all the performers had left. Now the city seemed to have finally settled back into her usual, steady rhythm.

He particularly loved the walk down Tremont Street where the city's artists and literati gathered. Behind the windows and doors, there was creativity and invention, free-thinking and expression. It seeped out onto the street and soaked the walls and the sidewalks, and although Ned felt invigorated by it, he felt shut out from the life he would prefer to be living.

Still, a visit to Cotton's was like salve to his soul and he would often make his way here when he was troubled or simply to remind himself of who he really was. Two storeys of everything an artist could ever need or want. The full spectrum of oils and watercolours displayed like the most beautiful rainbows. Canvases and all types and grades of paper, soothing to the touch and waiting to be brought to life. The finest sable brushes of every shape and size, soft and yielding to the touch. This was his sanctuary and on difficult days at the Atelier if he closed his eyes, he could summon up the unique smell of Cotton's and it would fill his head like the most wonderful perfume.

Thomas Cotton Jr. the proprietor was attentive and enthusiastic about every item in his store down to the humblest crayon. If he was ever frustrated that Ned more often browsed than bought, he did not show it, he merely enjoyed the patronage of any smart young gentleman who chose Cotton's over the other artists' suppliers in the city. Besides, Uncle William's practice was a very valuable customer.

'Mr. Miller, can I help you with anything in particular today?'

'Sadly, I have had little time to paint these last two months Mr. Cotton. However, I conclude a design commission I have been working on for some time very shortly, and I hope this will allow me some free time to return to my painting as this has been much

neglected of late.'

'That is understandable sir. I hope you will visit us again when the time is appropriate. Your uncle is well I hope?'

'Very well sir.'

'Please send him my very kindest regards.'

Ned knew Mr. Cotton was taking care of business by asking him to pass on his good wishes, but he also knew it was genuinely meant, Uncle William was warmly regarded and held in high esteem by all who knew him.

'Happily. Good day to you.'

As Ned was about to take his leave, a smell of oranges and spices reached his nostrils, followed by an unfamiliar voice from behind him.

'Excuse me, could you help me?'

Turning in response to the question, there stood the most striking looking man Ned had ever seen. Tall and distinguished Ned was immediately struck by his Prussian blue silk cravat, it was edged with black and Ned had never seen anything so fine. Set off by a solid black frock coat made of the most exquisite broadcloth and a waistcoat of midnight blue, he was a perfect pallet of blue and black – blue eyes, black wavy hair, all perfectly painted on a pale taught canvas.

'Charles Broadbent pleased to meet you.'

'Edward Miller. How might I be of assistance?'

'I have been despatched by my mother to buy a birthday gift for my sister. She sketches but now has a fancy to paint flowers and landscapes and I wonder if perhaps you could guide me on what materials will give her the best chance of success shall we say...'

He smiled kindly at the thought of his sister trying to graduate from her simple sketches to painting.

'I see your problem; it can be a little difficult to know where to start. Can I suggest a simple watercolour box and some cold-pressed paper to begin with. I think the free and forgiving nature of watercolours might encourage her in her early efforts.

'We are certainly keen to encourage her and I will gladly take your recommendations.'

Mr. Cotton will be able to guide you on a suitable purchase I am sure. Please forgive me, I must return to my office.'

'Yes of course, I am sorry to have delayed you. My card sir, thank you for your help today.'

'And mine, should you wish to let me know how your sister progresses.' Ned was surprised to find himself offering his card in return so readily.

'I would be most pleased to inform you of her

masterpieces!'

'Then it is settled, good day sir.'

As Ned left the store the warm smell of oranges followed him down the street. Why was he so intrigued by Charles Broadbent?

He glanced at the card before slipping it into his pocket.

Charles Broadbent Esq
Attorney and Counsellor at Law
20 Elliot Street
Rooms 45-50
Boston
Mass.

As he made his way back to the office, he smiled to himself at the meeting with this strange fellow, by profession presumably so capable, by nature so seemingly helpless.

A week later during the usual tedious breakfast at No. 11 a letter arrived for Ned.

'Post for you Ned? From your mother?'

'No uncle, it is not her hand.'

Ned opened the letter and Uncle William enquired no further.

Dear Mr. Miller,

I have taken you at your word and write to inform

you of my sister's progress. Sadly, it is as I feared, I see that she shows no natural aptitude for painting and to me her work bears little resemblance to the subjects of her compositions.

Fortunately, she appears blissfully unaware of her lack of talent, unfortunately this means she is prolific in her productions and I fear her disastrous efforts will eventually take over our home.

She finds such pleasure in her painting and I would seek to encourage her and so enquire whether it might be possible for you to give her some guidance that might set her on a more aesthetic path. I will completely understand if you are unable to agree to my request but I am sure an afternoon of your helpful instruction would be most advantageous to us all.

If you were so kind as to agree to my request, your reward would be to bring contentment to a brother who adores his sister and would wish to see her succeed, and if you would join me, supper at Parker's on School Street one evening, the turtle soup is second to none and their cellar stocks simply the finest French wines and Champagne.

I await your reply with anticipation.

Yours,

Charles Broadbent Esq.

Until Charles' letter had arrived, Ned had not

realised how much he had hoped to hear from him. He replied directly and the time was fixed for the next Saturday afternoon at three o'clock at Charles' home on Beacon Street.

He looked forward to it. Apart from Frank, he had made no friends of any significance since his arrival in the city, preferring a visit home for the company of his mother and his sisters instead. He folded the letter and continued eating his breakfast. The curious Charles Broadbent was unlike anyone he had ever met before.

CHAPTER 7

November 1872

In the two weeks Ned boarded at Pinckney Street, he had spent as much time as possible with Nancy, always under the watchful eye of Mrs. Dean of course. With Charles away in New York City for three weeks and Uncle William and Aunt May settling into their new house in Roxbury, he was free of all his usual social commitments. Even Pock was making sure that Frank was rarely able to lift his head above the rising tide of correction after correction, so he saw little of him these days.

This brief social void meant that Nancy was able to step easily into the centre of his world and by the time he was preparing to leave for Manchester, the die would be cast, she would have him.

No one could describe the beginnings of their relationship as a courtship in the romantic sense. They were drawn to each other, and it was true that they had both felt a powerful need to spend as much time together as possible since that first day in his room. Nancy's yearning for him was a manifestation of all she knew he offered her to achieve the life she wanted, she must keep him in her sight, not let him slip from her grasp.

As for Ned, he was repeatedly seized by the grip of her physical presence, his desperate longing to be with her perhaps mistaken for love. In reality, something strange and unfathomable lurked between them, an ocean too deep to cross. He would come to know that she was a wolf in sheep's clothing and that time would unclothe her true nature. This masquerade of love would eventually reveal itself for what it really was.

It became an obsession to paint her and so with Mrs. Dean's permission and the door always partially open, providing she did not shirk her duties, she could legitimately be his muse. Painting her lines, capturing the light as it touched her cheekbones and layering the burning hues of her hair became his daily joy but with every brush stroke, the artist did not take possession of his subject, it was she that took possession of him.

As she emerged on the canvas, she appeared to Ned almost as some wonderful celestial creature, that was until the angel spoke. It was not just the shrill timbre of her voice but her words carried a sharp edge, cutting, judgmental. Even when she spoke of things about which she knew little or that were not her concern. She was like someone who extols the beauty of a rose in bloom, but in being challenged by its loveliness, decapitates it merely so she can possess it and have dominion over its virtues.

Nancy sat herself comfortably on her own pedestal, setting herself above ordinary folk, even though that was her own moniker. Rarely did she speak kindly about anything or anyone except him and herself of course. He understood, she had been starved of kindness and simply did not have it in her to give, it would need to be nurtured.

Oh Lord, if she would just stay silent while he painted her the spell would not be broken but she would talk incessantly, fidgeting, a kettle constantly boiling over. He had to close his ears to the cadence of her thin grating voice because it had the power to almost paralyse the brush in his hand and painting her beauty became almost impossible in the presence of such ugly sonance.

His time at Pinckney Street was nearly over and he would be leaving for Manchester the day after tomorrow. Now, as he painted her for the final time, she started.

'Do you not think this green dress very dull?' She was looking down and picking at the skirt miserably.

'I have never had a new dress, just hand-me-

downs.'

He would not enter into this discussion, he already knew her well enough to predict its destination, he did not want to go where she wanted to take him this morning.

'Please do not move your head.'

She sighed and pushed on. *'It is so faded. It is one of Mrs. Dean's cast-offs you know and so unfashionable do you not think?'*

'The colour complements your eyes.'

She was not satisfied with his response. She would have to try harder.

'I cannot see how such a dour colour can complement anything. Are my eyes so dull and lifeless to you?'

Her eyes were in truth her most striking feature. They were like vibrant autumn leaves flecked with gold and black, but he would not tell her that, or he would be walking straight into her trap.

'No, that is not what I suggest.'

'Well then, what do you say?'

'All colours are dulled by these long dark winter days.'

'All the more reason then to wear bright colours. I have seen simply the prettiest silks and taffetas to

light these dark days as you call them.'

He let her go on.

'Purples and pinks are what the fashionable ladies are wearing and Madame LeBlanc is the talk of the city. Her designs are the latest from Paris and everyone says a dress by Madame LeBlanc is the one to be seen wearing in fashionable circles.'

'I know nothing of ladies' fashions but I do not believe that any dressing of silk or taffeta could make you look any more beautiful.' Again, he hoped the compliment would divert her.

She ignored his compliment *'Of course, buying a dress for a special occasion is always the most thrilling.'*

He had arrived at his destination and found himself softening to her pleas. She had played her hand beautifully as she inextricably tethered the purchase of an expensive gown to a special occasion, a wedding, an intention perhaps already understood but as yet unspoken between them.

With his stay at Pinckney Street coming to an end he felt a sudden sense of urgency. He put down his brush and looked into her expectant face.

'Will you dine with me this evening if it can be arranged with Mrs. Dean? There are things that need

to be said before I leave for Manchester on Monday.'

Nancy understood what the invitation meant and was content to drop the subject of the dress for now. The prize before her was so much greater, eligible men were in short supply since the war and she would do well to grasp the opportunity he presented for her; she could make something of him. She nodded and smiled so sweetly at him, there was goodness in her he thought, yes he was sure there was.

Charles' words came into his head '*My dear Ned, how I desire to see the good in all people as you do no matter how they scheme or disappoint, but that fancy cannot be mine, I am called to always seek the truth no matter how unpalatable.*' He put it to the back of his mind.

With the agreement and eager assistance of Mrs. Dean, a small table was set in the parlour that evening away from the main dining room. Ned had brought Mrs. Dean into his confidence, and in honour of the important occasion, she had gone to the greatest trouble to set the proposal table. A delicate bobbin-lace tablecloth, small crystal glasses and the silverware from her own hope chest were polished and laid out with care and precision. A few sprigs of winter heather in a blue vase brought an infusion of life and colour to the scene. Finally, her own wedding day napkins. Lost in her thoughts, she ran her thumb slowly across a pink rose embroidered at one corner, before folding it and placing it on the table. Stepping back to look, she thought it perfect.

He had written to his mother that afternoon to let her know of his intentions, but did not seek her blessing, he had decided on Nancy. Likewise, he had written to Uncle William and Aunt May to let them know of his marriage proposal plans. Neither would have time to reply before the deed was done and promises were made.

He knew Nancy's estrangement from her parents meant there was no need to seek their permission or indeed any blessing from her father, they would remain uninformed, Ned had no reason to think he would ever meet his in-laws.

In all this, he had felt the greatest burden to tell Charles of his news, and last of all he had written to him.

Saturday 9th November

My dearest Charles,

I hope my note finds you well and that by the time you read this you will have successfully concluded your business in New York City. It is a great shame that my time at Pinckney Street coincided with your trip as I would have enjoyed us being practically neighbours.

My lodgings have been more than adequate these past two weeks. I have enjoyed a very comfortable room on the third floor with delightful views towards Louisburg Square and Mrs. Dean has been hospitable to me beyond what was required of her for which I am extremely grateful.

I have been well employed during my stay and have enjoyed the free time to paint immensely. As you would expect I have not missed the daily routine at W. Adams & R. J. Morris for a moment although I feel the loss of my time spent with my uncle and aunt acutely.

I write with some news which I am sure will come as a surprise to you, it is indeed something of a surprise to me! This evening it is my intention to propose marriage to Miss Nancy Sullivan, a young lady in the employ of Mrs. Dean, and I have every reason to believe she will accept me.

These last two weeks we have grown very fond of each other and it is my hope we can build a fruitful and happy marriage. She is most encouraging about my painting and I believe will be a great support to me despite the self-inflicted unpredictability of my future.

She does not come from a family of any standing and the poor girl is completely estranged from her parents which would be understandable to you if you knew the nature of their circumstances, so I will be all her family to her.

I plan to leave for Smith's Point as planned on Monday and will make the house ready for Nancy to join me in a few months once we are married. No date is set for the wedding but this is something I hope we will be able to agree presently, perhaps an early spring date. It is my dearest hope that you will consider being my best man, there is no-one that I would want more to stand by my side.

It will be a small and modest affair but I hope it will be possible for my mother (her health allowing) and my sisters to come and of course my Uncle William and Aunt May. Unfortunately, my Aunt Adeline and Uncle John are too unwell to travel these days which is a great disappointment to me.

My dearest friend, I would value your blessing above all others, and I hope that you can find it in you to be happy for me even if this is so different from the future we talked of many times.

That you will often be our neighbour whenever you vacation in Manchester is wonderful and I hope we will spend many happy times together and that you will come to care for Nancy as I do.

Affectionately yours,

Ned

As he folded the note he felt relieved. No-one's support for his plans was more important than that of Charles. He would deliver it to Beacon Street himself to be waiting for him on his return next week.

The proposal that evening went according to plan, in fact he wondered if she had heard him rehearsing it in his room earlier, as she appeared ahead of him in what he was going to say, almost accepting him before he had even asked. There would be a ring and she would get her dress. She was satisfied.

However, if there was any joy in the moment of their promised union it ended abruptly, and Ned would later reflect that the events of that night were a bad omen which he should have heeded.

Just as they were finishing their supper as a newly engaged couple they were interrupted by a commotion coming from the street. There were loud screams and shouts, although they could not make out the words, and a distant sound like gunfire. Something was wrong. Then they heard Mrs. Dean shouting from beyond the parlour door.

'Oh, my Lord! Oh, my Lord! Oh no…

As Ned entered the hall he saw that Mrs. Dean and Arthur Drew were standing at the front door which was wide open. Beyond it he could see that there was a strange orange glow in the sky and the buildings and treetops were dappled by flickering lights. The air was filling with choking, acrid smoke that wafted in and reached down into their lungs.

'What has happened? Is there a fire?'

Ned pushed past Arthur, who stood rigidly in a trance-like state blocking the doorway, and the now muted Mrs. Dean, her hand clasped over her mouth for fear some undignified cry might escape her lips. Finding himself in a fast-flowing river of people he grabbed for the arm of an elderly man who was scuttling down the street as fast as his bandy legs would take him.

'Fire! There is a fire!' He stuttered.

'Where?'

'Summer Street they say but the wind is carrying it downtown at a lick, they cannot stop it!'

Ned held on to his arm, he wanted more information.

Just then the loud bang of a gas line exploding ricocheted through the air. *'Let go of me you devil! I do not intend to die this night.'*

Ned let go of his arm and looked towards the source of the light. He could see flames in the distance shooting at least fifty feet above the rooftops, jumping across the narrow streets from roof to roof, dense smoke billowing up into the clear night sky.

Nancy had now joined Mrs. Dean and Arthur Drew on the doorstep, and as he looked back at her in the hope of compass, instead he felt a foreshadowing of something strange and destructive that was nothing to do with the fire.

That night, thousands of people were out on the streets watching, as the blaze took hold of building after building. At midnight, the sounds of loud booming explosions were heard across the city, as buildings were blown up to create a firebreak. By early light, the flames dimmed and no longer reached so far into the sky. By noon, the fire had been stopped in its path.

Thankfully, it had come no closer to them than Washington Street and the Beacon Hill area was left untouched.

The church bells seemed to ring louder that Sunday morning as people gave thanks for being spared and sent up prayers for those who had perished in the fire. As the gossip circulated throughout the day it was clear that many commercial properties had been lost but that there had been limited loss of life as most of the buildings and warehouses affected had been empty.

'Can you fathom that they could not find the key-holders for the fire alarm boxes?...'

'Yes, they say it was at least twenty minutes

before the alarm was even raised with the fire department...'

'And not enough horses because of the sickness so all those poor souls having to pull the engines themselves...'

'I hear their water hoses were not even up to the job. It is a wonder that we did not all die in our beds...'

'It is a miracle that more souls were not lost.'

'Yes, thank God in His mercy.'

Any danger had passed them by although the invisible hand of the night's events held on to them all. Acrid smoke carried on the wind burned their eyes and the smell of scorched wood, oak and pine concocting a heady perfume, clung to their skin and hair and soaked their clothes.

An unnatural silence had settled on the city, all except the noisy popping and cracking of beams and supports as they cooled and split, and the distant sound of rubble tumbling as walls fell heavily, the fire having burned away their stitching.

There was no need to delay, Ned could leave for Manchester as planned.

When the time came his parting from Nancy was easy, she had the promise she craved, she would bide her time now until they were married.

They let go of each other easily.

Within an hour of his departure a note from Charles arrived at Pinkney Street.

'Nancy dear, a letter arrives for Mr. Miller from a Charles Broadbent Esq. It may perhaps be of an urgent nature so should I forward it to his address in Manchester? I would be happy to do so.'

'Do not trouble yourself Mrs. Dean, I know Mr. Broadbent and will visit him with news that Edward has already left.'

'You know the gentleman?' Mrs. Dean looked perplexed.

'I do, Edward has spoken of him many times, he lives but a few streets from here.'

Mrs. Dean hesitated *'Very well if you are sure'* and she handed the letter over into Nancy's safekeeping.

As soon as Mrs Dean left her, Nancy carefully opened the letter and read it.

Monday 11th November

My dearest Ned,

I am just returned home early from my business in New York City following the terrible events of these last two days. It is a relief to find that the ravages of the fire were not more profound and I thank God that the loss of life was not as grave as it might have been.

Having read your note, I thought better of visiting you at Pinckney Street in person as I would have liked, as I believe free conversation may have been difficult for you. So, I write to you now in the hope this letter will reach you before you depart for Smith's Point.

You are correct that I was indeed surprised by the contents of your note and as my dearest friend, I am most concerned about the wisdom and the speed of your decision.

I caution you to consider whether this is the right path for you and if marriage to Miss Nancy Sullivan is something into which you can wholeheartedly enter. By now you will already have given her your promise but I beg you to take some time to reconsider your actions, it is not too late.

I will await your reply and will not press myself on you Ned unless I receive your permission to visit you at the earliest possible occasion at Smith's Point.

I remain as always your dearest friend.

Charles

Nancy was shaking with fury, how dare Charles Broadbent interfere, by what right? As she slipped the letter into her pocket, she cursed him under her breath, she would consider what she would do with it later.

CHAPTER 8

March 1873

Today as every day, the dawn would find Amelia alone in her studio.

It was a small but bright room with two large picture windows looking out onto the garden. With honest white walls, wear-worn wooden floors and a small well-used fireplace, it was a functional space that served its purpose well. Amelia made no nod towards maintaining it and the clumsy Martha was never to enter to clean it. So, years of paint of every colour spattered the floors, dust was left undisturbed, and the furnishings steadily became faded and tired.

Still, surrounded by her work, this was her place of solace and peace and she spent most of her waking hours here. Hundreds of paintings and sketches were hung, propped up and piled up precariously, each one intimately known to her if not fully visible. To the eyes of others, it might look disorganised and haphazard, but she knew exactly where everything was.

Little by little, as she bothered with herself less,

Amelia was becoming as worn and faded as her studio. If the outside world were ever to be let in, her self-neglect would be evident.

Her hair rarely brushed let alone dressed, two shabby black dresses sufficing as her attire for every day, her body thin and wasted from lack of sustenance. Her meals were small and her stomach shrunken by it. There was no respite at all from the gnawing pain she felt in her gut and she was always exhausted. Sleep did not restore her, she would go to bed feeling tired, she would wake up feeling tired.

There was not much outside world for Amelia now. Moving as a shadow she rarely ventured beyond the garden walls feeling anxious about going any further. She had decided long ago that she would stay safe with her memories inside the garden boundary. Prison or sanctuary, it was all she wanted.

Lottie and Martha ran the house now and had found an equitable and satisfactory division of duties that worked for them both. Lottie took care of the cooking, the buying of groceries and the bottling and preserving of the fruit from the garden to take them through the winter. She had perfected the baking of delicious cornbread and her apple pie was every bit as good as her mother's.

Martha's domain was everywhere except the kitchen and the studio. She cleaned and polished, took care of the laundry, set the fires and tended the garden. She took great pride in her work and blossomed when complimented on the smallest thing like the pressing and folding of the linen or for a vase of flowers thoughtfully arranged. The two women, so different, were the left and the right hand of everything that needed to be done.

Days at Greenbrook were simple and routine and each passed by much the same as the next with visitors to the house few and far between these days.

Adeline was too frail to make the short trip to visit her friend and William's declining health meant he too made the journey to visit them less often. Very occasionally, ladies from the church would come for tea and Lottie would do her best to make it a happy event in the hope it would lift her mother's spirits but Amelia would just sit by quietly, listening to their chattering; somewhere else.

Amelia's children had left her, as they should, and had families of their own. All gone from her orbit now except for sweet Lottie who had devoted herself to her mother, weighing not an ounce of bitterness, she had put aside her own hopes of marriage and motherhood.

Even her Little Ned was to be married soon and would become more distant from her. Nancy would become the most important woman in his life and she felt the loss of her status intensely. She had sent him her blessing but she would not go to the wedding, she was too weary, she had no wish to spoil such a happy day.

Increasingly she seemed to live her days with the spirits of the past, her parents, her dead babies and even her lost husband. Most of all, her precious John, his handsome face always before her. Thankfully in these last few months his constant presence had tipped the scales in favour of comfort rather than pain.

Lottie appeared at the studio door.

'Mamma, can I bring some tea to warm you?'

Amelia looked up but did not answer.

Lottie approached her mother and pulled out a chair to sit next to her.

'What will you paint today?' she asked gently.

Amelia turned and looked at her daughter *'John is here again this morning.'*

'I think the cold plays tricks with your mind or perhaps you were dreaming? John is not here mamma.'

She took her mother's hand to reassure her. In her own hand, her mother's looked like a child's.

It was cold and bloodless and Lottie instinctively drew it to her cheek to warm it.

'Child, do you not recognise your own brother? Is he not unchanged?' Amelia looked towards the window and smiled in the way only a mother does when she gazes down on her first born.

Lottie followed her mother's eyes towards the window where only a sparrow sat on the windowsill industriously fluffing its feathers and preening itself. She was increasingly disturbed by her mother's visions but did not show it and continued to speak gently.

'Shall you paint a sprig of apple blossom perhaps? The pink buds and white flowers are so pretty but so fleeting. You should capture them quickly before the wind blows them away or rain spoils them.'

'Perhaps.'

Amelia was back from where she had been, her eyes now in focus but somehow dimmed.

'I miss John too mamma. We all miss him.' She looked at her mother so small and fragile and her eyes lingered on her auburn hair now cruelly streaked with grey.

'Can I brush your hair mamma?'

'Yes if you would like. Do you remember you used to do that when you were a little girl?'

'Ida and I would always quarrel over who would

brush your hair. I shall fetch your brush.'

Lottie returned with the same wooden brush she had used as a child, smaller and more manageable in her hand now. Standing behind her she began to gently pull the brush through her mother's hair, at first with stuttering progress as knots got in the way, but with slow gentle teasing, the brush began to flow more freely along the length of her hair. She felt like a child again, and yet her mother was now the child, as they changed places.

'Did I ever tell you that your brother was able to walk by the time he was but ten months old? He was always in such a hurry over everything and so fast on his feet even as a baby.'

'I remember that in a chase he always caught me. I could never outrun him no matter how hard I tried.'

They both smiled and it was silent except the soothing sound of the strokes of the brush.

'I feel the loss of John every day, I try not to, but I cannot help it.'

'I know mamma.'

'There! It is as lovely as ever' and Lottie ran her hand over her mother's hair relishing the feel of it once more.

'Thank you my darling. Do I remember correctly that you offered me tea?'

'*I did*' and Lottie hoped her mother did not hear the break in her voice as she spoke.

As Lottie closed the door quietly behind her the tears welled in her eyes despite her best efforts to hold them back. She knew her mother was on a journey to somewhere bewildering and empty and there was nothing she could do to stop it. For the first time in her life, she felt alone with no one of her own, even Ned would be starting a new life and she knew his precious letters would become more and more infrequent.

At the sound of Martha's heavy and ungainly footsteps on the stairs she peeled herself away from the door, straightened up, and went to the kitchen to make the tea.

Inside the studio Amelia sat and stared at the blank paper in front of her, and then from her mind's eye, she began to paint the apple tree nearest the stream. As the image began to emerge, the colours were vibrant and the fruit perfectly ripe and abundant. The tree was lit by late summer sunshine and beneath it, she herself stood looking up with her arms wide open, ready to carefully catch the fruit so that nothing would be spoiled or lost.

CHAPTER 9

June 1871

'The day is nearly done and by my estimation there is little to show for it! Take heed gentlemen, I shall not hesitate to have you work extra time to make up for your lack of productivity today.'

It was four o'clock in the afternoon and the day had seemed excruciatingly long. Even the tick of the wall clock seemed laboured as it pushed on to the end of the day.

Pock had been even more sour than usual, stressed by the completion of the Carver Street job, which was not progressing as planned. The client was exacting and discerning and Pock's usual oily charm had failed to win him favour. Pock blamed everyone except himself of course and the vent for his frustration and anger was always his students as they soaked up the effects of his failings.

The star of the once brilliant Pock was dimming, as fashions changed and clients became more demanding, he simply was not able or willing to move with the times. The growing derogation of his power was becoming evident for everyone to see.

Frank, always prepared to hold a looking glass up to Pock's inadequacies, came off worst and Ned had seen his friend's despondency reach new depths over the last few months. Still, tomorrow was Sunday and at least there would be a day's respite from Pock's bad mood and foul temper for them all.

He always did his best to try and cheer Frank and he had hoped that tomorrow he might join him and Charles on their trip to Rockport. The sea air and open spaces would do him good Ned had suggested, but Frank had thanked him and declined, as he had done on so many previous occasions.

All considered William Adams to be a fair and progressive employer, and the office usually operated from seven o'clock in the morning to half past six in the evening, although sometimes longer in the summer when there were more daylight hours for eyes to benefit from. He believed in the welfare of his employees and students and that he would get the best from them by investing in generous working practices so he allowed a half-hour-long break at midday for lunch or exercise and once a month everyone at W. Adams & R. J. Morris would be given a Saturday afternoon off. Today was not one of those Saturdays and so at just after half past six, Pock not having invoked the overtime he threatened, Ned and Uncle William stepped out onto the street to a beautiful balmy evening.

The walk home to No.11 was generally done with little conversation both men using the short walk to cast off the day. Ned found the silence comfortable and easy now, almost pleasurable. He had come to accept over the last three years that Uncle William was a quiet reflective man with little appetite for meaningless talk, so this evening, Ned was a little taken aback when he started up a conversation on their way home.

'Your aunt tells me you venture to Rockport tomorrow?'

'Yes uncle, it is our intention to take the early train to make the most of the day. I very much look forward to it.'

Uncle William cleared his throat. *'You travel with Charles I expect. Will his family be joining you? I know you are very fond of them.'*

'No uncle, just we two. I hope time away from the city will benefit him and the change of scenery restore his spirits somewhat. He has been burdened with an exceedingly difficult and distressing case these past weeks and I seek to lighten his load a little if only for a day. I have been encouraging him to paint and I hope a visit to Pigeon Cove might inspire

him to take up a brush.'

Uncle William did not answer immediately and Ned became aware of the sound of their footsteps on the sidewalk's granite flaggs. Counting the sharp beats, he waited for his uncle's line of questioning to resume.

'I think Charles a fine fellow if somewhat unconventional in his attire and demeanour. He is widely respected and from a very good family and I am sure he enjoys a large social circle of interesting and influential friends. It is a wonder that he can dedicate so much time to your friendship.'

Ned did not know how to answer.

Uncle William continued *'It does indeed seem a shame that such an accomplished man approaching his middle years does not yet enjoy the blessing of a wife and children. It is my earnest hope that this might be something that will come to him in time.'*

It was the significance of the unsaid words that weighed heaviest between them, both knew the true meaning of their conversation, neither would name it.

I am sure Charles would be greatly appreciative of your desire for his happiness uncle. As his dearest friend, I have learnt that he does not measure himself against other men nor generally find his contentment in the things they hold in high esteem, although he does of course seek happiness and fulfilment like any one of us.'

'Indeed, each man should take his own path in life and not seek to align himself with the ways of others, that only leads to tribulation.' His words were gently directed at Ned.

As they arrived at No.11, Ned was aware that it had been the longest conversation he had ever had with his uncle, such was his disquiet.

Supper that evening passed cordially without reference to their earlier conversation and Ned excused himself early, retiring to his room to gather his things together for the next day's expedition.

He woke early, still bothered by the remains of yesterday's conversation with Uncle William but pushing it to the back of his mind, he focused on the day ahead.

'Surely in this modern age we should be capable of inventions much more conducive to comfortable transportation?'

Ned smiled at his friend who sat uncomfortably in his seat, long legs like a spider's folded awkwardly, arms rigidly bent unable to stretch. He seemed too big in every sense for the constraints of the railway carriage and certainly did not go unnoticed by his fellow passengers. The woman sitting opposite them hardly took her eyes off him, averting her gaze quickly every time Ned's eyes met hers. Charles seemed either unaware or did not give a care.

Ned considered the object of the woman's fascination as he took a sideways look at his friend. He did look glorious, all around him dulled in his colourful light, the dark wood panelling of the carriage serving as a sober frame around the most joyous painting.

He wore a sack suit of sky-blue linen, a pale blue waistcoat, topped off with a straw hat around which was the most vibrant pink and blue silk striped band that complemented his bright pink necktie perfectly. Every line was crisp, every detail exquisite down to the beautiful mother of pearl buttons, as always he smelt of oranges and spices.

Despite the boldness and gaiety of Charles' attire, it did not overpower him, he commanded it.

Charles endured the train journey with as much grace as he could muster and finally they arrived to clear blue skies. Stepping down onto the platform, despite the oily pungent smell of the engine, Ned was sure he could catch the smell the sea rising above it and he felt exhilarated by it.

They set off on their walk to Pigeon Cove along the undulating coast path, the changing scenes of Back Beach Landing and Gull Cove to their right in all their glistening glory, finally passing Granite Pier and Sandy Bay which spread itself out like a pale blue tablecloth as far as the eye could see.

If Ned had thought that Charles' flamboyant appearance stood out on the train, the juxtaposing of his colourful attire now, with the backdrop of such a rugged natural landscape, induced people's blatant staring even more. Still, Charles would graciously meet their eyes with a smile, followed by a tip of his hat.

Hot and a little weary from the exertions of their walk they decided to dine at the newly opened Ocean View House Hotel and to avoid the heat of the midday sun. The cool light dining room was elegantly decorated in whites and blues and seascape paintings lined the walls although none were as fine as Ned's. Palm trees in colourful planters placed around the room added a breeziness to the space and large ornate chandeliers were hung with crystals like icicles that played a cheerful but discordant tune and flung fragments of rainbows onto the walls and ceiling.

They were enthusiastically greeted by the slightly pompous maître d' who had clearly acquired the airs and graces of his patrons but had none of their breeding. He would find the gentlemen one of their best tables even though they were extremely busy he said and it had sounded to Charles like he offered this as some kind of favour rather than simply doing his job. The maître d' called over a rather timid looking waiter who led them to a table near the window from where they could take in the spectacular views. This waiter, as it was everywhere they went, was highly attentive to Charles' every need, hardly noticing Ned at all. He did not mind, one of the reasons Ned knew they were the greatest of friends, was that he was never jealous or begrudging of the special treatment Charles attracted everywhere they went.

They dined on oysters, broiled cod with parsley butter, followed by vanilla ice cream and all the while enjoyed the slightly over-attentive service of the nervous waiter. *'Is everything to your liking sir? Is there anything else I can bring you? Shall I bring you a fresh jug of iced water?'* All directed to Charles while Ned sat by quietly smiling to himself.

Now as they sat drinking their coffee and Ned took in the sea view for the hundredth time he said with some note of mischief *'Now I very much hope Charles that you will finally venture some painting this afternoon. If this vista does nothing to inspire you, I am not sure what ever could.'*

'My dear fellow my abilities will never be sufficient to do any level of justice to God's creation. My destruction of perfection would seem a wicked

venture to me. However, I promise I shall be the ideal artist's companion. I shall remain quiet when required, offer praise when it is due, and take the utmost pleasure in your evident talent.'

Despite Charles' summing up, Ned was not going to be put off.

'How will you ever know what you are capable of if you do not at least try? You may have artistic hidden depths that you have not yet discovered.'

'Dearest Ned I truly believe that you think I can do anything, but you should understand that I do not seek to master everything, why would any man? I am content to receive joy and inspiration from many things that are not the labour of my hands or intellect. I assure you; I shall be your most appreciative spectator.'

Ned knew he would never verbally out manoeuvre Charles and resigned himself to the current state of play. As he looked across the table at his friend, last evening's conversation with Uncle William came to mind, and then he ventured where he instinctively knew he should not go.

'My heart and soul are filled to the brim when I paint and I honestly think it the antidote to a dull and mundane existence. Of course, painting is my great passion but I also seek all the usual human comforts of man…'

Charles reflected on Ned's words as he looked out of the window.

'Can I assume you talk of love?'

Ned nodded.

'I think the virtues of true love may be overrated and indeed rarely achieved. As I have looked around, I have never witnessed the depths of love as depicted in Shakespeare's Romeo and Juliet and besides, all such great love stories appear to end in tragedy and disappointment. I think perhaps more commonly people subscribe to the idea of romantic love whilst complying with society's traditions of marriage and companionship. This seems a narrow view in my estimation.

To care for another person, for their happiness to be your happiness has nothing to do with social conventions or indeed contracts. I consider that marriage is generally the cart before the horse, and the horse, being love, may never catch up! Please do not misunderstand me, I can allow myself to believe in the institution of marriage as it can bring many benefits, but I cannot constrain and limit my belief in love and its freedom to roam wherever it may choose.

I spend my life searching for truth, seeking proof of events and character, but ask me to stand in court and prove love, it is impossible. I could no more look at a couple married for fifty years and say "there is love" than I could prove that a mother loves her child although nature dictates it. It transcends evidence, it defies logic, it flies in the face of all that is contrived by man. It is its own thing, not of our making, but a gift if you are fortunate to give and receive it.'

Ned had never heard Charles speak this way, and in doing it, he had revealed something of himself. Ned knew he would honour his friend's candour and speak of it no more.

'Let us raise a glass to love then, wherever it freely roams and finds its home, let no man stand in its way.'

'I will drink to that. Now, we should make haste, there are masterpieces to be painted.' Charles laughed and raised his glass, then summoned the waiter over to pay the bill.

They spent the rest of the afternoon at Pigeons Cove. Ned found his friend a comfortable boulder to sit on, although Charles questioned whether there was such a thing as a comfortable boulder but sat happily anyway.

Ned settled himself comfortably too and carefully opened up a Pochade box on his lap revealing the rainbow jewels inside. Painting *en plein air* was his greatest joy, all his senses fed and his subject set out before him in all its glory just waiting for him. The light, the colour, the movement all in the moment ready for him to capture.

Birds swept and dived and fishing boats scattered the horizon where the blue of the ocean met the blue of the sky, and as the sun on the water brought thousands of flecks of light to the scene, he was more than ready to take on the challenge. As Ned painted, he whistled to himself happily, while Charles sat tossing pebbles into the water, the two of them a picture of contentment on a warm summer's afternoon.

As they parted later that evening Ned reached into his Pochade and took out the Pigeon Cove watercolour handing it to Charles. *'To remind you'* he said.

Their day at the cove would be one of the happiest Ned had ever spent.

CHAPTER 10

May 1851

31st May 1851

My dearest Amelia,

I regret it has taken me so long to write, I am sure you have been concerned about me and how I am prospering on behalf of our family.

The situation here is difficult and the living conditions are hard as you might imagine. There remain great opportunities for those who are brave and enterprising like myself but the prevailing lawlessness and constant threat from the uncivilised heathen natives here make it harder than I had expected for a decent man to make his fortune.

I have had a small setback, the details of which I will not burden you with now, and therefore need you to secure further merchandise for me so that I might continue trading and pursue other favourable business ventures that present themselves to me.

I enclose a manifest of the goods I require listed by wholesaler along with details of the related weights and prices. You will see that the entire *order totals less than $100 and I believe that some items might be secured for even keener prices than I have indicated particularly from A.T. Stewart & Co. who are happy to offer me discount. I also enclose all the details you need to make the necessary transportation arrangements and as I already have existing accounts with the suppliers, I anticipate that the arrangements will be easy to make.*

In support of our family, I hope your brother might be prevailed upon to offer up the funds required and that he will assist you in securing this merchandise and its transportation. As I know he has reason to travel to New York City for business frequently, I would hope a visit to the wholesalers could happen expediently and the next available shipment opportunity might be secured.

You can reassure him that his investment will be returned to him with healthy interest in due course and I hope he would see this as both a reasonable request from his dearest sister as well as a highly advantageous business opportunity for him.

Please be encouraged my love, with receipt of these goods and the industrious application of my sales talents, I would hope to return to you and our family within the next two years, a rich man, and for us to have the best of everything that money can buy.

Please write to me by return to confirm receipt of my letter and to let me know that the merchandise has been arranged. Also, by what date I might expect it to arrive in San Francisco for collection.

Make haste my love as the future of our family is in your hands.

I hope you and the children are all in good health and please pass on my fondest regards to my aunt and uncle.

Your loving husband,

Walter

He folded the letter placing it carefully in his pocket ready for it to go by the Express Line first thing in the morning. It was true that it would take almost half of his remaining funds to pay for carriage to the post office on the corner of Pike and Clay in San Francisco and then its long onward journey, but he had no choice.

Fortunately, fair weather ensured an Expressman's journey to San Francisco was expeditious at this time of year, apart from the usual risks of ambush by Indians en route. Then, if there was favourable weather for his letter's onward progress, by the Pacific Mail Steam and then the Atlantic Line, the letter should be with Amelia in a month. If she and William made haste to arrange the shipment of his merchandise, he hoped he would receive it by the end of September.

This would ensure he had everything in place for a very profitable winter of trading, although he was also giving serious consideration to whether he could establish his own company of Expressmen, why not? He was paying a hefty three dollars just for the carriage of his letter to San Francisco and the ever-growing demand for faster and more efficient mail routes was something he knew he could profit from handsomely. He could easily start up his own Express Line business to San Francisco, he would only need one healthy young fellow and a strong mule to get started. With placer-gold seemingly already harder to find, he knew there were a growing number of disaffected prospectors no longer able to sniff out the pay dirt to make their fortunes. They were resigned to working for a pittance in the hard rock mines, to making someone else rich. He was sure it would be easy to find someone as enterprising as himself, someone who shared his hunger for success.

It was a hot afternoon and he decided to stay out of the blazing sun in the relative cool of the tent. He was exhilarated by the promise of the letter in his pocket despite Thursday's terrible events, so after a brief look around at the reality of his somewhat barren tent, he lay down on his cot to continue thinking through his plans for the future. He closed his eyes and felt for his gun, he would not be caught out again.

From the very beginning business had not been as brisk as he had hoped, the days passed at a slow pace and it was taking much longer than he had expected for the pinches of dust to add up to anything significant. He had scraped his way to just over ten ounces of gold dust and knew he could get up to fifteen dollars an ounce if it was clean, but he had held on to it too long and now it was all gone.

Sales of the more significant items of merchandise had been few, so he had only traded in dust on the smaller items, not securing the shiny gold nuggets he had dreamt of. With poor sales, his merchandise levels had remained stubbornly high, that was, until last Thursday.

Now lying on his cot, despite his efforts to divert it, his mind doggedly dragged him back to that terrible day that had started uneventfully but which had turned out very badly.

It had been just before seven o'clock at the start of another hot and humid day and he had been outside the front of the tent setting out his wares arranging them to look as appetising as possible - a daily futility on his part. A dull spectrum of buckets, pans, kettles, tin cups, and flatware hung from hooks at the tent entrance, while blankets, bolts of canvas, flannel overshirts and cotton trousers were stacked on a wooden trestle table.

As he was about to go back into the tent, a man coming down the trail called out to him.

'Good day to you friend.'

Walter had never seen him before.

'Good day, how can I help you?'

The man was advanced in years, at least three score Walter thought, unusual for these parts where youth and vitality were necessary for survival. His skin was the colour of a saddle and the limp folds of skin around his eyes hung so heavily that his eyes were almost completely hooded, although Walter could see that one was clouded and had the appearance of a part-cooked griddled egg. Three yellowed teeth protruded down under his untrimmed moustache and Walter was not sure that he had any lower teeth at all.

His shirt hung dirtily over angular shoulders from which the meat had long been lost and his trousers slumped on his body with no curve or fat to hold on to. He smelt sour. Despite his appearance, he could be a customer, so Walter was helpful and charming with a clear eye firmly fixed on profit.

The man stumbled a little as he approached. *'Could I trouble you for some water before we talk business?'*

Walter pulled out a stool from inside the tent opening so the man could sit, pouring him some water from his flask, which the man greedily accepted. Then he waited impatiently for him to recover and speak his business.

'Thank you, you are most kind, I do find myself feeling a little faint in the heat this morning.' He stood up, and without a word, picked up the stool and set it down under a shady tree a little way away from the tent. Walter followed to continue their conversation and to keep an eye on his stool.

'I come on behalf of my son who has been most fortunate these last few days. So successful that he seeks to establish a more permanent pitch and so sends me to arrange canvas, tools, cooking utensils and all manner of things to make a hard-working man's life more comfortable. He has the means to pay I assure you; he has a gift for spotting the pay dirt where no other man can find it.' At the mention of this, Walter could almost see the glint of gold in his cloudy eye.

'I will be very happy to help you and encourage your son in his labours. Shall we write a list and I can gather together all that he requires for collection later?' He was about to fetch paper and pencil from the tent but the man caught hold of his arm to hold him back. He was stronger than he looked.

'No need friend, the list is short but of significant value, I am sure you will be able to commit my requirements to memory.'

Walter did not resist him and stood ready to take the man's order.

'Tell me friend, what brings you to these parts? Have you family left behind somewhere in this world?' He spoke very loudly and Walter suspected he was a little deaf.

Walter was keen not to delay their business with unnecessary and unwelcome small talk so he tried to hurry him along.

'I do, and as you will understand, they rely on me to conduct my business proficiently and expediently. It is their future I seek to secure.'

'Yes, yes, I must make haste in giving you my order. Time has slowed my mind and made it prone to wander.'

Walter waited and said nothing as he did not want to encourage this line of conversation.

'Now let me see, where should I start? I am minded to start with the whiskey!' He laughed, air whistling through the gaps where his teeth should have been. Then to Walter's dismay he began to sing loudly and tunelessly, clapping his hands and stamping his feet.

I have been a wild rover for many's the year

And I have spent all me money on whiskey and beer
But now I am returning with gold in great store
And I never will play the wild rover no more

> *And it is no, nay, never*
> *No, nay never no more*
> *Will I play the wild rover*
> *No never no more…*

On and on he went, louder and louder, until finally he ran out of verses.

Before the man had the chance to start up another song Walter quickly asked, '*How many bottles of whiskey would you like?*'

'*Let me see, hmmm…*' He looked down at his filthy fingers, the tip of his small finger on his left hand was missing, '*darned coyote*' he offered as explanation as he began to count aloud, slowly and noisily.

Walter was dismayed. Not only was this going to take a very long time, not one other customer had come to the tent during his time with the old man, not even one of his regulars from a neighbouring camp, another sign of his failing venture.

The old man had not needed to use his fingers to count as at last he said '*Two.*'

Walter was disappointed, perhaps this was not going to be his big sale of the day.

'Now, what else can I help you with?'

He thought the old man looked distracted and twitchy.

'I do not feel so well friend. No, I do not feel too well at all. Look here, do you see my hands tremble and not a drop of drink this day or yesterday. I think we must conclude our business tomorrow.'

Then the sound of hooves and as Walter turned he was hit full in the face with the butt of a rifle. As he lay in the dirt, dazed, he was sure that he saw the old man brisk as you like, jump up on a heavy-laden mule behind a younger man. Saddle bags bulging with what he was soon to learn was his whiskey, tobacco, molasses. Everything with the highest portability and value, all gone.

As his senses began to return to him, with blood pouring from his brow and dust congealing in his throat, he managed to find his feet and stagger back to his tent. At the rear, the tent wall had been slit from the ground up to the height of a man. The thief had worked quickly and quietly under the cover of loud raucous singing, and it was hard to see that anything had been disturbed, there were simply empty spaces where his merchandise used to be. He checked under his cot for his gun and was relieved to find it still there, along with the little money he had, but the dust was gone except for the small pouch he kept in his pocket just for the feel of it.

He pushed his recollections of that day out of his mind, he must focus on the future and success. He would not be caught like that again, although there was no protection to be had from his crooked neighbours who chose to turn cloudy blind eyes to trouble, he would have to rely on his own wits.

The next afternoon an Expressman would be lying in a ditch on the route through to San Francisco, throat cut, letters from that morning's mail bag scattered to the wind. *Mr. Jacob Swain, Mrs. Susanna Wilde, Mrs. Amelia Miller...*

Walter Miller had four dollars and fifty cents and less than an ounce of gold dust to his name, he was alone in the world now, but did not know it.

CHAPTER 11

28th March 1873

The day had arrived, Nancy would finally be Mrs. Edward Miller.

She could not have been more pleased to leave Mrs. Dean's employ, the last four months had passed slowly and she had found it hard to apply herself to anything useful much to her mistress' perpetual frustration, although it was true that Mrs. Dean now offered Nancy a greater respect due to her engaged status.

Nancy was clever and resourceful, skilfully securing everything she needed from Mrs. Dean by including her in all the details of her wedding dress and veil, like she was family. Mrs. Dean fell into it. She would never play the role of the mother of the bride and Nancy cruelly exploited this to the full, allowing Mrs. Dean to believe she was valued and appreciated for her help, even that there may be some affection between them.

Visits to Madame LeBlanc's had been frequent and after long tortuous discussions, and many changes of mind, the future bride had settled on a gown of the palest pink watered silk embroidered with tiny roses, a faithful tribute to the latest fashionable designs from Paris. A short court train of pleated silk with silk-knotted trim would ensure she would sweep her way grandly up the aisle.

The long tulle veil was fastened with orange blossom woven through her hair forming a sort of coronet, and as she gazed at herself in the mirror, she was satisfied that she looked as regal as she felt.

However, the colour of the day did not match the vibrancy of her gown. It was a grey and lifeless spring day and clouds obscured all evidence of the sun, as they deepened, it looked like it would rain.

They would marry at eleven o'clock at the Church of The Advent on Bowdoin Street. Nancy thought it an ugly building but it was prominently placed and they would be seen by many passing by so she was content. The scale and grandeur of the church would add importance to the event, even though it would be a small affair, just eleven.

Ned's mother and his Aunt Adeline were too unwell to travel but Lottie, Mabel and Ida would come, Alice would stay behind to care for their mother. Nancy had already concluded that Lottie would be the main thorn in her side, the others she could manage, but Ned regarded Lottie's opinion too highly and she did not care for that.

Ned's friend Frank would be there and then of course there was the completely flawless Charles who would be bringing his sister Sarah. Thank the Lord their parents were away touring Europe or she would have had to suffer even more tiresome Broadbents.

As Mrs. Dean helped Nancy to fix her veil, her hand lingered, lost in the silkiness of it beneath her fingertips. Joining Nancy's gaze in the mirror she smiled.

'I think you are ready my dear.'

Nancy smiled back at her, the cold insincerity of it, obscured by the blurred reflection.

'I remember my wedding day very well although such a beautiful bride as you I did not make. I do believe though that my Mr. Dean thought me handsome.'

'I am sure he did' Nancy said in a throw away fashion, she was far too self-absorbed to give any care to what Mrs. Dean was saying but then caught herself *'Yes, to be sure I expect he thought you the most beautiful bride Mrs. Dean.'*

'I have something for you that I hope you will do

me the pleasure of accepting.'

Now she had Nancy's full attention.

From her watch pocket, Mrs. Dean took out a small red leather box and held it gently in her hand like it was a small, injured bird. She said nothing but her face told of re-visiting an intimate memory.

'There was a time when I had hoped we would have children but God in His infinite wisdom chose not to bless us with a family. My dearest hope was to have a daughter...' she looked down at the box *'and that I would be able to pass this on to her, but I have no one in the world of my own and such a pretty thing as this should be seen. If you will accept it I hope it will bring you luck.'*

She placed the box in Nancy's already eagerly outstretched hand. Lifting the lid, inside was the daintiest gold four-leaf clover brooch, no bigger than a thimble. It was studded with tiny rubies, emeralds, sapphires and diamonds and in the centre was a single pearl.

Although Nancy was a little disappointed at its size, it was exquisite and she could see that it was very finely made. Besides, jewels were jewels and she had none of her own, nothing more than coloured feathers and ribbons.

'Thank you Mrs. Dean, that is most kind of you. Will you fix it to my bodice?'

'Yes of course my dear' and as a distant melancholy rose up in her, fingers fumbling a little, she fixed the brooch in place. As Nancy stood back and admired herself in the mirror she felt the transformation from girl to woman. She would do the bidding now, she would have the authority she craved, she felt powerful.

CHAPTER 12

November 1872

If Nancy had approached her wedding day with a sense of victory in sight, it was not so for Ned.

His uneasy feelings in the days following his proposal to Nancy had necessarily been subsumed by the lengthy list of things that needed to be done. He had arrived at Smith's Point on that cold November day only to be met with a flood in the studio. There had been heavy snow during the previous week the weight of which had clearly found a weak point in the roof and had fallen through into the studio below. The melted snow had seeped into the rugs and floorboards and climbed the curtains. Everything smelled damp. The agent was apologetic and arranged for the roof to be fixed the next day, while Ned began the process of drying out the studio, but it was not the warm welcome he had hoped for.

After three days, fires lit in all the rooms day and night, the walls finally began to reflect back some warmth. Watertight now, no longer freezing cold, for the first time he felt able to venture out to explore his surroundings.

He took the short walk down to the shore. Past the rowan tree, through the old broken-down wooden gate, along the path of stiffly frozen saltgrass, through the cedar canopy until he reached the rocky outcrop that marked the boundary of the land and the sandy shore below him. He stood frozen, not by the chill wind blowing in off the sea, but by the majesty of the scene before him.

Even shallow breathing iced his lungs and he had to pull his collar up around his face so that his breath could warm his inflow of air. A numbing cold rose up through his boots until there was no heat left to be found in his body and his bones became stone cold, his back beginning to ache from the chill that crept in. Still, he was content to go back to the house now that he had a taste of what was to come, there would be so many days ahead to take in the beauty of the Point.

As he turned into the biting wind to make his way back he smiled as he thought of Charles, he would hate this, it had none of the comforts he needed. He was so much more suited to the tranquillity of gentle repose under the shade of a tree on a warm sunny day.

He had still received no reply from Charles to his letter about his engagement to Nancy and he was disheartened by his silence. Perhaps he had been delayed in New York City and had not received his letter yet. Charles already knew he would be at Smith's Point from the 11th and it was only the 14th so he was sure it was just a matter of time, nevertheless he was unsettled by it and it was still playing on his mind when he arrived back at the house.

Closing the door behind him he took off his overcoat and hat, rubbing his hands together, stamping his feet to try and bring some heat back to his extremities. He went to the kitchen to make tea and then climbed the stairs to his study.

The fire was burning low and he refuelled it liberally with cedar logs sending sparks spitting into the air. He settled himself at his desk and took out a sheet of paper to write to Nancy. He would let her know that all was fine at the house - no need to mention the leaking roof - and that it would make a fine and comfortable marital home for them. He would make arrangements to send her the money to buy her wedding dress and all the comforts needed for the house. She could choose her own linens, quilts, and tableware. Nancy would come to him with nothing and he knew he would need to provide it all.

He would assure her that he would interview for domestic help in due course to assist with the running of the house and the cooking, but anticipating Nancy's protestations, he would be clear that there would not be the luxury of a full-time live in servant and she would need to take her share of managing their home. For now, there was no hurry and he was enjoying living simply and alone, preparing his own meals as they were.

Over the next two weeks his life fell into a pleasant rhythm. Snowfall permitting, he would walk down to the sea most mornings as soon as it was light and then would cocoon himself in his studio greedily using as many daylight hours as possible to paint. He already found himself bewitched by the ever-changing light of the sea and the sky, he thought there could be nowhere more beautiful on earth.

He would dine early at candle-lighting and then spend his evenings reading, often Laurie would visit him, but that did somewhat depend on whether Ned felt like company and also the ferocity of the chill wind at this time of year.

Ned had still not received a reply from Charles and he was beginning to become worried. He knew the trip to New York City would not have delayed him as much as these last three weeks and if there had been a letter to Pinckney Street, he was sure Mrs Dean would have forwarded it to him and Nancy would have written of it. So, he wrote again.

30th November 1872

My dear Charles,

I write again having received no reply to my letter of 9th November regarding my engagement to Nancy Sullivan.

I trust that you and your family are in good health and hope that no difficult personal circumstances have been the cause of your silence on this matter.

I am settled here at Smith's Point these last three weeks and I am very much pleased with the house. I paint every day and delight in the location more than I can express in mere words. I understand now why you commended the area to me and why your family have been charmed by so many summer vacations here on these shores. I will be ever grateful for your assistance in helping to secure such a piece of heaven.

The house and its location will inspire my painting and it will make a most satisfactory home for us. When Nancy joins me in the spring, I hope the brighter, warmer days will help her see beyond the flaking paint and somewhat tired furnishings. I am sure she will do what only women seem to know how to do, in making a comfortable home, although I am not sure that this is necessarily where Nancy's talents lie.

The wedding is set for eleven o'clock at the Church

of The Advent on Bowdoin Street on Friday 28th March and it is my dearest hope that you would do me the honour of being my best man.

I await your earliest reply my friend, there is no other soul that could be dearer to me except in marriage, and so it is my heartfelt wish that you might be by my side.

Your affectionate friend,

Ned

Over the following days although happily employed by his painting, Ned remained distracted by the absence of any communication from Charles. Finally, a letter arrived.

6th December 1872

My dearest Ned,

How relieved I was to receive your letter today which I think must have been delayed by the difficult weather.

I regret that you did not receive my note of 11th November sent in reply to yours of 9th November. I had hoped that this would have reached you before you left Pinkney Street but failing that, assumed Mrs. Dean would be kind enough to forward it to you.

When I received no reply from you, I was hesitant to write again or send word for fear that I had offended you or overstepped a line in our friendship, something I would never want to be guilty of.

As you never received my letter, with caution, I repeat my concerns here that I am troubled by the speed of your decision to marry Miss Nancy Sullivan and whether this is the right path for you. I cast no aspersions on Miss Sullivan but simply seek to counsel against the haste of your actions. If this is what your heart desires, I respect your decision, but there is still time to reconsider if you have any reservations.

I do not seek to press you on this, but weather allowing, I hope I may visit you at Smith's Point on Sunday 14th December to speak with you about your plans. I would expect to arrive at around two o'clock and perhaps, if I could prevail on your hospitality, you might offer me supper and a bed for the night.

If this arrangement is agreeable to you please send word to confirm - perhaps by telegram if you are able to arrange it - so as to ensure I am in swiftest receipt of your reply.

I remain as ever your dearest friend,

Charles

As arranged, Charles came to the house on the fourteenth. In so many ways it was as if no time had passed, but in other ways, there was a distance between them to be crossed.

With obvious delight in seeing each other again, Ned proudly and enthusiastically, showed Charles around the house and studio. Charles thought the work Ned had done during his short time at Smith's Point was beyond anything he had painted before and told him so. There was something about the way he captured the light and the animation this brought to a static image, every scene appeared more magical when it came from Ned's brush.

Charles stood back and carefully studied one particular painting that caught his eye. Ned had painted a rowan tree that could be seen from the studio balcony. He had captured the sparkling snow-laden landscape and the raging sea beyond perfectly but it was the rowan tree that seemed to be reaching out from the canvas. Branches extended like arms of welcome, laden with snow, but through which its blood red berries glistened like jewels.

'This is sublime Ned. I think it may be your finest yet. You know a rowan is supposed to be the threshold between this world and the next?'

'Yes and my protection against witchcraft too apparently, something I hope to never need!'

'You truly have a rare gift. I wonder, would you consider selling this painting to me?'

'Sell it to you? With all my heart I would gladly

give it to you as some small token of our friendship and gratitude for your many kindnesses.'

'The words "small token" do not lend themselves in any way to this magnificent painting Ned. I could search the world and never find a painting upon which I would more gladly gaze.'

'Consider it yours!'

Charles' composure was shaken momentarily. 'You are sure?'

'I am sure.'

That evening they dined on a simple supper suited to Ned's limited cooking abilities and then pulled their chairs to the fire for warmth.

They talked for hours but Charles found it hard to prove his case in the courtroom of the heart, where there were no laws or rules he recognised, a place where, by his own admission, he could bear no witness to logic or proof.

Ned was settled on marrying Nancy, he had given her his word, still Charles could not reconcile himself with his friend's intentions. Did he seek to follow society's conventions afraid to be outside them? Was he fearful of living a life alone? Was he to be this girl's unwitting saviour from a wretched life? She was beautiful Ned had said, but was so little a thing enough to secure his heart? At every line of questioning, Ned turned him back, Charles had rested his case but had lost.

By the time they retired for the night, they remained as united in their friendship as ever, but at odds regarding Nancy. Charles agreed to be Ned's best man and through clever negotiation on his part, payment for the painting was replaced by the offer and acceptance, of paying for a reception for the whole wedding party at Parker's.

When Charles left the next morning, he took with him his deep concern for his friend's future and when the painting arrived a week later, those feelings were re-ignited. As he carefully unwrapped it he was once again moved by its beauty and when he read Ned's inscription on the back, he wept.

As for Ned, after Charles' visit he had been left with a feeling he could not name but when the day of the wedding came, he knew *drowning* was the word. He was out of safe harbour and adrift at sea.

CHAPTER 13

September 1880

Ned could hear raised voices coming up from the kitchen. Unable to make out the words, he had experience enough to know that there would be consequences, so he was on alert. Still, he vainly tried to re-absorb himself in this evening's book. Then Nancy burst into the room in a highly agitated state and he knew this was the unwelcome prelude to a fight.

She charged across the room to where he was sitting in his armchair near the fire.

'Mary will have to go. She is lazy and impertinent and I would expect that you would not want your wife to be spoken to in such a cheeky way. She is constantly complaining and over-estimates her value to this household. I will not tolerate it.'

'I have not found her to be so.' he countered carefully without taking his eyes from his book.

'You have not found her to be so? It is clear that she keeps her sassy remarks for me and that she is nothing but polite and accommodating where you

are concerned.'

Closing his book quietly he turned and looked up into her face *'I can only say that I have not witnessed such disagreeable behaviour on her part, or a reluctance to carry out her duties, which she appears to do perfectly adequately.'*

Her eyes had narrowed to black slits and she was biting her lip hard enough to draw blood and he knew that her attack had begun to turn in his direction. *'I think that is because you do not care to look. You lock yourself away in your studio from morning to night with little thought for the running of this house or for your wife's travails. You hardly seem to notice my hardships or pay me any attention at all except when I sit for you.'*

This was a very old and often repeated line of complaint on her part. The house was small and they lived simply, there was little for her to concern herself with except to mete out orders to Mary.

'We often dine together, we spend most of our evenings together, I encourage you to walk with me and enjoy the beauty of our surroundings but to no avail. Even after all these years you appear to have no interests or hobbies to occupy you. If there had been something that would interest you and lift your spirits, be sure I would have encouraged you, but I have seen no such desire.'

'Well, it is clear that my expectations of what married life would be are very different from yours in every respect. I did not suppose that I would be merely an object to be drawn or painted at whim by a husband who shows little interest in his wife except when she is on canvas.'

There was truth in her words and it stung him. *'Believe me when I say that I am sorry that marriage to me is such a disappointment to you.'*

His contrition took none of the fury out of her words *'I did not expect that I would be shut up here with you every day with no amusement and that our only visitors would be Charles or your family.'*

'Do you not come and go as you like?'

Ned knew that what she really meant was that she wanted the freedom to do as she pleased and he expected that the likes of Silas Browne would come into their lives again. It was only a matter of time, but for now, she found herself without the necessary affections of a man. If she knew anything of Charles' part in cutting her off from her lover she would have even worse things to say about him. She must never know; Browne must remain the cruel lover who heartlessly abandoned her affections.

'Do we not have a comfortable home? Have I ever discouraged you from entertaining your own friends here?' She had none. *'I do not expect you to wait*

on me or subjugate your desires and ambitions in favour of mine. Your mind and your body are your own to use as you choose and I do not seek to promote some old-fashioned view of a woman's place in the world. You are free to explore whatever interests you and nourish your mind in any way you wish.'

'How pretty and noble your words are! As long as you have your painting and your friends and family, I do not believe you give a care for anything else, including your wife.'

Truth stung again. Nancy was a fact in his life but brought nothing to him that he had hoped for or wanted and he blamed himself. In all his fine words his motives were not entirely selfless. Despite the terrible trial she had put him and Charles and Uncle William through, it would still serve him well for her to have her own interests and friends, even lovers, as long as they were not the Silas Browne's of this world.

'I have given you everything I promised you from our marriage.'

'You have? I wonder that there would be any woman who would be satisfied with my lot. No parties, no jewels, no attention from my husband, not even any children.'

There, she had said it. She would no more want to be a mother than he would want her to be the mother of his children, but she wielded it as a weapon anyway. She sought to wound him in any way she could. They both knew she had no love in her to give to a child or indeed any natural inclination to put anyone before herself.

A child would be a miracle; there was no intimacy between them and they did not share a bed. Ned had learnt early in their marriage that the kind of love she wanted to give was not the nature of the love he wanted to receive. Hers was not born of kindness and giving but of possession and control. Still, there was guilt, as he knew she suffered for the lack of it.

Ned did not respond but she was determined to escalate their fight and with a sweep of her arm knocked the book from his hands. She would have his full attention. *'It is no wonder you have nothing to say, you are frequently guilty of treating me with coldness and disregard and have nothing of the qualities required to be a good husband. No woman could endure such cruelty.'*

'I have no intention of being cruel and I am sorry you continue to be so disappointed in me as a husband. I have tried to the limits of my ability to satisfy you but you remind me again that I have failed dismally. Let us not fight, it serves us both ill.'

'With every word you say, you reveal yourself as a weak pathetic man.'

'If it is weak to prize peace over war then I am

happily a weak man.'

'There is no strength in it, no virtue in being a peacemaker, if that is what you seek.'

'It is.'

She was ugly when she was raging like this. Any small piece of her that appeared sweet turned sour like milk and despite her beauty, there was never a more worthy grotesquerie than she in moments like these.

'If you gave me one ounce of the admiration and appreciation you give your precious Charles, I would be happily weighed down with it. I ask, why is it that you seek his company so readily but not mine? I am your wife! He has never hidden his dislike for me, he has done everything possible to turn you against me; I got in the way of him keeping you to himself! Believe me, no amount of money or charm can blind me to that man's peculiarities, I see what he is.'

Her words about Charles again summed up all that was stupid and vulgar about her.

'Please do not speak ill of Charles again.'

'Or else husband?'

'It is unedifying and beneath any civilised person, to speak so wildly and inaccurately about such a good and honourable man. I thought your discomfiture was to do with Mary? You are the mistress of this house and if it be your decision,

let her go but remember, she is far from home with no family and has committed no misdemeanour, so be assured she will leave this house with a good character reference.'

She began pacing the floor again, hands on her hips, eyes raised to the ceiling.

'You seek to divert me. I will not have it!'

'I seek to address your original complaint, it is for you to decide what is right, what is fair.'

'Be warned husband, you push me too far, I will not stand for it. Perhaps I shall leave you and this house, how would that be? How harshly you would be judged.'

'I fear it may be you that would attract harsh judgement in such circumstances, but still, I do not seek to keep you here against your will.' Ned stood slowly and deliberately as a signal that their discussion was over.

Spinning round to face him, she spat in his face. Immediately she knew she had gone too far.

It was too much for Ned, all his senses were afflicted by the poison that flowed from her, still she stood her ground defiantly and waited for a reaction. Without looking at her he took a handkerchief from his pocket and wiped her spittle from his face and then cast her poison into the fireplace. He steadied himself and walked to the door. He did not turn to look at her, but looking down, almost as if addressing his own hand on the doorknob, he spoke quietly but firmly.

'I will leave you to make your decision about Mary but I believe her to be most unjustly maligned by you and that will be on your conscience. I shall take my leave of you now and wish you goodnight.'

That night in his room, a deep and troubling sleep took him over, the like of which he had never experienced before. The light from a disembodied lamp entered his otherwise dark room as he felt everything solid retreating from him. Then he was no longer in his bed but in a place he did not know, where shadows without form moved and crept around him.

A sweet and pungent smell, both delicious and detestable, filled his nostrils and seeped into his brain. His body felt cold and weighed down but his footsteps were light and silent on the soft ground below his feet as he carried his burden.

A silent swaying canopy above him rose and dipped touching his head and his shoulders gently, and as his exertions forced the air from his lungs, all the while thousands of tiny red insects crawled on his skin and then dropped from his fingertips like rain.

The smell of the earth, the whisper of the

sea, followed him down deeper and deeper into the blackness where no eyes could see. Rest was found there.

Ned woke late the next morning soaked in sweat but thankfully, with the promise of the new day, the monstrosity of last evening had been swept away. Peace was recovered and the house was quiet and calm except for the sound of birds excitedly chattering outside. He knew Nancy would already have gone into town and he felt the relief of their time apart so that her fury could subside, they would both benefit from it. He pulled on his robe and went to his studio opening the doors onto the balcony. He breathed in the fresh sea air, and the wakening sunlight dispelled the last remnants of sleep, he was restored.

CHAPTER 14

August 1873

The contents of today's letter from Lottie had disturbed him greatly and he had immediately settled on visiting Greenbrook as soon as possible.

On sharing the news with Nancy, she had acted out some level of concern for his mother's continuing poor health but this did not extend to accompanying Ned on his visit home, he would go alone. It suited him.

Nancy did little to hide her disinterest in his family and the boredom she felt in their company, it would do him no favour to have to carefully manage her sensibilities, so there would be some relief in leaving her behind.

Nancy had only met Ned's mother once. As Amelia had been too ill to attend their wedding Ned had taken his new bride to visit her shortly after their marriage, where they had passed three very pleasant days at the house, or at least Ned had. Nancy had made no secret of counting the hours until their departure.

Amelia's joy at seeing him after such a long time had been palpable and in turn he had realised too just how much he had missed her company. Apart from Charles and Lottie, there was no one that felt more like his own, not even Nancy. Time with his mother felt like home.

Lottie had been excited to see them too and had welcomed her new sister warmly into their home. Alice, Mabel and Ida all visited with their children over the course of the three boisterous and happy days and the sisters took great pleasure in telling Nancy stories about Ned as a child while she feigned interest in the details all too convincingly.

The weather had been kind and they had spent time in the garden and taking walks into the town while the children had climbed, chased, jumped, and dizzied themselves running between their mothers and aunts and uncle. They had picnicked under the apple tree nearest the stream and Lottie had delighted her nephews and nieces with the somewhat exaggerated story of Uncle Ned falling from the tree, she gave them all of the hilarity and drama, none of the horror. Ned had played his part in the telling of the tale by re-enacting the events of that day and bewailing his aching back whilst hobbling about theatrically making the little ones scream with laughter.

Their visit had also allowed Ned to spend precious time alone with his mother, and although she had put on a convincing performance of normality, he had seen the change in her as the shadows of her malaise steadily crept over her.

The cause for alarm in Lottie's letter had been, that for the first time, Amelia was not getting out of bed. Lottie had continued that, three days earlier their mother had woken feeling extremely tired almost unable to open her eyes and with her usual stomach complaint more troublesome than usual, so she had thought a day of complete bed rest might restore her. One day had turned into two and now three.

She did not ask him to come but Ned needed to see for himself, to speak with her doctor. As it was already gone noon, he would not travel to Watertown today, he would go to her first thing tomorrow morning.

This afternoon he would use the time to complete the portrait of Nancy. It would be a welcome distraction, not demanding much of him, this portrait was after all a perfunctory thing, rather than something about which he cared.

Nancy had petitioned him relentlessly in the months following their marriage for a painting to celebrate her status as a new bride and mistress of the house. So contrived was it in its genesis that he came to it reluctantly and without joy, he was learning that resistance was of no merit where Nancy was concerned, early surrender to her wishes was prudent.

It was a wholly artificial and unnatural composition staged by Nancy herself. The bohemian red glass vase of roses on the table beside her, the open window to illuminate and flatter her skin, the single rose casually laid in her lap. She had even wanted him to paint two white doves at the window but he had refused something so incongruous and forced. Even the four-leaf clover brooch Mrs. Dean had given her was dismissed as too bright and naïve for such a scene of sophistication and grandeur; she would wear the large gold locket Ned had given her as a wedding present instead.

She had an ideal of herself as a fine beauty and

indeed the composition of her face was sublime but he had already come to see the sum of her beauty in a different way. The look of her, what came from within, was cold and hollow but he had come to know that it was transformed on the canvas when the greater glory of a landscape or seascape gathered her in. She was of beauty, not beauty itself.

Still, today as she sat looking towards the window, to the undiscerning eye she looked radiant. The pale pink of her gown matched the blush of her skin as if she were washed in a sunset light. Her long slim neck rose up from her lace collar like a sapling breaking through snow, rising and stretching towards the sky, the sun illuminating her face as he transformed her into a marble goddess.

He had painted the folds of her dress with pigment laden strokes of vibrant pink and with a wetted brush had delicately pulled out the colour from the darker strokes before they dried. The process brought luxurious depth to the folds and soft light to the silk capturing the feel of it not just the look of it.

As he added the final details to her eyes with fine brush strokes of black and burnt umber he saw that she stared out at him from the canvas, not with the open look of a bride in the first flush of love, but as a disappointed lover perhaps already resigned from love.

He stood back to take in the almost finished painting, he could see that he had achieved a satisfying weight and substance to her form, she would be solid and present there in the room with anyone who looked on the painting. Not lightly surfacing the canvas, but of it, Mrs. Miller immortalised.

As always, she found it impossible to stay quiet *'What time shall you leave tomorrow?'*

'Before seven o'clock. I shall not wake you.'

'And how long will you be away?'

'I hope to return home by the last train on Wednesday evening.'

'I would not think that your mother would want to keep you away from your new bride for two whole days.'

'My mother makes no such request of me; I use my own judgement about how long it would be wise to allow for my visit. I anticipate there will be things to attend to.'

'Ah, then perhaps it is I that would hope a new groom would not want to be parted from his love for so long.'

'I shall return to you before you have even noticed me gone I am sure, you will have Mary for company by day, you will not be lonely.'

'In giving me that answer sir, I think you have little understanding of a woman's heart.'

'Of that I am sure I am guilty.'

He always gave in too easily and it left her frustrated and dissatisfied. To her it was another sign of his weakness, he was not her match.

'There, it is finished.' He put down his brush. *'I hope you will be pleased with it.'*

She stood, and stretching her back, sighed loudly.

'Let me see it. You have been most unkind in not showing me your progress these last few days.'

She did not seek the artist's permission and now standing beside him on the other side of the canvas, looked with fascination at her reflection. Taking a step back she took in the glory of the painting, not interested in the success of it in celebration of his talent, but in checking that her beauty had not been diminished in any way by his lack of it. Tilting her head from one side to the other, finally she said *'It is an exceptionally good likeness my love and I think will create a great impression on those who gaze upon it. It will do very well thank you. I am happy with it.'*

And with those words, Ned knew he had no care for her happiness with it, it was done and he was released from it.

The next day, as he approached Greenbrook, he was instantly transported back to his childhood. He had always loved the symmetry of their pretty white house, its simple lines and low pitch roof, adding to its solid and reassuringly sturdy impression. It had been a place of safety and refuge for them all.

Left and right of the porch, white and purple asters still frothed in a disorderly way as they always had but crabgrass now claimed every crevice and crack in the path, a forlorn sign of recent neglect. All the windows were open - his mother liked a breeze to chase through the house – and the smell of freshly baked cornbread wound its way out to greet him. He was home.

Lottie was at the door before he could even knock, like she had expected him to arrive at that very moment. Framed against the green front door, arms open wide, ready to catch apples.

'Ned you came.' He saw the relief in her face.

'Of course, how could I not? How is our mother?'

'She seems a little better today and sat out in her chair this morning for a short while although she could not bear it for long. You are truly like the prodigal son returned brother, her spirits will be greatly lifted by your visit, like no other could do.' There was no jealousy in her voice. *'Come into the kitchen for some tea, then you can take some to mamma, she will be so much more delighted by the sight of your face at her door than mine!'*

As they sat facing each other across the kitchen table he watched his sister as she poured their tea, that pretty girl with the halo of golden curls, now aged and careworn by life. As she placed his cup in front of him he covered her hand with his and squeezed it. She smiled at him but they said nothing, both with full hearts, both empty of words.

As he stood at his mother's door she called out. *'John?'*

He stepped over the threshold *'It is Ned mamma.'*

As he approached her, everything was exactly as it had always been except she seemed so small in her bed, like a child.

She stared at him in disbelief. *'It really is you. My darling boy your mother is so happy to have you home. Come sit by me.'*

He set her tea down on the bedside table, next to the portraits of her dead babies and John and pulled a chair close to her bed. She reached out and touched his face and then traced her finger along his hairline pushing back a curl of hair.

'You look well, marriage favours you. How is Nancy? Is she here?'

'Nancy is well mamma but could not come with me this time. She sends her fondest regards to you and hopes you in better health soon.' He lied.

'That is kind of her.'

'Tell me how you are. We are concerned that you seem more unwell these last few days. What does the doctor say?'

'I need no doctor, I have had many babies before and once this one is born, I will be well again.' She looked down and laid her hand gently on the mound in the blanket.

Ned was stricken by her words.

'It will be a boy I think. Your father will be pleased to no longer be in a house full of women.'

'Why do you mention my father?'

'Why would I not? He has been most considerate and kind these last few weeks, so loving and attentive, is that not wonderful? You are so like him my darling.'

'But my father is not here mamma, you were dreaming again perhaps?'

Amelia hesitated before answering *'I was not dreaming but perhaps it is true that he is not here now'* and she glanced around the room anxiously.

'It is just you and I mamma.'

She did not appear to hear and looked away from him towards the open window. He followed her gaze but there was nothing there. He would send Martha to fetch the doctor immediately. He would also write to Uncle William in the morning.

'I do not wish to tire you further, I will leave you to rest and will come back later with some supper, we can dine together.'

As he got up to leave, she reached for his hand and held it with more strength than he thought she had in her body *'Stay away from the tree my darling.'*

With no understanding of what she meant,

he nodded to reassure her.

'Rest now mamma.' She smiled at him and closed her eyes.

There was no shared supper that evening, she was gone, out through the open window and free at last. In the depths of his grief that was how Ned chose to see it.

CHAPTER 15

November 1883

Ned opened the door to Charles, who stood on his doorstep a tower of black from head to toe, snow glittering on his overcoat like a scattering of stars against a dark sky. Stamping his feet to keep warm and blowing on his numb fingertips he protested *'How long does a man have to stand in the freezing cold? I shall turn to a pillar of ice if you make me stand here much longer.'*

'Come in, come in! We shall have you warm in no time.'

Flakes of snow showered everywhere as he removed his hat and coat. Casting off the blackness, underneath his attire was as vibrant as ever, the centrepiece of which was a fine dark blue wool waistcoat that had a row of red jewel-like glass buttons down the front. Charles always left Ned feeling a little underdressed.

They climbed the stairs to the parlour *'The fire is lit and awaits you! It is so good to see you my friend.'* Ned ushered Charles to his own chair nearest the fire, it was by far the most comfortable and away from any draughts, Ned took the one opposite.

'Tell me, how are your parents?'

'They do very well although the long cold winters are not conducive to their health these days. They find their summer visits here in Manchester restorative and I believe they plan to spend more time here if possible away from the bustle of the city. They send their kindest regards to you.'

'Please return mine to them. I hope that I might then see more of them this summer if we are to be frequent neighbours.'

'Beware, my father always has you in his sights as a chess partner! Remember, you could surrender many hours of a summer's evening to his grip if you weaken your resolve.'

'I consider myself forewarned! And how is Sarah?'

'Sarah is in good spirits despite all her health endures. She stays positive and busy and remains in high demand! The commissions for sketches and watercolours for greetings cards are more abundant than you can imagine and she finds such joy in it. I still say it was an exceptionally good day when you first came to Beacon Street and took her under your wing. You saw what I did not and I am forever chastened that I had any misgivings about her abilities. Although had I not considered her lacking them, you would never have come to give her lessons

of course!'

Ned smiled. *'I think her to have always had a good eye and sound technique but had there been any shortfall at all in her talents, I believe someone of such a sweet and positive nature would always have painted with a delightful optimism that transcends any skill that is lacking. Please give her my fondest regards.'*

'With the greatest pleasure, any word from her Mr. Miller is received with enthusiasm, she remains a great admirer of yours.' Charles smiled gently, and catching Ned's eye, they both understood.

'So, my friend, I knew that only you would be foolish enough to take on such inclement weather as this. The snow covers the path and all around it, so it is a wonder that you could find your feet to get here.'

'It is such a short journey from the town and the carriage was able to bring me to within a hundred paces of the house, I am happy to endure it! Besides, I find such a journey settles the mind. There is something profoundly calming when all detail is erased from sight by snow, like I am the only words being written on a blank sheet of paper.'

Words to Charles were as paints on canvas to Ned.

'Please do not worry yourself, a carriage returns for me at three o'clock so I will take my leave of you before the light begins to fade for safe passage back

to town. How is Nancy, is she here?'

'She is but I believe will again absent herself from our company this afternoon. Nancy continues to prefer spending time in her own rooms, or on pursuits that take her away from our home, so we spend ever lessening time together.' Ned's words hung in the air uncomfortably.

'It is clear she seeks to avoid me both here and when you visit Boston as she never accompanies you. Charles dropped his voice to a whisper. *'I assume she still knows nothing of my involvement in resolving that terrible Silas Browne business?'* Charles was shaken by the mere memory of it.

'She knows nothing of it and please do not think that there is any misdemeanour on your part that would give her cause to avoid you, I fear that Nancy's issues are all of her own making, it appears to be her way. We both know that I have not found marriage to be anything of what I had hoped and this is true for Nancy too, although it is hard to know what a man would need to be, for her to be satisfied with her lot in life.'

'The delicacies of love are happily a mystery to me.' Charles tried to lighten the mood.

'That may be true, but you are my wisest counsel in this whole world, and I do not forget your words of warning to me on telling you of my engagement. You saw better than I what lay ahead and I lament my

misplaced ego and asinine approach to marriage.'

'It is often easier for others to look into our hearts than to know our own. We need not talk of what troubles you, tell me that you have been prolific in your painting and are much pleased with your labours.'

Ned appreciated the change of direction in their conversation and took Charles' lead.

'I am encouraged just this last week to have four paintings displayed with Williams & Everett. Mr. Williams is most effusive about my seascapes and assures me there is a raging fashion for them. It is apparent, those who live in towns and cities have a desire to have a view of the sea, even if it only hangs over their mantlepiece!'

'Very much less expensive than renting your own summer house!' Charles laughed.

'Indeed! Mr Williams is confident that my paintings will be well received. He displays them in the most superb setting. Have you ever been to the gallery?'

'No, I do not think that has been my pleasure.'

'It is on the corner of Bedford and Washington Street. You should take Sarah even if just to see the paintings on the ground floor, I am sure she would enjoy it greatly, it is the most inspiriting experience to go there. I know Frank intends to go, perhaps you

and Sarah might join him? It has the most wonderful ambience with fine wood panelling, the grandest staircase leading to the galleries on the upper floors and a towering carved chimney piece that extends all the way to the ceiling. I tell you Charles, it is the perfect setting to display paintings, I could happily spend a week there!'

'On your effusive recommendation, we shall go for certain. Sarah will be cheered by such a pleasurable outing and always enjoys Frank's company.'

'Both Mr. Williams and Mr. Everett are very well connected and I believe my association with them could serve me very well. There have also been discussions about an exhibition, if I am able to build up an adequate body of work that is, we shall see.'

'I am delighted to hear that but remind you, as I have so many times before, that I have many wealthy and influential acquaintances who seek a fine artist for portraiture. I would be happy to make introductions and I am confident that this would result in a legion of profitable commissions for you.'

'Thank you Charles but as far as I am able, even as the man of meagre means I am, I seek to serve my art not for it to serve me. I do not wish to appear ungrateful in any way but the prospect of long hours painting a precocious spoilt child holding

its manicured pet or a matronly lady who fancies herself as the next Mona Lisa would sink my spirits. It is the scene that commands me, or the joy of a moment that inspires me to paint, I find pieces of silver blur my vision and stunt my talent.'

'I consider myself truly chastised! I understand, I simply desire that you might feel comfortable and free from financial burden, such a talent as yours should bring riches.'

'Well on that you are in concord with Nancy although her desire for my financial success comes from a more selfish position. Painting already brings me riches beyond measure, but nothing that will fill my pockets to overflowing, much to her disappointment.'

Charles noticed that Ned was shifting uncomfortably in his chair.

'I have taken your chair, please let us exchange, it will give you some relief.'

'No, no, my back just needs some stirring, if I sit still too long, it settles painfully. I have learnt its ways over the years and how to overcome it. Shall I call for Mary to bring us some hot chocolate?'

'That would be most welcome.'

They passed another enjoyable hour in each other's company until Charles glanced towards the clock on the mantlepiece and sighed *'I fear I must leave you, the light will be lost within the hour, and my carriage awaits!'*

Ned sent his friend off into the snow with a promise that he would visit him at Beacon Street within the month.

'I thought he would never leave.' Nancy's thin irritated voice came from behind him.

'We had much to catch up on.'

'Talking about me I suppose.'

'Charles always enquires after you Nancy, that you are well, why would he not?'

She scowled at him and sighed loudly, there was nothing to be gained by being in the same space as her today, so he would leave her to herself.

He lit the lamps, closed the blinds and settled himself by the fire in the parlour, but staring into the flames, Charles' departure had left him feeling empty and lonely. By his nature he savoured time alone and sought blissful solitude at every opportunity unless his companion was the sea, or a bird, or some other inquisitive creature. Lonely was different, like a space opening up inside him, nothing to fill it.

After eating the supper of cold meats and pickle Mary had laid out for him he must have dozed in the chair because he was awoken by

Laurie knocking at the door. *'Come in my friend'* he could hear himself saying, not aloud, but in his head. They drank beyond reason and the night drifted away, sometimes in ways that reached the heights of sweetness, sometimes in the depths of all that was sour.

Two days after Charles' visit with Ned at Smith's Point, Elizabeth Broadbent stepped from a carriage onto the frozen sidewalk outside the Williams & Everett gallery. She was a tall and handsome woman and expensively dressed, people noticed her. Her gown of magenta-coloured fine merino wool and the dark green velvet Dolman with fur trim were intricately appliqued with tiny beads of peacock blues and greens. A fur muff and fur brimmed hat - her protection against the biting cold - completed the elegant ensemble.

She was noticed from inside the gallery too and was met at the door by Mr. Williams. Ready to assist her, he was at her most humble service. He was tall and thin with a long angular face and a beak-like nose but his face was kind and friendly dark eyes looked out at her from under his bushy grey eyebrows.

He bowed gracefully and without any of the usual limitations of movement for a man of his advanced years. *'Good day madam, welcome to Williams & Everett. I am Mr. Williams co-proprietor of the gallery; can I direct you in any way? Perhaps there is something in particular you are looking for today?'*

'Thank you Mr. Williams, I look for a painting for my drawing room, something exceptional. I believe I will know when I find something fitting and would be grateful if you would be available to wait on me then.'

'Of course, please take as much time as you need, I am sure we will have something that meets your requirements. To assist your visit, you will find the paintings of more established artists on the ground floor, on the upper floor you will find the works of a number of new and exciting talented artists. Williams & Everett has a long-established reputation for discovering the celebrated artists of tomorrow.' He gave her a wide confident smile that revealed every crooked tooth in his mouth.

'That is very reassuring Mr. Williams, I am sure I will leave your establishment highly satisfied.'

Elizabeth felt he had stayed just within the boundaries of helpfulness without being brash and he was clearly proud of his establishment which made her smile to herself, she liked that.

She did not linger on the ground floor but slowly climbed the staircase with its beautiful winding balustrade and intricate carvings until, at the turn of the stairs, a sign pointed the direction to the galleries above. As she reached the top step she was met by a wonderful soft light that gently and evenly illuminated the wood panelling. Paintings stretched as far as her eyes could see around a large square room off which were smaller anterooms. There was a hush and the only sound was the tap of her boot heels and the soft swish of her skirt on the wooden floor.

She stopped at a painting of a smiling young girl sitting by a window. She was about three years old and looked like her own daughter. A scene of a carefree child with so much ahead to look forward to, it was enchanting, but sorrowful for her. She moved on.

Having made it halfway around the gallery, she passed the opening to one of the anterooms and as she looked in, she knew she had found them. In an ocean of dark and muted colours there they were. Splashes of white, the softest pinks, blues, and greys of nature but not of man. She stepped in approaching the four seascapes that hung together, scenes she recognised from her times in Manchester of sunset light, of storms, of morning light; they were magical. There was his signature, *Edward W. Miller.*

Having summoned Mr. Williams they stood side by side in front of the paintings.

'Madam, I believe you have made an excellent

choice. Mr. Everett and I consider Edward Miller to be a most talented artist with a distinctive style, we are proud to display his work here at the gallery. Is there one of the four that you particularly favour?'

'I think them all exquisite and impossible to choose between but perhaps the scene at sunset, oh dear no, perhaps the scene at sunrise, the colours are so beautiful and would complement the blue of my drawing room.'

'I think either would look most elegant in a drawing room madam.'

'I agree, so I shall take both.'

Mr. Williams was a little taken aback by her swift decision but gathered himself quickly. *'Both would be delightful I am sure.'*

The price was agreed and arrangements were made for the delivery of the paintings to Beacon Street the next day.

'I am most pleased Mr. Williams and shall tell my friends of your establishment and your excellent service.'

'That is most kind madam, we are always most grateful for any commendations.'

'One final matter, I am sure it is not necessary to mention, but my name should not be known to the artist should he enquire. I wish to remain an anonymous admirer of his fine work.'

'Yes of course madam, be assured.'

'Good day Mr. Williams and thank you for your kind assistance.'

'Good day madam.'

16 November 1883

Mr. Edward Miller,
Smith's Point,
Manchester,
Mass.

Dear Mr. Miller,

I hope this letter finds you in good health.

I am delighted to inform you that yesterday we sold two of your paintings (catalogued nos. EM3 & EM4) and I am pleased to report that the buyer was delighted with her purchases and I think may look to acquire more of your work in future.

Might I request that you visit the gallery at your earliest convenience so that we can arrange payment details with you for the sale of your art, which after Williams & Everett's usual commissions, amounts to a total of $105.00.

I hope you are content with the sale price we have achieved on your behalf and please do consider whether you have other similar works that you might display here at the Gallery.

I would also welcome the opportunity to recommence our recent discussion about a possible exhibition of your work in the upper gallery.

Yours sincerely,

H.D. Williams
Williams & Everett

CHAPTER 16

August 1869

Ned had looked forward to visiting Beacon Street since first the date was set, and now as he walked up the street paralleling the wrought iron railings of the Common, counting the house numbers, he found himself looking across the street at the Broadbents' home.

To his mind it was the most handsome townhouse on the street. A four-storey Federal-style building, simple and symmetrical in its design, with evenly spaced tall sash windows sandwiched between black slatted shutters and a first-floor wrought iron balustrade that ran its full width. Its cornicing and embellishments were all plain and yet more elegant for their intentional simplicity. All except the transom light which was a complicated weave of metal and glass that wove itself into the shape of a lady's lace fan.

On paper, Ned knew Pock would criticise it as too plain, in reality, he would have to admit that it was exactly as it should be and worked perfectly.

He crossed the street and up the stone steps to the front door. He was about to knock but found himself momentarily distracted by the mirror-polished brass door knocker, it was large and ornate, the strike plate embossed with the scales of justice. As he lifted the hammer and struck the plate, he thought the sound eloquently embodied the solemn weight of justice; all who entered would know the hallmark of the house.

Through the door he could hear the quick light tap of heels on marble tiles, and as the door swung open, a young housemaid stood smiling at him.

'Good day sir, how may I help you?'

'I am here as an invited guest of Mr. Charles Broadbent and Miss Sarah Broadbent. I am expected at three o'clock, but my apologies, I am a little early.'

'Are you Mr. Miller?'

'I am.'

'Please come in sir, I will let them know you are here. If you would wait in the library I am sure they will be with you presently.'

She led him to a door on the left of the large entrance hall, and as she opened it, he was met by the smell of beeswax and the vanilla-perfume of old books. There was also a vague, pungent, musty smell but he could not place it. *'Please take a seat sir.'* She smiled again and left him closing the door quietly behind her.

It was an impressive room. There was one whole wall of books, which appeared perfectly ordered, with the shelves stretching from floor to ceiling and a sliding ladder to reach the highest three rows.

A white marble fireplace was the centrepiece of the room and over it hung the portrait of an eminent looking gentleman. Ned recognised the eyes so it was likely a Broadbent, Charles' grandfather perhaps? Two well-worn leather armchairs flanked the fireplace like bookends, seats sagging, many derrieres having found comfort and respite in them over the years. Between them on the floor, a wicker basket inside which was a mis-shapen cushion, also well used and crumpled.

On the other side of the room near the window was a mahogany desk on which stood the most unusual chess set he had ever seen. He decided to take a closer look, and just as he picked up the Queen to study her decoration, Charles Broadbent burst through the door.

'Mr. Miller, how good to see you. Do you play?' Ned, feeling like he was trespassing, replaced the piece quickly on the board. *'No, not really, but this is surely the most magnificent set, it would make you*

want to play.'

'My father is the greatest advocate for the game. Two things I have known since a child, I was required to be just and fair in all my relationships and obligations but perhaps equally important, I must learn to play chess!'

Charles approached the desk and picked up one of the pawns and studied it turning it over in his hand. *'My father believes that a man who can play chess well, will always find a way to stay one step ahead of his opponents in life, a material advantage he would say. However, utmost he is always a champion for those considered the pawns in life.'* He carefully placed the piece back on the board.

'My sister is excited to meet you today and very much looks forward to her lesson. She awaits us in the drawing room if you are ready.'

'I am sorry I am a little early.'

'Are you? She has been ready this last half hour so please do not concern yourself on our account. You will find her the sweetest child with never a complaint passing her lips despite her unfortunate circumstances. You see, she does not walk I am afraid, I wanted you to be aware so that your face does not show surprise when you first meet. She is completely content with her lot, but on her behalf, I feel for the loss of her freedom and liberty acutely as you might imagine.'

'Thank you for telling me, may I enquire the cause of her incapacity?'

'A childhood accident. She was but five years old, when she tripped and fell down the stairs chasing Beau, her dog. We had just moved to this house and she and Beau were both excited, running from room to room, unfamiliar with its spaces, its dangers. Beau was chasing a ball and Sarah was chasing Beau. In a moment, the course of her life changed, as did ours. Not a soul in this house will ever forget the sound of her screams and I can attest that these last ten years have not lessened the memory of the sight of her little body lying twisted, well, like a discarded rag doll.'

Ned could see that Charles was moved by the retelling of such a terrible event and the vision of the cruel chain that linked ball – Beau – Sarah – fall.

'I am so sorry to have brought such tragic recollections to mind, please forgive my insensitivity, I should not have asked.'

'Not necessary my friend and do not mind me, it is the plight of the Broadbent men to be tender-hearted, a burden we all gladly embrace. Come, she will become impatient!'

Sarah was every bit as sweet as Charles had described and for the third time Ned was met by the steady blue gaze of the Broadbent eyes and a wide, open smile. She was propped up with cushions on a blue velvet chaise longue, twice her length, she did in fact look like a doll.

There was a desk in front of the window on which her painting materials were laid out ready and beside it, a chair with metal-rimmed wooden wheels and an upholstered seat and arm rests, a leviathan for such a little creature as she.

'Mr. Miller, I am so pleased to meet you, I have been counting the hours since Charles told me you had kindly agreed to come. He thinks me in need of instruction and believes you are the man for the task.' She smiled at her brother.

'I hope I might be of help; it is always a pleasure to encourage others in discovering the joys of painting.'

'Charles tells me you are an architect by profession, I think that must be a most fascinating world, how wonderful to create something that will stand for generations.'

'Indeed. I am not yet qualified however, I train under the generous sponsorship of my uncle, and hope in time I may become as enthusiastic about architecture as he is.'

'I am sorry that my interest lies in only painting flowers and landscapes and not something more laudable, I fear you may find it rather dull to offer me instruction.'

'On the contrary, my mother is a fine

watercolourist, and particularly accomplished in painting flowers. I spent many happy hours in her studio as a child and learnt from her to fully appreciate the joy of capturing God's glorious creation through painting.'

'Ah, well then I hope your time instructing me will not be too much of a trial! I was most pleased with my birthday gift and have already begun experimenting with the paints, I would be pleased to show you. I think Charles was nervous that I might gift one of them to him and insist he hang it in his room!'

'Heaven forbid!' Charles laughed.

'Charles, will you help me to my chair?'

'Of course darling girl.'

He swept down and lifted her into his arms like she weighed nothing but said *'I believe you get heavier by the day! What have you been eating?'*

She laughed at him and tweaked his chin.

He set her down gently in her chair wheeling her around to face the desk so she could reach her brushes and paints. As he bent over her, locking the wheels in place, she whispered something in his ear which seemed to upset him. He paused momentarily looking into her face giving her a silent nod in response, then straightening up he cleared his throat to dislodge the emotion in his voice *'There, the artist is ready! I shall take my leave of you now. Shall I order some tea for you?'*

'Yes please Charles, or would you prefer coffee Mr. Miller?'

'No, tea would be much appreciated, thank you.'

'I will return at five o'clock and look forward to critiquing your work little one! Mr. Miller will you dine with us this evening? Our mother and father are so looking forward to meeting you. I can assure you; never will you meet two people more interested in just about everything, I know they will want to interrogate you thoroughly about the world of architecture. I hope you will say yes.'

'I fear I am a little underdressed for dinner.'

'No matter, we do not stand on ceremony in this house.'

'If you are sure they are happy to extend the invitation, I should be delighted to stay, thank you.'

Sarah gave a little clap of her hands.

'That is happily settled then.' Charles left them leaving the door a little ajar.

Ned pulled up a chair beside Sarah. Her wheelchair was cumbersome, and the armrests prevented her from sitting as close to the desk as would be ideal, but they managed the best they could. He was surprised to find that she had a good measure of talent, but she doubted herself, so he took care to gently encourage her throughout their time together.

He demonstrated simple techniques as they painted first a creamy-white rose and then a lilac-coloured sweetpea taken from the vase on the desk. He found Sarah had the desired light hand for preparatory sketches and a good sense of proportion, she also showed a natural understanding of colours and shading, he was sure she had much of what she would need to be a competent watercolourist.

Their compositions were staged of course and he thought how different the experience would be for her to paint in the open air, not a cut flower, but a living flower lit by the sun or a tree blown by the wind. Like Charles, he felt for her limitations and that the freedom of body and limb were not hers, perhaps though there may be a way he could help. He had an idea.

As the mantle clock struck five, Charles was at the door.

'Is it safe to come in?'

'Of course it is safe! Come see my work.'

Charles picked up the painting of the sweetpea studying it intently. *'I think you to have potential darling girl.'*

'That is what Mr. Miller says!'

Charles gave Ned an appreciative smile.

'Then it is just as well that such an accomplished painter as Mr. Miller was able to come today and show you what you could not see for yourself.'

Ned suddenly realised what had been at play. Charles had never doubted her talent but had used her suggested lack of it to get him to visit Beacon Street. He had been completely and happily duped in a very good cause.

'We all agree then, you shall have a great future as an artist! Now come little one, you should rest before we dine this evening' and he swept down and lifted her from the wheelchair.

'Thank you Mr. Miller, you have been a most generous and patient teacher and I have so enjoyed our afternoon, I very much hope you might come again. In the meantime, I promise I shall practice like a good student.'

'Shall we save our conversation for later when we dine? My back breaks standing here with you in my arms and you would yet have me carry you up the twenty-eight stairs to your room!'

'Of course, I am sorry.' Sarah tightened her arms around Charles' neck and kissed his cheek.

'Until later Mr. Miller.'

'Until later Miss Broadbent.'

Through the open door Ned watched Charles

carry his precious load up the stairs, laughing all the time, until they were out of sight and sound.

As they sat down that evening to dine, Ned was captivated by the ambience of the room. The walls were covered with green and metallic gold-striped wallpaper and the three large windows were hung with dark green velvet curtains that pooled generously onto the wooden floor beneath them. A large gilt mirror hung over the fireplace softly reflecting the light from the chandelier and candles and pastoral paintings lined the angled walls quietly telling their stories. Despite its obvious grandeur, they had made it a comfortable, intimate space.

John and Elizabeth Broadbent were everything that Ned had anticipated and they could not have made him feel more welcome in their home. They were as unapologetically inquisitive as Charles had warned and no amount of detail was too much for them, they were interested in it all.

During the soup course they learnt about his life growing up in Watertown and this continued through the salad course. Then during the *Salmon a la Hollandaise* and roast duck with apple sauce courses, Ned learnt about the Broadbent family history all the way back to their Massachusetts Bay Colony roots.

The ham timbales brought questions about life

at W. Adams & R. J. Morris, the latest designs and fashions in architecture, the rapid expansion of Boston's housing stock and the ambitious plans for Back Bay. The discussion consumed them all right up until the last spoon was laid down after finishing the *Mousse au Chocolat.*

Ned witnessed their passion for social reform, anger over the ongoing blight of segregation, their deep concern for the poor and less fortunate. '*To whom much is given, much will be required*' Elizabeth Broadbent quoted the Gospel of Luke without any note of piety but with a genuine sense of responsibility. Although she did not live the life of a free spirit as his mother did, he could see so many similarities and they shared something that united them, they were both the heart of their family.

In John Broadbent, Ned observed a devoted father with his children, something he had never experienced himself. It was clear that despite all his accomplishments, his prestigious legal career, his influential friends, in this room tonight, he was first and foremost a loving father and husband.

It made Ned aware of the open space inside him, the one that Walter Miller had put there. He may have been little more than an idea of a man to him, but in his heart, he had always hoped that it was the most impossible of circumstances that had stood in the way of his father returning to their family, to him.

'Would you like some cheese Mr. Miller? I can highly recommend the Cheshire.'

'Thank you Mrs. Broadbent, I will.'

John Broadbent looked around the table contentedly *'Sarah tells me she very much enjoyed her lesson with you today Mr. Miller, we are very grateful to you for making the time to give her some instruction.'*

'It was my pleasure and Sarah shows great promise.' He looked across at Sarah and smiled reassuringly at her.

Suddenly John Broadbent pushed back his chair and stood up. Without saying a word he went to the bureau by the window, opened the drawer, and took out a small portfolio of papers.

'John, is something the matter?'

He still said nothing as he returned to the table and laid the portfolio down carefully pulling loose the knotted purple ribbon fastening it. Then, reverently as if he were handling something rare and precious, he lifted the first sheet of paper and before revealing it, looked on it with pleasure. Then the next.

He walked around the table to where Ned was sitting and handed the first sheet of paper to him.

'I think this to be an excellent likeness of my wife do you not think?'

It was a charming sketch, simple, but it had every necessary line and shading needed to capture its subject perfectly. *'It is indeed charming and well-drawn sir. By Sarah's hand I presume?'*

'Indeed, it is.'

'Oh John, do let Mr. Miller finish his cheese.'

'And this one...' he handed Ned another drawing. It was a sketch of a dog, a Beagle he thought, dark melancholy eyes. *'...our lovely boy Beau, Sarah captures his sweet nature perfectly I think. What do you say Mr. Miller? Is it not fine?'*

'It is most fine sir and Beau is a very handsome fellow.'

'I have more. I would like to frame and hang them but Sarah will not allow it.'

'Oh papa, please stop! They are not worthy of framing.'

'Yes please sit down John.' Elizabeth Broadbent reached over to where her husband was standing and laid her hand gently on his arm. It was a silent signal to him that she understood what it all meant.

'Yes of course, please forgive me Mr. Miller, but you can perhaps see that I already believe my daughter to have a wonderful talent. Please eat, eat, I do not

wish to be the cause of your indigestion!' He took back the sketches and returned to his seat at the table placing the drawings carefully back in the portfolio.

'Do you play chess?'

Charles shot Ned a wide-eyed look across the table.

'A little, but not so that I could give a proficient player any real challenge.'

'I believe it to be one of man's finest inventions and I consider I have spent some of my most enjoyable evenings playing chess. I find it both relaxes and stimulates the mind. Unfortunately, Charles has little time to play these days.'

'Sir, have you forgotten that we only played this last evening and on Wednesday evening too?'

'Indeed we did, although I think perhaps you give me favour with your moves, to expedite the game more quickly perhaps?'

'I can neither confirm nor deny that accusation!'

'Your face says guilty!'

'Mr. Miller, despite my son's somewhat nonchalant attitude, it is a wonderful game and I lament the lack of opportunity to play more frequently. For many years I would meet with my friends William and Rufus at their offices to play. I was by far the worst player but I always savoured the

challenge.'

'My father refers to Rufus Choate, U.S. Senator, Attorney General, great orator... One of the finest legal minds this country has ever known.'

'And impossible to beat at chess! He was taken too soon and I miss my friend greatly. I would very much like to establish such a group of friends to meet here at Beacon Street. Charles you would naturally be expected to join with us' he smiled in Charles' direction *'but we would welcome more novice players too if you would like to consider it Mr. Miller.'*

'Thank you sir, I shall certainly give it some thought and think you can be assured that, unlike your matches with Mr. Choate, you are guaranteed to be the victor!'

'Well, I hope that if that should be the case, I will show the same humility in victory as in defeat, although I am rather more used to the latter!'

The evening passed far too quickly, and as Ned walked home that evening, he felt content for the first time since he had arrived in the city. The longing for home seemed to have vanished in just one evening, under the Boston stars tonight, he finally let go of Watertown.

CHAPTER 17

28th March 1873

A small crowd had gathered in anticipation of the bride's arrival and as Nancy stepped down from their carriage outside the church she could tell from their faces that they were impressed by what they saw.

Mrs. Dean followed her out of the carriage holding on to her train tightly to save it from the dirty sidewalk that was now becoming wet from the rain that had begun to fall.

'Please be careful Mrs. Dean, you hold too tight, you are pulling me backwards, I shall fall.'

'I am so sorry my dear.'

Holding the train high with one hand, with the other Mrs. Dean turned her attention to straightening out the wrinkles in Nancy's dress and adjusting the folds of her veil. She was becoming more and more nervous and in her clumsiness her ever-fidgety fingers dislodged a few petals of the orange blossom that was woven into Nancy's hair. *'Mrs. Dean! You are too heavy handed!'* Nancy looked down with dismay at the petals that had fallen like snowflakes at her feet, now dirtied and spoiled.

As the rain began to fall more heavily, discomfiture outweighed the curiosity of the bystanders, who now dispersed as quickly as they had gathered much to Nancy's annoyance. *'Let us get inside, my dress will be spoiled.'*

The wedding party was already seated at the front of the church and although she tried to ignore it, she was disconcerted by the rows of empty pews as she walked down the aisle. The only other seats taken were by two old ladies in the back row who had decided to come in and watch, or to get out of the rain, she did not know which. In their dull lives, something to talk about later she thought.

As she took in the sight of her groom standing at the altar with Charles by his side, it suddenly struck her that he was not very tall, she had not noticed that before. No matter, next to Charles most people would appear short she supposed.

Arriving beside him, he turned to look at her, he was more than adequately handsome she thought. He had very pleasing wide-set dark eyes, a slightly weak chin perhaps, but nice teeth.

The ceremony passed in a perfunctory way, vows were recited, a ring was given and received.

The bride and groom did not look at each other, eyes firmly fixed on the excessively fat minister who perspired profusely all the way through the ceremony, no-one seemed to notice that their eyes never met.

When Ned finally turned to kiss his bride, it felt odd, awkward even.

The rain had stopped so the main wedding party decided to make the short journey to the Parker House on foot. Charles and Sarah would go ahead of them in a carriage and so it was with a significant measure of impatience and ill-humour, that the bride waited her turn while Mrs. Dean and Aunt May helped Charles to settle Sarah comfortably and safely in a carriage.

Finally, the bride and groom climbed into their own carriage to make the two-minute ride. As they sat beside each other Nancy spoke first.

'Well, we are married. Are you happy husband?'

'I am. Are you?'

'I am very happy to be Mrs. Edward Miller my love.' She reached for his hand.

'It is strange is it not to be one moment single and the next married?'

'Does that trouble you?' She gave him a quizzical look.

'No, no, I simply note the significance of a moment

that changes one's future so profoundly.'

'A wonderful moment.'

'Yes of course. I think as your husband I have been remiss in not telling you how beautiful you look today. Will you forgive me?'

'You are forgiven husband' and she reached over and turned his face to hers and kissed him. The second kiss felt as strange as the first to Ned and he diverted her from a third.

'I am sorry that my mother and Aunt Adeline could not be here on this special day. We shall visit them very soon I promise.'

'There is no hurry, I will have much to keep me busy setting up our new home, and I think I should like you to myself for a little while.' She tightened her grip on his hand.

'It is one of my dearest wishes that you should have a family who love and care for you. You are not alone anymore Nancy.'

'You are all I need for my family. We shall be everything to each other.'

As they pulled up outside Parker's Charles was standing outside the entrance with a smiling Sarah in his arms.

'I do think it would have been better if she had stayed at home. It creates a spectacle and everyone is looking. What was Charles thinking?' Ned felt his

stomach turn at the ugliness and stupidity of her words but was careful not to show it in his face.

'I think it is simply what love makes people do, they are happy to put themselves aside, for another's happiness.'

'Well, I think that a foolish kind of love, Charles looks absurd, people are looking on them both with pity and it will do his reputation no service.'

They had been married for less than fifteen minutes and their marriage morning was already far away from Tennyson's *golden morning of love*, Ned could feel the light fading on their union before they had even begun.

With everyone gathered at the hotel Charles led the way into the large foyer. It was handsomely decorated and furnished and its marble tiled floor sent the sound of their footsteps ricocheting around the walls.

The maître d' *would be delighted* to show them to their table, and as the wedding party snaked its way through the dining room to the accompaniment of the pianist's rather melancholy rendition of There's Music in the Air, diners clapped and smiled warmly at the colourful procession. For anyone who cared to look they would see the self-congratulatory smile that crept across Nancy's face as she felt her status grow. Just yesterday not one person in this restaurant would have looked in her direction, today she was a lady of great attraction, her moment perhaps only tainted by the interest Sarah was attracting as Charles carried her in his arms.

Awaiting them on the far side of the dining room was a small alcove. In this intimate space white tulips and pink cherry blossom spilled from silver vases that punctuated the crystal glasses set out along the length of an oblong table. To one end was a towering three-tiered wedding cake, so exquisite and fragile, it was as if it was made entirely from lace. Seating place cards were set out neatly, and it was not lost on Nancy, that she had not been consulted on any of it.

They began to take their places. The bride and groom were seated at the top end of the table and Uncle William and Aunt May at the other. Lottie was placed directly to the right of Ned and Charles to Nancy's left, much to her irritation.

The wedding breakfast menus '*On the Occasion of the Marriage of Mr. & Mrs. Edward Miller*' deliciously announced Chef Anezin's *Oysters, Green Turtle Soup, Ham in Champagne Sauce, Lamb Cutlets with Mushrooms and Cream Meringue* followed by *coffee*. All accompanied by the famous Parker House rolls and a selection of fine French wines to be moderately consumed.

Despite Uncle William's efforts to put them at their ease, Frank and Ned's three sisters were visibly intimidated by their surroundings. Surreptitiously looking around the table to ensure they had selected the correct silverware for the appropriate course, then eating in slow motion, hoping it would add elegance to their masticating. Never had they experienced anything so grand. The food, the surroundings, the clientele of writers, politicians and businessmen. They were overawed by it but Nancy, unlike the rest of them, had an appetite to become very accustomed to it.

Throughout the meal, Nancy endeavoured to avert her eyes from Charles, but with Ned to her right almost constantly engaged in conversation with Lottie, it was only a matter of time before he caught her eye.

'*May I offer my congratulations to you Mrs. Miller.*'

'*Thank you.*' Nancy did not want to enter into conversation with him.

'*Ned is the finest fellow I have ever had the good fortune to meet and I am sure he will bring all his great qualities to being an excellent husband.*'

'*I hope that to be so. I understand that you have not yet had the good fortune to find yourself a wife.*'

'*That is true. No suitable candidate for such an*

onerous task as becoming my wife has ever presented themself!'

'I am surprised, there must have been many a young lady who would have been enthusiastic to become a Broadbent.'

'Thankfully, I appear to find myself quite well suited to a single life.'

'That is indeed fortunate.'

'You look forward to making your home in Manchester I expect? It is the most charming place and there is so much to be enjoyed there. I find the coast to have some of the most breath-taking walks and I have always found it to be such a pleasure to be within the sound of the sea.'

'I am sure it will do very well although I am not partial to quiet living and prefer the gaiety and sophistication of the city. It is my hope that our time at Smith's Point will be quite brief and that we will return to the city and all its attractions in good time. If my husband is to be a success he needs to move in the kinds of circles that I expect are not to be found in Manchester.'

'Well of course Ned seeks to make a home in a place that will inspire his painting, city living and moving in the social circles you suggest would leave him lacking in this respect I fear, something I am sure you understand.'

'I understand very well what Ned desires but we are a married couple now and the needs of both must be satisfied. I am confident, that with time, he will seek the same things I do.'

'Indeed, I am sure that a successful marriage is dependent on the shared desires of both parties being met. Disharmony in this respect is surely the route to failure.'

Charles decided not to pursue their conversation any further, but the disquiet he already felt was growing, he was concerned for Ned even though he knew it was not his place to interfere.

Ned had been engaged in happy and lively conversation with Lottie and they had been laughing over stories from their childhood. Still laughing, Lottie caught Charles' eye across the table and noticing that he looked like he needed his spirits to be lifted, brought him into their conversation.

'Did you know Charles, that when Ned was a child, our mother would find him sliding down the banister singing loudly in the middle of the night? It would give her the fright of her life. We all thought it very funny, especially as he has the most awful singing voice and does find it hard to strike any recognisable note, awake or asleep!'

Charles smiled *'I have not heard you sing Ned, is*

it true, do you sing badly?'

'Most dreadfully, although I very much enjoy the spirit of it, I fear others are suffering because of it!' Ned was leaning across Nancy who clearly did not think the story funny or entertaining and did not join them in their mirth.

'He has a voice that would make any dog howl!' As she spoke the pianist was playing *Jeanie with the Light Brown Hair* for at least the third time that afternoon. *'You would most definitely not want to hear him sing this one!'*

'That is unkind sister, surely you applaud my effort and enthusiasm, even if I lack the talent!'

Mabel had been talking to Ida and Frank, but picking up some of what was being said at the other end of the table said, *'Might you be talking about Little Ned's nocturnal adventures?'*

'We are!' Lottie laughed.

'Poor lamb, he kept us all entertained, even if he had no idea he was doing it! Do you remember when mamma found him sitting on the pantry floor in the dark eating peaches out of a jar? He had emptied three that were destined for much worthier recipients than he, much to mamma's annoyance. No one could ever stay angry at Ned though.'

Ned was almost blushing at the retelling of these stories, but these tales of their childhood bound them together and it made him feel happy, although miss his mother.

Mrs. Dean was seated between Sarah and Uncle William and was having the most enjoyable time. She thought Sarah a very engaging young lady, she had been most generous in her compliments about her dress and the pearl necklace she was wearing which was a gift from her mother. She had shown great interest in her critiques of Anne Bradstreet's poetry and they talked for a good while about the Harriet Beecher Stowe books they had both read. Today she had almost felt like she was part of a family, something she had not felt since she lost Mr. Dean.

'Tell me Mrs. Dean, was Ned a considerate boarder at your establishment?' Uncle William asked with an inquisitive smile.

'He was indeed Mr. Adams. Well-mannered and not a trouble to me at all. Although all my boarders are gentlemen of good character. I also do not take any foreigners seeking accommodation and believe this helps to ensure an equanimity between all my guests.'

'I have great admiration for you Mrs. Dean, I am sure that running such an establishment is not without its challenges, especially for a woman without the support of a husband.'

'I sorely miss my Mr. Dean, he was a good and

honest hardworking man, but he was not one for giving up on things and neither am I.'

'I have the greatest respect for that Mrs. Dean.'

Mrs. Dean blushed at the recognition and appreciation of her stoicism.

'Can I take this opportunity to thank you for all you have done for Ned and, well, for the opportunity it gave him to meet Nancy. It is my dearest wish that theirs will be the happiest of unions.'

Mrs. Dean's cup was full to overflowing.

William Adams glanced around the table eyes finally settling on Ned. He looked so like his mother and it stirred in him the deep love he had for his nephew. He cleared his throat and stood to the ringing sound of the crystal glass in his hand as gradually the remnants of conversations around the table dropped away and everyone looked in his direction.

'If my dear sister had been here today I know she would want me to say a few words on behalf of our family. Ned, to all who know him, is a kind and decent young man and we are all extremely proud of him. I know, that had May and I been blessed with our own son, we could not have been more grateful for it to be a young man like Ned. You begin a wonderful new chapter in your life today and I hope you and your lovely bride Nancy will be as happy in your marriage as I have been in mine.' At his words,

Aunt May dropped her eyes to hide her sudden discomposure.

'Please raise your glasses to the happy couple. Ned and Nancy. To happiness, health and good fortune.'

Ned watched his uncle sit down and saw the briefest exchange of an intimate glance between him and Aunt May. He knew they had been quietly there for him these last four years never asking anything of him. If they had considered him like a son in their home, felt like parents, he was glad.

Charles had booked Ned and Nancy a hotel suite for the night and then the next day they would travel on to Manchester. Ned's sisters would be staying with Uncle William and Aunt May for the night and then would return to Watertown in the morning to report in minute detail on the day's events to their mother.

By four o'clock all the guests had departed except Charles and Sarah who were waiting in the foyer with the bride and groom for their carriage to arrive. They stood in an awkward triangle, all tired from the day, Sarah settled on a couch beside them.

'Well, I think it is time we take our leave of you. I know the manager here and he has promised me their finest suite so I hope that all will be to your satisfaction. Nancy you truly have made the

most beautiful bride...' She thought Charles would go on, but he said nothing more. She took the compliment but was not blind to the lack of any other commendations or accolades.

Charles stretched out his hand to shake Ned's. *'Well, my friend, be a good husband! I travel to New York City tomorrow for a few days but I will send word on my return and perhaps I can visit you at Smith's Point soon?'*

Nancy felt invisible at this point.

'Of course, I, we, shall look forward to it. Thank you for everything Charles. We are so grateful for all your kindnesses and generosity.'

'It is nothing.' and he held Ned's gaze.

'Well goodbye Charles' Nancy interjected abruptly, she was keen to bring their lingering goodbye to an end.

Charles understood her signal, smiled, swept Sarah up and they were gone.

'Come my love, let us go and see this wonderful suite Charles has promised us. Let us walk slowly, see how everyone looks at us, we truly must make the most handsome couple.'

As they stepped through the door of their suite they were met by the peppery smell of fresh flowers. The lamps had been lit and a light cold supper had been laid out for them.

'See what treats we have!'

Ned watched his bride as she looked around the room taking in the opulence and all the modern conveniences. He himself had never seen anything so luxurious and there was even a hot and cold bath in the bedroom which connected with their sitting room. The chairs were upholstered in plum coloured velvet and the carpets were so thick it felt like walking on feather pillows. On the surface, the way she looked today, she could belong here he thought.

In these most lavish of surroundings, a modest leather trunk, contained all that Nancy brought with her to their marriage.

As they sat at the small table near the window to eat their supper Nancy's eyes continued to survey their surroundings and with everything she saw her expectations for their future seemed to grow.

'Is this not the most exquisite tea set you have ever seen? This would do well for our guests...'

'Is this chair not the most comfortable you have ever known? and the colour so rich...'

'Did you feel the weight of the curtains? No east wind could ever overcome them...'

Ned nodded at the relevant points and did nothing to stifle her ambitions as she spoke as if they would live in a mansion.

The clock was ticking as his anticipation and nervousness grew at what lay ahead. Contrary to how he was feeling, Nancy seemed to grow in confidence with every mouthful of cold roast beef.

When later she withdrew to prepare herself for bed he reflected on the day. It had changed his life forever. He longed to go back. When he entered their marital bed for the first time, he felt he had become someone else, a different man. Here was his wife, clouds of white linen and lace against pale skin, auburn hair the tangled net in which he would be caught.

She did not wait, she kissed him with confidence as he lay down beside her, and he was swept along. Like honey that attracts the fly, he was trapped.

In the darkness now her voice came to him quietly and close in his ear.

'Are you content husband?'

'I am.'

'You are not disappointed by me tonight?'

'I am not.'

'You know that it is my greatest wish to be a good wife to you.'

'Thank you.'

'We are truly husband and wife now are we not, now that we have shared ourselves with each other?'

'We are.'

'How wonderful that you are as content as I am.'

'I am.'

'Goodnight my love, sleep well.'

'Goodnight.'

Sleep did not come to him.

CHAPTER 18

April 1884

Williams & Everett had invested considerable time and money in promoting Ned's exhibition *'From the Wilds to the Sea'* to their established clientele and had called on the full breadth of all their business connections. Colourful posters had been prominently sited across the city for the last four weeks and they had advertised widely in Boston newspapers including features in the Globe, the Times and the Portland Daily Press.

Ned had worked hard over the last few months to build up his body of work all the way fighting his instinct not to live by the clock. Expectations were high for the exhibition and the gallery would be showing thirty of Ned's landscape and seascape paintings and sketches. They had been assiduous in handsomely framing his work and as Ned walked the gallery now to review their hanging, he was satisfied that they had been displayed and lit to their best advantage.

The collection included five paintings that featured Nancy at the heart of their composition.

Catalogue no. EM 6 *Storm Watcher* - Nancy standing by the shore, wind whipping her auburn hair around her face.

Catalogue no. EM11 *Distant Tides* - Nancy standing by the studio window looking out to the sea beyond.

Catalogue no. EM16 *Afternoon Rest* - Nancy slumbering under the rowan tree in her green dress.

Catalogue no. EM20 *Girl with Bluebells* - Nancy picking seaside Bluebells by the beach.

Catalogue no. EM27 *Reflection* - Nancy looking at herself in a rockpool.

As he stood in front of *Afternoon Rest*, he looked at her through a stranger's eyes, she appeared as an angel. Undeniably a beautiful and ethereal other-worldly creature, he knew her to be the perfect anchor for the glorious wild and free scenes she inhabited, all around gravitating towards her. She brought an alchemy that turned his paintings into glittering gold, but she lived to him as this shining woman only in his paintings, alive more keenly perhaps here in the innocence of sleep.

'I hope that you are pleased Mr. Miller?' Mr. Williams' voice came from behind him.

'I am most pleased Mr. Williams. I think you have

hung my work most thoughtfully and to its best advantage. Thank you.'

'I am delighted that you are satisfied. Many of our most highly valued clientele will be visiting the gallery this week and we have every reason to believe it will be a most successful exhibition.'

'That is most encouraging.'

'We shall open our doors on the hour. May I enquire whether you would like to be made known to our customers or whether you would prefer to observe with anonymity.'

'I prefer to remain anonymous Mr. Williams.'

'Of course, that is understood Mr. Miller.'

Ned decided to station himself in the lower gallery, close enough to the reception desk so that he could observe visitors as they arrived, while remaining hidden from their sight. He settled himself on a couch against the corridor wall that was at right angles to the reception area and began the wait. As his eyes travelled the walls he was mesmerised by the eclectic selection of etchings, engravings, paintings, and chromolithographs that lined them.

To his left, through an opening to an even larger room, the walls were hung with landscape photographs that took their viewers on a journey to far off places. Everywhere he looked, elaborate gilt-framed looking glasses punctuated the hangings and bounced their soft light around the gallery, guiding points of light to the aesthetic voyager.

He checked his watch, five minutes. He checked again, eight minutes. Ten minutes and no one had come through the doors, he began to feel like an imposter. Why would people come to see his work? Then finally the shop bell rang and a very well-dressed couple entered the gallery. Mr. Williams' business partner Mr. Everett almost leapt from his spot in his enthusiasm to greet them.

'Mr. & Mrs Lane, we are so delighted you were able to come. We think you will be most pleased with the exhibition of Edward Miller's work. His is a most exciting talent and is attracting a lot of interest amongst discerning collectors. May I show you to the upper gallery and then I would be happy to wait on you and assist you in any way.'

'Thank you Mr. Everett, we always consider your valuable opinion when adding to our collection.'

'That is most kind of you to say and we are glad to be of service to you. If you are ready, I would be happy to escort you to the upper gallery.'

Ned was watching them climb the stairs when the shop bell rang again. This time Mr. Williams stepped forward.

'My dear Mrs. West, it is a pleasure to see you.'

Again, after warm words of welcome, he escorted her up the stairs to the upper gallery passing Mr. Everett on his way down who also stopped to exchange exuberant greetings with her.

The shop bell rang again, and as Ned looked in the direction of the door, he smiled. It was Charles and his mother. In response to the bell, Mr. Everett hurried down the stairs to welcome them, mis-judging the bottom step and almost stumbling in his haste. Ned emerged from his hiding place to greet his friends.

'Elizabeth Broadbent' she extended a gloved hand to Mr. Everett. *'Charles Broadbent, pleased to meet you'* he removed his hat.

'Welcome to Williams & Everett, is there anything specific I can help you with today? he hesitated as Ned joined them not sure whether to give away his identity *'or might you be here for the Edward Miller exhibition of works?'*

Looking in Ned's direction Elizabeth spoke first *'We are already a little acquainted with Mr. Miller and are great admirers of his art, we think it a very astute decision on the part of Williams & Everett to display his work.'* It was Elizabeth Broadbent that was astute in not giving away the closeness of their friendship and risking any assumption of favourable bias.

'Indeed madam, we enjoy a long-established reputation for identifying the finest artists of the future.' A well-rehearsed line. *'Would you like me to show you to the upper gallery where Mr. Miller's work is displayed?'* He smiled in Ned's direction.

Charles interjected *'Perhaps Mr. Miller would be kind enough to escort us? It would be a pleasure to have the artist show us his work in person.'*

'Would you be happy to escort the Broadbents Mr. Miller?'

'Yes of course, I would be delighted.'

'That is happily agreed then. However, please do let me know if you require my assistance at any time and I will be happy to help.'

Ned led the way.

'Thank you for coming today.'

'We would not have missed the opportunity to see so many of your paintings at one time.'

'That is kind.'

'On the contrary, selfishly, we simply seek to treat our eyes!' Charles slapped his friend's shoulder.

'I am sorry that Sarah was not able to join us today. I hope her cold is much improved?'

'She is much better and almost restored to full

strength. She was so disappointed not to have been able to visit the exhibition but we assured her that you will have others for her to enjoy in the future.'

'Indeed, I hope so, if this one goes well.'

'If this one goes well? It will be a triumph!'

'Charles, I do find you show more than a little partiality where my artistic talents are concerned.'

'You are considered an artist of the highest calibre in the Broadbent household and Sarah definitely considers herself to have had the finest teacher.'

'I know her watercolours are in high demand for greetings cards but I would like to think that there will be a time when her work might be considered for an exhibition of its own.'

'She has produced enough work over the years for at least a dozen exhibitions!

'They should be seen and enjoyed.'

'Well, at least she has given in to father over the years, there is a permanent exhibition at Beacon Street with every spare inch of his study walls now covered with her work, only the painting of my grandfather remains and that may be on borrowed time! She paints almost constantly since she has had her own studio space, and the special easel you had made for her to attach to her chair, that changed everything. So clever how it articulates just as she needs - those brackets and hinges and all -it has given

her so much freedom. So ingenious of you.'

'As you know, it was by my design but the engineering and construction were the work of Frank's hands, fine workmanship on his part. It was such a small thing but I am glad she continues to get so much use and pleasure from it.'

'It was kind of you and Frank beyond measure.' Elizabeth said in a soft broken voice. *'Now tell me, is Nancy here? I am sure she is excited to see you receive the recognition and appreciation you so justly deserve.'*

'Yes, she awaits us in the upper gallery.'

'How wonderful, I so look forward to meeting her after all this time.'

As they reached the top of the stairs, Elizabeth's curiosity overtook her as her eyes immediately searched the room for Nancy. There was a couple standing in front of a sunset seascape deep in discussion and another lady of mature years who was studying a painting of a woman standing windblown by the sea. She could not see anyone who could be Nancy and gave Ned a confused look.

'Is she here?' She asked for a second time.

'She is, please follow me.'

He led them down the gallery and then stopped unexpectedly. They were standing in front of one of his paintings. It was of a woman sleeping under a tree. Her head was tilted back exposing her long neck, her back curling to the shape of the trunk. Her hands lay in her lap, palms open, like she was receiving a blessing and her green dress was spread out around her disappearing into the grass like they were one and the same.

'Here she is. This is Nancy.'

Elizabeth gave her son a concerned look.

'Is she not beautiful?'

Elizabeth nodded. She was.

'Ned, why has she not come? I do not seek to criticise but surely she would want to support you on such an important day as this?' Charles spoke calmly but was hiding the anger he felt on Ned's behalf.

'She had a prior engagement impossible to cancel. I am not disheartened, Nancy has little appreciation for art or things of any virtuosity or substance, her pleasures are found in the more trivial and superficial I am afraid, it is just her way. She will I am sure be delighted however, if the exhibition is a commercial success, her contentment is usually measured in dresses and trinkets!' He laughed to himself but Charles and Elizabeth were saddened by the sound of it.

They remained in front of the painting, all

looking at its subject, all lost in their own thoughts and conclusions about Nancy.

Elizabeth Broadbent had no comprehension of how a wife could make herself so separate from her husband's needs and sensitivities, she must have her reasons, she could not make sense of it otherwise. Once again Charles felt the sorrow of their disastrous match acutely and a sense of bleakness that all his instincts had been right about Nancy.

The gallery was beginning to fill up and the room hummed with hushed but animated voices. As he looked around him at the scene, Charles sought to lift the melancholy that hung over them all.

'Well, my friend I think you are creating quite a stir and personally I find it a pleasure to be in a room with so many people with such discernment and good taste as mine!'

Ned laughed *'Charles it is a comfort to me that you find yourself amongst your peers!'*

As they walked the rest of the gallery, Elizabeth had already resolved to purchase the painting of Nancy under the rowan tree. This time, not because Charles had asked her to, but because she wanted it for herself. In some peculiar way, she thought that she may be able to influence and steer Nancy in the things that were lacking in her if she was present in her house, even just as a painting. Besides, the painting was wondrous and she felt strangely drawn to it, like it was trying to tell her something.

Throughout the day, Mr. Williams and Mr. Everett were fruitfully employed waiting on interested customers and enthusiastically assisting their purchases. The exhibition was going very well.

Having decided to make her purchase, Elizabeth Broadbent had absented herself from Ned and Charles and had discreetly sought out Mr. Everett to make the arrangements. Catalogue item EM16 was hers.

After such a good day Ned walked through the door at Smith's Point feeling happy and content. It could hardly have gone any better. He knew Nancy would be delighted with the success of the day and it augured well for the whole exhibition.

She was waiting for him. *'Well, what news do you have for me? Was it all we hoped for?'*

'It was. There was much interest and enthusiasm for my work especially the seascapes which drew great admiration.'

'Yes, yes, but what of the purchases?'

'According to Mr. Everett, five paintings and two sketches were purchased and interest was registered

on a further three. It all bodes well for the week.'

'That all sounds very good, what a clever husband you are.'

'You are happy then?'

'I am.'

CHAPTER 19

September 1851

15th September 1851

My dearest Amelia,

It is regrettable that I have received no reply from you to my letter of 31st May which I now think perhaps did not arrive with you safely.

I am sorry to report that my circumstances have become unbearable these last three months and in the absence of any reply from you and confirmation that the merchandise I requested has been sent, I resolve now that I must return home despite all my efforts to make a success of my venture.

I seek to dispose of my last remnants of merchandise in these next two weeks and make arrangements to leave this place before the cold weather arrives and makes travel more difficult. By my estimation, the funds I will raise from my merchandise clearance will be sufficient for my passage back to New York City where I plan to visit with Henry and his family for a few days before my onward journey home. I have a business proposition for Henry which I believe would be highly advantageous to him and which I hope he would be favourably disposed to investing in.

God willing, you should receive this letter by mid-October following which, I hope that I shall be returned to you and the children by Christmas for the happiest of reunions.

You will find me a changed man my love. These past months have been cruel to me beyond measure, and my one and only desire now, is to be back home with my family whose love and devotion will surely restore my spirits.

Please write to Henry to inform him of my intended visit with him in December and pass my fondest regards to my aunt and uncle who I am sure will be heartened to hear of my return.

I trust you and the children are all in good health.

Your loving husband,

Walter

As Walter looked around him at his diminished merchandise he once again lamented his bad luck. He had deserved better.

Sleep had eluded him since the robbery and never able to give himself over to the oblivion and vulnerability of unconsciousness he was left exhausted. The days all rolled into one, from dawn to dusk, he kept watch and prayed for the miracle of a change of fortune or a letter from home. However, the inevitability now of his destiny if he stayed was clear to him, and this letter to Amelia carried his reluctant but necessary surrender.

The small leather-bound bible Amelia had packed in his belongings, which for so long had languished disregarded and unwanted under his cot, was now his source of daily comfort. He had read the parable of the Sower over and over again believing he had sown into good ground and so he awaited his promised harvest one hundredfold. He lived by the parable of the Talents and believed God would reward his enterprise and fearlessness with the blessings of profit.

Also bookmarked were verses that he believed God intended for him.

This Book of the Law shall not depart out of thy mouth, but thou shalt meditate therein day and night, that thou mayest observe to do according to all that is written therein. For then thou shalt make thy way prosperous, and then thou shalt have good success. **Joshua 1:8**

For I know the thoughts that I think toward you, saith the Lord, thoughts of peace, and not of evil, to give you an expected end. **Jeremiah 29:11**

The blessing of the Lord, it maketh rich, and he

addeth no sorrow with it. **Proverbs 10:22**

He chose not to heed God's word in Matthew 6:24 or even 19:24, surely God sought to prosper him, not to consider him vain or in servitude to money. Camels, needles, he was blind to the warnings, they were for other men, not for him.

The sound of Amelia's voice came to him so often in these troubled days, sometimes as a comfort, more often as a rebuke. He was reminded that in the instruction of their children and as a lesson to herself, she would proffer that in humbling yourself in the sight of the Lord, He would lift you up from the depths of despair. He had never seen any virtue in humility, it made men weak and powerless, there was no room for such passivity if you wanted to be a success in life.

As he placed the bible back under his cot he straightened up and stretched his back. As he rubbed it, he could feel his protruding ribs, the skin moving loosely over the surface where meat and muscle used to be. Lack of nourishment and sleep had left him weak and shrunken and his hands seemed to tremble constantly.

His head pounded most days and a sound like the rush of waves breaking on the shore filled his ears. With hair now more grey than brown, but at not yet forty years old, he looked and felt like an old man.

He thought of John so like him in his physical features, a bitter reminder of everything that he used to be and now, everything he had lost. When he returned home, he resolved he would spend more time with John, who he believed was unhealthily attached to his mother. A young man of nearly thirteen now, it was time for Walter to instruct him in the art of business as his father had done with him at that age. He was lifted by the thought of it, *W. C. Miller & Son* would be the continuity of the family enterprise; John would bring the youth and energy and he would bring the experience and business acumen.

Tonight, Walter felt so tired and weary that for the first time he longed for home above everything else. He sought the comforting love of his wife, the admiration and respect of his children, and the restoration of deep peaceful sleep in his own bed more than anything in the world.

Greenbrook, the house that he had felt was so inadequate and meagre, now appeared in his mind's eye like a palace. The garden like Eden, a sacred divine place. Why had he never seen it before?

The day he had left, he had done it so lightly, as if none of what he was leaving was of any great consequence in the greater scheme of his life. Now he felt alone and frightened and tonight it seemed to him, that everything he really wanted, was there on Spring Street.

He dreamt a peaceful dream of home that night. His children ran to him smiling and Amelia lovingly embraced him *'Husband it is a happy day to have you home safe.'* They dined on roast chicken and apple pie. They laughed and shared stories and Walter made his children gasp in awe at tales of his exciting travels and adventures.

The next morning dawned as a fine and dry day and Daniel Brown anticipated an easy journey ahead. There had been severe retribution dealt to the native Indians for the attacks on his fellow Expressmen over the summer and, for now, ambushes were rare. The massacre of Indians was encouraged and generous bounties were often paid, so the hunt was always on, and fear grew and took root in the Indian settlements stifling their desire to spill white blood.

Daniel was saddled up and mounted by seven o'clock and on his way to the first of his five collections of the day. Checking his manifest; the first was Walter Miller, he knew the camp, he could be there in half an hour.

As he rode up to the tent, he had expected Mr. Miller to be outside waiting, but there was no sign of him. He dismounted and tethered his mule to the nearest tree, then pulling back the heavy flap, he entered the tent.

He stood at the opening and called out but there was no reply.

As his eyes adjusted to the strange light inside he was aware of the dull fizz of mosquitos and that the air smelt sour like stagnant water.

The front section of the tent was completely empty except an animal trap, not set. Towards the back there was a small pile of hardware stacked up on a table and three bolts of canvas leant heavily against the tent wall. In one corner woollen blankets hung from hooks and in the other there was what looked like a pile of clothes beside which was a kerosene lamp still lit from the night.

Daniel Brown was angry, a failed collection would cost him dear today, he cursed Walter Miller. He would take something for his trouble and reaching up unhooked two of the blankets. He was entitled to them. The nights were cooling and an extra blanket for him and for his mule would not go amiss.

As he threw the blankets over his shoulder a large black Borer Beetle fell from their folds landing on the leg of his pants, he hated crawlers, and frantically slapped at the scurrying bug until it fell to the ground and he was able to squash it under his boot.

Stumbling backwards, his leg brushed against

something hard and rigid. He looked down and saw a pale bloodless foot sticking out from under a grey blanket. As his eyes travelled the length of the cot, they finally rested on the face of an old man, eyes open, smiling. He did not need to touch him, or stand near to feel his breath, he knew he was dead.

Shame he thought. No point letting his things go to waste though so he gathered up what he could carry including the gun which he prised from Walter's stiffened fingers.

As some small gesture of respect, or at least to stop a dead man's eyes staring at him, he pulled the blanket up over Walter's face, but he did not pull the letter from Walter's other inflexible hand. There was nothing to be gained in taking that now and no point in giving anyone the false belief that he was alive.

Daniel Brown mumbled a short prayer, tipped his hat briefly, and then left.

Walter Miller 1815-1851. Husband, father and eternal optimist. R.I.P.

CHAPTER 20

August 1879

It had been a perfect summer so far. Long sunny days, cool nights, and clear evening skies full of stars. Ned had been able to spend nearly every day painting outdoors, taking advantage of the dry weather, and the subtly changing summer light from dawn to dusk.

Most of his days were spent in solitude except for the wildlife that seemed to take a keen interest in his activities; a mischievous raccoon or perhaps an inquisitive robin were often his only spectators.

He reflected that he and Nancy had stayed true to themselves, because after six years of marriage, they still had nothing in common with neither one of them moving towards the other to bridge the space between them. The knitting together over time that most married couples might expect had never happened and they had found nothing to bind them other than the dull ties of mundane routine.

He had no interest in superficial social

gatherings or the pursuit of the right people and time spent with his family or an evening spent with Charles, Frank or even Laurie was always his preference. Blessing or curse, he felt no need to prove his worth to strangers or impress them with his clothes or belongings, he only valued the opinion and acceptance of those he loved and respected. If he never attended another tedious party in his life it would be a relief, the theatre of God's creation was more than enough to satisfy his need for entertainment.

Nancy steadfastly remained the opposite. She had no interest in the natural world, or in walking simply for the pleasure of it, even the sea held no allure for her. He often wondered what went on in her head, to him, she seemed interested in nothing of any commendation only that which was frivolous or transient. However, despite her almost permanent look of disdain where he was concerned, she did seem more content these days and whatever the reason, it was a relief to him.

They argued less, in part because she absented herself from their home so frequently so the opportunity was lacking, but also because she seemed almost indifferent towards him nowadays. It was not in a hateful or unkind way, she simply said little if their conversation began to venture into anything meaningful or turn sour in any way and would step away from him with disinterest.

He knew he held fault in it all but he had resolved long ago that there was nothing within his possession that would change the direction of their lives and so they drifted on benignly year after year, together but separate.

Nancy was at least still prepared to sit for him and today she had agreed to stay home for the day. He had his composition worked out and he planned to paint her in the garden under the rowan tree.

Now standing at the window of the studio looking out on the scene the light was perfect and he was eager to get started.

Just then Nancy appeared at the studio door behind him.

'You said to be ready for ten o'clock.' He turned and there she stood looking expectant and clearly feeling very impatient. She was wearing his favourite green dress, an exquisite and superior replacement for the hand-me-down green dress she was wearing the first time he saw her. That was definitely something Nancy had a talent for, despite their modest income, she always seemed to be able to dress beyond their means. He assumed she must have a most talented and inexpensive seamstress at her disposal.

'I did.'

'Well, I am ready.'

'Yes of course. I am sorry, I find myself a little behind the clock, I will be ready within the half hour. Perhaps you could wait for me in the garden? Take a blanket to spread on the ground to save your dress from spoiling as I plan to paint you sitting on the grass, under the rowan, leaning against its trunk.'

She sighed. *'I hope you will not keep me too long today; I am tired and I do not care to sit on the hard ground for hours, nor for the sun to spoil my complexion.'*

'The tree will shade you.'

Exasperated, she threw her hands limply in the air, then left.

As he prepared a palette of Chinese White, Chromium Green Oxide and Viridian, Cadmium Yellow and Aureolin, Alizarin Crimson and Red Ochre, coming from below the studio window, he could hear her talking to herself. He could not catch the words but he was sure she was complaining about him.

As he concluded his preparations and made his way down the stairs to join her, he hoped that the pretty day might soften her spirits and the hard lines of her face, finding her of a more amiable disposition because of it.

With his hands full, he pushed open the screen

door with his foot and stepped out into the garden.

He was about to call out to Nancy but caught his words, she had fallen asleep under the tree, and his instinct was not to wake her. He set down his things and quietly moved towards her, the soft yielding grass under his feet the silent accomplice to his hushed approach.

As he stood looking down on her she did not stir.

Her head was tilted back against the trunk of the tree which accentuated her long slim neck. Her hands lay in her lap open and relaxed. Her face tilted up towards the canopy of branches was mesmerising in repose, and the specks of light breaking through the leaves lit the gold in her eyelashes and illuminated the blood that flowed beneath her cheeks and lips.

She looked like a sweet, innocent girl not a cynical, hardened woman. This Nancy was the one he craved even if she was not real.

Ned decided not to wake her and to work quickly to capture the candid moment. He sketched her outline quickly but with no compromise of accuracy or skill. As he added paint to paper, she stirred and slowly opened her eyes, blinking in the dappled sunlight.

'Good afternoon.'

She gave him a confused look.

'You have been asleep.'

'Why did you not wake me? How can I pose for you if I am not even awake?'

'There was no need for you to contrive a pose, when I found you asleep I simply sought to capture the scene of a beautiful slumbering woman, unaware of her watcher.'

'No woman would want to be admired without her knowledge, what would be the point of that? Any woman would question a man's intent in stealing such secret glances and besides, it would seem ignoble to me to take advantage in such a way.'

'I am sorry, I did not wish to upset you.'

'It is too late; it is done now. You have profited from my compromised state, so perhaps you will at least release me from my uncomfortable position, I must stretch and ease the stiffness in my limbs.'

'Of course, let me not delay you any further, I am sure you have things you need to attend to.'

Saying nothing, she stood and brushed the grass from her dress.

'Indeed, I do. I shall go to town this afternoon I think.'

'Very well, I shall see you at supper then.'

'I may be late, do not wait for me. Good day sir!'

and she was gone.

Like a pianist who plays by ear, he had been able to capture with his eyes, all that he needed to complete his painting. His mind would hold her image there even now she was gone.

Ned spent the rest of the afternoon on the painting only pulling himself away from it when his hunger pains became too much of a distraction.

As he entered the kitchen his eyes adjusted to the dim light, the window shutters were closed, thankfully blocking out the light and the stifling heat of the day. Mary had set out some welcome sustenance for him on the kitchen table, and as he lifted the white linen napkin, the smell of the cured ham, cheese and cornbread only increased his hunger. The day's post was also on the table but he did not recognise the hand, he would eat first, then open the letter.

Feeling revived and with his energy restored, he picked up the letter and prised open the envelope; now the hand was known to him.

Wednesday 20th August 1879

My dearest Ned,

It is with the deepest regret that I am compelled to write to you today. I must meet with you to inform you of certain grievous events of the last nearly two years, which have now reached an impossible climax.

Do not worry, your aunt and I are in good health and there is no ill news of your sisters, but there is an issue of grave consequence to you that we must discuss urgently and I hope that you will be able to visit me in Roxbury at the earliest possible opportunity.

It is most important that you do not tell Nancy of my letter, nor that you intend to visit me, this must remain between the two of us.

All will become clear when we meet. Please come soonest.

Your affectionate uncle.

With puzzlement, he looked at the disguised hand on the envelope and then read the letter again, but on the second reading, it was no less alarming. It was full of deep consternation and knowing that nothing ever seemed to disturb Uncle William's equilibrium, he believed it must be a most serious matter.

'...*It is most important that you do not tell Nancy of my letter, nor that you intend to visit me...*'

He would go first thing tomorrow morning and would tell Nancy that he was visiting with Frank for a couple of days.

The next day, all the way there, his uncle's words turned over in his mind. Why did he mention Nancy? Did this trouble concern her in some way?

On arrival at the house in Washington Park he was taken directly to his uncle in the library.

William Adams rose slowly and stiffly from his chair and set aside the book he was reading, Loring & Jenney's *Principles and Practice of Architecture*, which Ned knew him to have studied many times before. There were not new things to be learnt perhaps but old familiar things to be revisited and enjoyed he thought. It was good to see him and Ned often imagined his uncle happily spending his days in this room now that he was fully retired from the practice and more limited by his declining health.

He held out his hand in welcome.

'Ned, I am so happy to see you. Please sit. I am sorry to cause you concern by requesting that we meet urgently.'

'No, it is I that should apologise uncle if there is anything that I have given you cause to be concerned about. Please, unburden yourself.'

'I know that it will come as a surprise to you to learn that Nancy has been corresponding with me on matters that I can hardly bear to reveal, however after her latest letter, I am afraid that I have no other choice.'

'Why would Nancy be writing to you?'

'I will explain. Nancy first wrote to me about two years ago suggesting problems in your marriage, the indelicacies of which, she seemed keen to divulge.' Uncle William cleared his throat before he continued.

'She said she had felt the need to share this with me so that I would understand the difficult circumstances she found herself trapped in.'

Ned interjected *'Uncle I assure you I do not mistreat my wife in any way.'*

'I know that Ned and remain assured of your good character and fine qualities however, although I did not believe any ill of you, Nancy was keen to suggest that if I would not heed her pleas she would find others to listen. She suggested that if I would help ease her sufferings, she would be prepared to stay silent.'

Ned could not believe what he was hearing. *'I cannot fathom that she has such hate in her heart towards me.'*

'She suggested that her sufferings would be eased by fifty dollars which would secure her some of the comforts to make her life more bearable. I am sorry nephew, but against my better judgement, I sent the money.'

I have seen no post arrive from you unless you

disguised your hand.

'She uses a postal address in the North End. I have been sending the money by post care of Mrs. V. Taylor at Endicott Street.'

'Why would Nancy be visiting that neighbourhood? It is not safe or indeed suitable for a woman alone.'

'Ned, I do not know what her associations are with such a neighbourhood or Mrs. Taylor for that matter but each subsequent letter suggests that she safely receives my payments by means of this address. After her first letter, when I did not hear from her again for six months, I had hoped that any matter of difficulty was settled between you, but then another letter came.'

'This time she alluded to your friendship with Charles Broadbent in the most vulgar terms and again suggested that others would be interested to know that you were more inclined towards his company than hers.'

Ned's eyes dropped to the floor.

'You already know that I make no judgement on your friendship with Charles and believe him to be a decent man, but I also believed that others may have an appetite for such salacious accusations and so I sent Nancy the one hundred dollars she requested.'

'You sent her one hundred dollars? I am so sorry

uncle.'

'Then came another letter six months ago, and based on its unsavoury contents, I sent another one hundred dollars to Nancy. I told her it would be the last payment and that I would not continue to be blackmailed. I had hoped that the use of such a word might encourage her to consider the gravity of her actions but it would appear that was to no avail.'

Ned was stunned into silence.

'This week, I received this.' He handed Ned the letter to read for himself.

Ned's head pounded as he read her ugly words: *unnatural, clandestine, abandonment…* She would do it; she would go to the newspapers about Ned, about Charles. She would play the part of the poor victimised wife, do whatever was required to get what she wanted – the dresses and the trinkets. She would talk to whoever would listen. His hands were trembling and in his distress he tore up the letter.

'I am so sorry uncle that you have had to read such terrible lies. Her words are grotesque, I have never mis-treated her in any way and I assure you that my relationship with Charles has never been anything other than honourable and proper.'

He saw his uncle's cheeks flush pink.

'Can you forgive me? I fear my judgement in this

matter has been poor but I sought only to protect you as a father would.'

He had been the very best of fathers to Ned.

'Thank you uncle, you are in no way to blame for any of this, but we must decide quickly what can be done. I must speak with Charles; he will know what to do.'

'Would that be wise?'

'How I wish wisdom could be the solution here, but I fear it will take something extraordinary and perhaps less noble to stop her, Charles will advise me.'

'Whatever you think best. I will not respond to this letter or any others I receive from her until I hear of your plans.'

The two men sat in sad silence. After a few moments Ned was the first to speak.

'I have reason to believe that, while the accusations of my indiscretions are completely unfounded, where Nancy is concerned that may not be the case. I have chosen not to listen to rumour or gossip which often has no veracity, but increasingly she finds her company and entertainment away from our home and out of my sight.'

Uncle William pondered his words.

'But what proof?'

'Well, Nancy has no proof, only wild words that

she hopes to profit from.'

'That is true but please be careful nephew, bad news travels quickly, and the truth has little to do with slowing its speed. Once the word is out, there is no way to silence it.'

'I will be cautious uncle. A conversation with Charles at the earliest opportunity however is crucial, and if I may impose on your hospitality tonight, I will send word to him this afternoon and visit him first thing tomorrow in the hope he is free to meet with me.'

'Of course. Your aunt will be delighted that you are to stay and that she will be able to fuss over you.' For the first time there was the glint of a smile.

'Thank you uncle, for everything.'

Uncle William waved his hand in dismissal.

CHAPTER 21

One night in 1871

A strange and weak light was coming in through the Atelier windows, hard to define in hue but somewhere between orange and lilac, neither one nor both. It was fading, but like an ambrotype, the dimming of the light brought the city scene through the window into a sharper focus that strained his eyes.

There was a growing chill in the air, his hands and feet felt cold and rigid, a raw chill cutting into his bones and Pock was on his feet and pacing the floor, his usual irascible self. He was in a bad mood most days now as the tide of his fortunes continued to turn at W. Adams & R. J. Morris. Every word had a sharp edge, every movement had frustration in it, even his pocked skin looked redder and angrier by the day.

His only pleasure continued to be the despondency of his students, especially Frank's, whose gloom he seemed to cling to like a leech.

'Mr. Miller, you would serve this practice well to spend less time looking out of the windows and more

time employed in finishing the Park Street design. You are aware of the impending deadline are you not?'

'Yes of course Mr. Dawson.'

'Well then, what is your excuse for such a lackadaisical approach to your work?'

'I have none sir, I fully understand what is required of me.'

'You leave very little time sir for any adaptions or corrections that may need to be made, that is bad planning in my book.'

'I anticipate that there will be little to be changed.'

'You are very confident sir, we shall see.'

Ned's heart sank as Pock now turned his attention to Frank for his daily sport. Ned was more than a match for Pock, who despite some small undeniable quantity of talent, was in essence a stupid and ignorant man. Frank was another matter, bound by fear and a lack of confidence, he struggled to deal with Pock's cruel games which affected him deeply.

If they had been creatures, other than human, they would be a snake and a lamb. Unevenly matched, the snake the predator with the advantage of cunning, speed and a poison to paralyse. The lamb the prey but with the elevations of gentleness, sweetness and a lack of guile. Every man to the last would seek out the lamb for company.

The problem for Frank was that he thought nothing of himself, made himself small, did not see the fine things others recognised in him.

'Mr. Jones, when can I expect to review your corrections?'

'I would expect by the finish of the day sir.'

'I hope so. It will be a fine day indeed when you manage a successful drawing at first attempt, it will save us all so much time.'

'Yes sir.'

As Ned looked on at his friend with sadness, it seemed as if he began to grow in size, as the room shrank away from him. The sky continued to darken and the light disappeared, he **was** growing, Frank was becoming a luminous giant his head pushing upwards towards the ceiling.

As Frank grew, Pock shrank.

Down and down Pock went, getting redder as he grew smaller, until finally he was no bigger than a juicy red strawberry. Despite his reduced size, his voice was not diminished, and it boomed even louder making the windows vibrate.

'Jones! You useless idiot, help me or you shall regret it.'

Ned looked at Frank who was now so tall he was bent double as the ceiling height constrained him.

'Jones! I order you to help me or I shall make sure you never work in this city again.'

Staring down at his feet, Frank did not move or speak.

'Jones! A curse on you and your beggarly family.'

With those words Pock sprang from the floor like a blood-hungry flee, first onto Frank's desk, then onto his arm. With teeth like needles, he began to bite Frank with ferocity over and over again, sucking the goodness of his blood greedily.

Frank began to cry and his tears fell heavily to the floor, pooling and then reaching to the furthest edges of the room. Unable to go any further, the waterline began to rise around Ned's ankles, then his knees, then his waist.

Ned was shouting '*Stop! Stop!*' But there was no sound.

Then the pencil he was holding snapped in his hand under the pressure he was exerting on it, then softening and wrapping itself around his fingers, it thickened and writhed violently.

As Ned reached out his hand to help his friend, the serpentine pencil sprang from his wrist and snaked its way towards Pock coiling itself around his neck. As it constricted, slowly it squeezed the life out of Pock, snake overcoming snake, until finally eyes bulging and starved of breath, he fell into Frank's rising flood of tears and sank until he appeared only as a tiny red speck below the waterline.

A moment of silence was broken by loud knocking and Uncle William's voice came to Ned's ears.

'Ned, are you in distress? Terrible sounds come from your room. May I enter?'

With great effort Ned opened his leaden eyes, he was in his room, standing at the washstand by the window.

'Ned, may I enter?'

Rousing himself quickly Ned replied *'I am sorry uncle, all is well, I think perhaps it was a bad dream. I am sorry to have disturbed you and Aunt May. Please forgive me.'*

Ned could feel his uncle hesitating on the other side of the door, close, not four feet away from him, but invisible.

'If you are sure you are quite well.'

'I am sure, all is well, goodnight uncle.'

William stared blindly through the closed door to Ned's room beyond and then reluctantly released his grip on the handle and went back to bed.

Ned looked down at his wet feet and to where the upturned water jug had poured out onto the rug. Around his wrist, his stock tied tightly, cut into his skin. He searched but could not remember, he could though feel the aftershock of the night's events coursing through his body, the echoes of something dark and disturbing. Frank, Pock, something circled in his head but he could not grasp it.

As he lay down wearily on his bed pulling the tumbled covers over him, his heart banged loudly in his chest, until finally the relief of dreamless sleep overtook him.

CHAPTER 22

March 1884

In all their eleven springs at Smith's Point, Ned had never seen the crocuses grow so profusely. They lit the vista with a carpet of yellow and purple stretching out cheerfully from under the rowan. They were in that fleeting perfect state of being, vivid unblemished velveteen petals, spikes of vibrant glossy leaves, all untouched by the elements or creatures of destruction.

He felt energised by all the symbols of spring especially after such a brutally cold winter and a nearly three-month covering of snow. The seasons each stirred a different feeling in him, all had their place and virtues, but as he breathed in the spring morning air, it was like sweeping clean his lungs for the first time in months.

The day held promise for him.

Before he began painting, he would read Lottie's latest and intriguingly bulky letter. He settled himself in the chair by the window and opened it. A sheet of paper folded inside the letter fell to the floor. He picked it up and on opening it the face of his sister was smiling out at him. By whose hand was this sketched? It was unmistakably Lottie and quite charming. Flattening out the creases, he propped it against the table lamp beside him and began to read her letter.

Wednesday 12th March

Dearest Ned,

How delighted we were to receive your last letter. It sounds like the bad weather has brought many challenges for you and Nancy at Smith's Point but I am relieved to hear brother that you have been able to maintain a sufficient supply of groceries from the town and that you have remained in good spirits throughout.

I know it to be difficult for you to be caged up for so long and understand that you have missed being able to take your walks as often as you would like. However, it is my hope that there may be many winter landscape paintings in the Miller studio that we will be able to enjoy very soon.

The boys are doing very well. Both excel at school although Edward continues to be distracted from his schoolwork by his desire to paint! He hopes very much that his uncle considers him to have some talent and at his insistence, I include a recent sketch he did of his mamma. Although I would like to believe that my nose is not quite so large and that my face not so round, I think he captures something of my look. He was so delighted with his efforts that I could not help but praise him abundantly! He is as sweet and kind in nature as you brother like it was pre-ordained that he would live up to his namesake.

John on the other hand continues to seek physical adventure as his pleasure. I believe the boy must have springs in his limbs. He is never still always finding a tree to climb or a river to jump. He is exhausting but joyous to us in his lightness of spirit and happy nature.

Everyday I thank God for the blessing of my two boys, brought to me late in life perhaps, but filling my days to overflowing.

Luke does very well too and sends his warmest regards to you and Nancy.

We hope that you might visit us soon, the boys ask me almost daily when you might come and you can be assured there will be an enthusiastic reception for their favourite uncle. We of course look forward to seeing Nancy too if she might accompany you? It has been such a long time since we last saw her and please pass my sister our warmest regards. Although I know nothing of it, I am sure she is busy in her own pursuits and social gatherings, which keep her happily occupied and entertained.

For all that I have already mentioned, it would be

so good to see you brother but there is also another important and pressing reason for asking you to come which concerns our mother and father.

As you know, since mamma's passing I have left her studio practically untouched. I have convinced myself over the years that this is not in the desire to create a shrine to her, more that it is a place I go to for reflection and peace in the midst of busy family life.

The time has come when Edward would benefit from his own space for his drawing and painting and so it seemed the right and proper time to pass the studio from mamma to her grandson. Over the last week I have been gathering together our mother's things and be assured, I will keep them all safe, nothing will be discarded. Most of her paintings have gone to our sisters' homes and adorn their walls and I know you already have your favourite pieces of hers but remaining were all her most personal mementos.

Yesterday in clearing out her bureau I found a keepsake box at the back of one of the drawers. It contained a memory of each of her children, a lock of hair, a sketch of a baby's hand or foot, a sock or mitten. Even the babies lost to her, our unknown brothers, their existence preserved with some small pitiful proof of their being.

Folded neatly underneath were three letters she had kept. The first, the letter from Samuel Dudley informing her of John's death. The second, a letter from our father dated September 1851 and the third a letter mamma wrote in June 1857 in response to his letter but which she never posted. I will not share the contents of these letters with you here but I hope you understand brother why I would welcome your visit at the earliest opportunity. I think only you can help to make sense of what I have read and the things our mother never revealed to her children. When you see the letters, you will understand why I felt it important that we were together to read them.

I will eagerly await your reply and pray that it will confirm the details of your visit with us.

Your loving sister,

Lottie

He would settle it with Nancy that he would visit with Lottie and her family at Greenbrook for a few days, he knew she would not come with him, but he would extend the invitation to her anyway.

'*My sister writes to me of her family.*'

Nancy did not look vaguely interested and her eyes did not even flicker in his direction.

'*They are doing very well by all accounts.*'

'*I am delighted to hear it.*' She did not try to hide the derision in her voice.

'*She invites us to visit. The boys would very much like to see us and Lottie has a family matter she is eager to discuss.'*

'Us or you?'

'Us.'

'I do not believe that your family would ever seek my company, it has always been clear to me that they do not consider me worthy of you.'

'I do not believe that to be true. They have always welcomed the opportunity to get to know their sister. I think perhaps it is you that does not seek their company, whatever your reasons for that might be, it would bring me happiness to know that you had their love and care. You still appear to have no friends even after all these years here in Manchester.'

'It is true that I do not have friends that I choose to bring to this house, they would find it so dull but be assured, I have plenty of friends.' She was defiant and combative as always.

Ned knew that she intended to wound him. Her weapon against him was guilt and he felt it pierce him. Everything she sought for her happiness he had not been able to give her and he knew a share of the fault to be his. Practically an orphan, did she not deserve to be loved, to be cherished?

He tried to suffer everything sour that came from her lips as some small atonement for all the ways he had failed her in marriage.

'They will be sorry to hear that you will not be

visiting but I shall write today to let them know that I shall come. I will leave on Thursday and return home on Sunday.'

'I know you do not seek my blessing for your trip and I have grown accustomed to being an afterthought in all your arrangements. It is nothing to me, go, do as you please.'

'I am sorry, I know I continue to disappoint you but it is not my intention, please forgive me.'

'Be assured, I will never absolve you of your failings as a husband, you must live with it.'

In his dismay, Ned knew there was nothing more to be said, she was not for changing.

Lottie was right, his nephews did welcome him with unfettered enthusiasm. They were like two coiled springs Lottie trying her best to anchor them to the floor without quelling their excitement.

Finally, after two tired children were put to bed, Ned and Lottie entered their mother's studio. Ned was immediately struck by the bare walls and uncluttered surfaces, the room now a blank canvas untouched by her brush. In its now almost barren state, it was so much bigger than he remembered but one thing remained the same to his eye, the light. The high ceiling and double aspect of the windows, spread the light in the room evenly and without obvious shadow, he knew it had brought a special illumination to her painting.

They sat shoulder to shoulder on the couch where their mother would take her rest. In the latter months of her life she would often nap here, then somewhat revived, return to her painting. Instinctively, Ned's hand smoothed the worn tapestry on the arm of the couch, trying to connect with something of his mother.

Lottie lifted the leather-covered box onto her lap, turned the key in the lock, and opened the lid. Inside were eight precious packages wrapped in white paper and tied with green ribbon. Each bore her child's name *John Walter Miller born 25th February 1839, Alice Mary Miller born 14th April 1840* all the way through to *Edward William Miller born 4th May 1851*. Beside each name she had painted a tiny flower. For John she had chosen a simple white daisy, for Alice a tiny pink rose bud, for Ned a blue violet, a symbol of faithfulness and humility. They were testament not only their mother's extraordinary talent but to her gentle heart.

One by one, Lottie carefully set down the packages beside her on the couch, mindful not to crush them or disturb their perfect packaging.

To Ned's surprise, Nancy came vividly to his

mind, no mother to care to preserve the joy of her birth. He felt sorry for her.

Lottie unfolded the letter about John's death and together they silently read it revisiting its horror, understanding the significance and the turning point it marked in their mother's life and their own. Their adored brother, their General, their hero. Lottie refolded the letter and kissed it before setting it down beside her.

'This is the letter I told you about. It was written by our father in 1851 but it would seem our mother never received it at that time, perhaps it was lost, she did not respond for nearly six years and then never sent the letter.'

Ned took their father's letter from her.

'...It is regrettable that I have received no reply from you to my letter of 31st May... my circumstances have become unbearable... in the absence of any reply from you... I resolve now that I must return home... I seek to dispose of my last remnants of merchandise in these next two weeks and make arrangements to leave this place before the cold weather arrives... God willing, you should receive this letter by mid-October following which I hope that I shall be returned to you and the children by Christmas for the happiest of reunions...You will find me a changed man my love. These past months have been cruel to me beyond measure, my one and

only desire now, is to be back home with my family...'

Ned could not take it all in. Had his mother ignored his father's request for help? Had she turned her back on her husband and denied him the opportunity to meet his father? He searched Lottie's face for answers.

Finally, she spoke. *'I did not believe that our mother would disregard such a desperate plea from her husband and the father of her children and she did not.'*

She handed Ned the third letter. *'I do not know why she never posted this, perhaps she lost heart, thought it would never reach him.'*

14th June 1857

Dear Walter,

You will not be surprised to learn of my shock in receiving your letter dated 15th September 1851 some nearly six years after it was written.

Had I received the earlier letter to which you refer and your request for me to arrange the additional merchandise for your venture, I would not have disregarded it, despite the challenge to my better judgement it would have presented. You are my husband and I have tried to hold fast to the vows we made before God.

As I write now, there has been no other

correspondence received from you and as you did not return to our family as you planned, I must conclude that your intentions changed and you decided on some other course for your life that did not include your wife and children.

In truth, I never expected you to return and you were lost to us many years ago. You can be assured that I have raised our children to respect the memory of their father and have tried my best not to offer up any resentment towards you. I hope that this might be a comfort to you wherever you find yourself in your new life.

Over these last six and a half years since you left, I have had countless days and nights to consider our union, and I reconciled long ago that ours was not a good match for either of us.

The strong feelings we shared in the early days of our marriage were not founded on sound reason or a relationship that had the qualities to last the course. It was not love. I know what it is to love, it has been felt by me most especially whenever I look into the faces of my children.

Every day I am grateful to God for the blessing of the children you gave me including the two angels we lost and it is my dearest hope that I have been a good and loving mother who has given her children the care and devotion they deserved from the moment I brought them into this world.

By the way of your distant living, your enterprises and schemes, I have had to be both mother and father to our children. I do not resent this, but I do think it wrong that it was required, that I should need to bridge the separate needs children have of their mother and father.

I have also reflected with honesty that you have been dissatisfied with me as your wife. Please know that I deeply regret that you were not content in our marriage and that you felt the need to pursue a life that took you away from me. You were never settled or fulfilled with me and for this I am truly sorry, but I could no more change myself to fit you, than you could to fit me.

In a spirit of truth and honesty I must absolve myself with one last confession.

In the spring after you left, there was another child, Edward William Miller. He takes your name but he is not yours. He is a beautiful child and as beloved to me as all our children although perhaps held closer to me as he will never know a father. His real father is of no consequence now and has no place in our lives, but I did love him once as he did me. God knows my transgression and by His grace, I pray I am forgiven. I hope you can find it in your heart to forgive me too.

I bear you no ill will and pray that God will prosper you. Be assured I will take care of your children and continue to raise them to be good and honest people.

God's speed.

Amelia

Before Ned could speak Lottie said, *'you **are** my brother.'*

Ned stared at the letter.

She touched his arm. *'You are fully my brother. You are as dear to me as my own husband and children.'*

He smiled at her *'I know, do not worry, I am secure in that and there could be no dearer sister to me. But all that I thought true is not and I consider it is an ill-fated man that loses a father not once but twice.'*

'The memories of my father are vague but I do remember that I felt no loss when he left us and that my only desire for his return was that he would bring me gifts. Uncle William has been more of a true father to us, never asking anything of us in return, always there and constant.'

'You are right, he is the best of them, we could not have asked for anything more from a father.'

'I genuinely believe that our lives have been better without Walter Miller.'

Ned nodded; he knew it to be true.

'But what of my real father?'

'I fear that secret died when our mother left this life.'

'Poor mamma, how she suffered, raising us all alone.'

'She did, but despite Walter Miller's shortcomings and absence, she had a life full of love and we all adored her. In some ways, I envy you, you were born out of love, I know now that is not something I could say about myself.'

'Dearest Lottie, only you could turn a tragedy into a blessing in such a convincing way. I honestly believe you will always try to catch me when I fall.'

'Depend on it brother.'

CHAPTER 23

August 1879

Charles opened the door to Ned without his usual warm smile, his face without any expression at all; an empty vessel ready to receive whatever was about to be poured out.

'Come in Ned.'

Ned crossed the threshold into Charles' office. He had never visited him here before but it was everything he had imagined. Rows of leather-bound law books, oak panelling, rich-coloured silk rugs and drapes, exquisite furniture, the smell of beeswax and oranges. In his turmoil it felt like a welcome cocoon of calm.

'Please sit. Can I get you some tea?'

'No thank you, I think it better that I waste no time in giving you the details of the reason for my visit.'

Ned sat down wearily in the chair in front of Charles' desk.

'I deduced from your note that you need to speak to me about something of a grave nature concerning

Nancy.'

'Indeed. My uncle summoned me to his house in Roxbury urgently.'

'Your uncle? Is he in some difficulty?'

'I fear he is because of his desire to protect me.'

'Protect you from what?'

'From Nancy's accusations and threats.'

'You need to enlighten me, why would Nancy be threatening you or your uncle, about what?'

'I can hardly bear to say; it is so ugly. It may be better if you read the letters my uncle has been receiving from her these last nearly two years.'

Ned took the letters out of his pocket and slid the shabby pile across the desk to Charles including the fragments of the final letter which he had torn up.

'I have placed them in order from first to last. You will see how she continues to raise the stakes.'

Charles nodded but said nothing. He read the letters one by one and as Ned watched his face he detected no emotion or shock at their contents. Finally, he pushed the letters back across the desk to Ned.

'Who is Mrs. V. Taylor?' It was not the first question he had expected Charles to ask him.

'I do not know her and Nancy has never spoken of

her.'

'Is it possible that Nancy could be writing these letters under duress from Mrs. Taylor or an associate of hers?'

'It is possible I suppose, I had not considered that. As for their content, over the years you have come to know that Nancy disliked our friendship from the very beginning. She does little to hide it, unjustly attacking your character without cause, repeatedly accusing me of seeking your company over hers. It is true that it is hard to find any pleasure in spending time with her, but that is true for her too and she takes herself away from me and our home to visit so-called friends in town as often as she can these days.'

'Do you know anything of who she visits when she goes to town or on to the city?'

'I do not, although rumour and gossip circulate from time to time. She is never forthcoming with information about her friends and chooses not to bring them to our home. I have not blamed her for this, I do not seek the company of the kinds of friends she would want to keep, and so it has suited us both to keep our social lives separate.'

Charles sat back in his chair fixing his gaze on Ned. *'You and I know the truth and that she has no evidence or reason to believe there has been any wrongdoing or inappropriate behaviour on our part but this does not lessen her threat. Exposure of something that is a lie is as powerful as exposure of something that is true. There are many newspapers for which unsubstantiated gossip brings great profits and once in print it cannot be retracted. These accusations must have shocked your uncle. I am very sorry that he has become involved in something so unpleasant.'*

'Be assured, he is settled on our good character but feels that he has been foolish in submitting to Nancy's threats so readily. He has paid all her demands except the final one.'

'He has not been foolish, he sought to protect you, but perhaps he has been a little optimistic that one payment would not lead to another and another.'

'What can we do?'

'Here is what I suggest. You should ask your uncle to respond to Nancy's last letter. We need to gain some time and stall her threats while I conduct my investigations. Please ask him to reply to let her know that he will arrange the payment but will need two weeks to access the funds given the amount she asks. I think Nancy, or indeed whoever might be coercing her, will not risk losing such a significant payment for the sake of waiting another two weeks.'

'Yes of course I shall go to him now. What investigations?'

'I have a man who is extremely capable and discreet who will be able to find out more about our

Mrs. Taylor, I believe any solution to this terrible business lies there.'

'I am so sorry Charles.'

'It is not for you to be sorry but I am not without my concerns. Keep these letters safe and of course you should tell no one else about this, not even Lottie. If we are able to keep it between the three of us we have a better chance of containment. Although does your Aunt May know?'

'No, Uncle William has not shared the horror of this with her.'

'That is good. Well then, I will arrange my investigations and you should let me know that your uncle has replied to Nancy. Ned, it is especially important that any correspondence between us should not reference this matter in any way, consider everything now with the potential to be used as evidence or to incriminate.'

His words fell on Ned like lead *'I understand.'*

'I will send word as soon as I have any news to report.'

'Thank you Charles and again I am sorry.'

Charles stood, bringing their meeting to a sudden end, then ushered Ned to the door. As he was about to take his leave, Ned thought Charles was about to say something, but he said nothing. Without even a '*goodbye*' Charles opened the door and Ned stepped out into the corridor, the door shutting quietly and solemnly behind him.

Ned returned directly to Washington Park and recounted the details of his meeting with Charles to his uncle. As agreed, his response to Nancy's last letter was sent that afternoon. Then they waited.

Two days passed slowly, both men lost in their thoughts, chained by the fear of what might happen next. Aunt May sensed there was something wrong but accepted that it was not something she would be brought in on, men's business she thought. So, she focussed on spoiling her nephew, all talk between them of nothing that mattered.

On the third day a telegram brought news.

Monday 25th August

Mr. Miller,

Please attend my offices tomorrow at ten o'clock to further discuss our business.

Charles Broadbent Esq.

Ned understood the formality and brevity of Charles' communication, it must be so, in case it was to fall into the wrong hands.

He had not slept for three nights, now again sleep eluded him despite his exhaustion, his aching head tumbling his thoughts constantly. He played conversations with Nancy over and over in his head, there must have been signs, she must have revealed things which he just did not see. In his mind's eye, with hindsight, he could see now what he had missed.

Regular visits to town of course, her often flushed complexion on her return home and her inability to rouse herself in the mornings sometimes sleeping until midday. Her continued allusiveness about her friends, her withdrawal from conversation with him not wanting their exchanges to go too far or to reveal too much, her fine dresses. It had suited him to be blind to what was in front of him, to not listen to gossip, to not question her absences. He accepted he was a fool and he blamed himself.

The morning brought dull skies that depressed his spirits even further and by the time he arrived at Charles' office on Elliot Street at just before ten o'clock he carried the weight of a condemned man. Climbing the stairs to the second floor, he was on his way to execution or reprieve, he did not know which.

On opening the door to him, Ned searched Charles' face for some clue about what was to come next, but again he could not read it.

Neither of them spoke and Ned did not wait to

be offered a seat, quickly taking up his position in the chair in front of Charles' desk like before, while Charles settled himself on the other side.

'What news do you have?'

'I believe my investigations have ascertained the source of our problem. Mrs. V. Taylor, if that indeed be her name, is the wife of Mr. Silas Browne of 25 Endicott Street. It is as you know not a salubrious neighbourhood and most of the properties there are used for industrial purposes or are tenanted. No.25 operates as a house of prostitution, a brothel. Your uncle has been sending payments to No. 7 Endicott Street, and I understand that Mrs. Taylor has an arrangement with a tenant there to receive post for her. They sought to throw us off by giving a different address, but in essence she is the madam at No. 25 and her husband the barkeep.'

'What has any of this to do with Nancy? What is her connection to these people?'

'I believe Nancy to have been unknowingly duped by Mr. Silas Browne.'

'How so?'

'He is a handsome and charming man by all accounts and is known to have been far from faithful to his wife. My man did not establish the frequency of their meetings, but there is record of their association this last two years from reliable sources and he was witness to a meeting between Nancy and

Mr. Browne just yesterday. I am afraid that it is clear that Nancy's relationship with him is of a romantic nature.'

Ned took it all in.

'We have a man here who is able to determine a profitable opportunity when it comes along. I believe he saw Nancy as that opportunity. We also have a man who understands the power of alcohol and other substances to ensnare and corrupt the vulnerable. I conclude that perhaps in the vulnerability of being in love, he trapped her through addiction, made her dependent on him.

There is no suggestion or evidence that she was involved in the activities of the house in any way, nor that she associated with the women working there, I believe he took her in with his proclamations of love and there is no reason to think that she knew Mrs. Taylor to be his wife. Nancy is the unwitting victim here as much as you and I. He has exploited her affection and taken the things she has told him in confidence and during occasions of intimacy, to use them in the most despicable way to line his pockets.'

Ned almost forgot the precarious situation he and Charles were in. His first feeling was for Nancy, sorrow that she had been preyed on in such a contemptible way, taken in by this man who had so callously exploited her affections.

'So, the letters were not really of her own volition.'

'I think not.'

'Is there something that can be done to stop this poison now we know its source?'

'By the nature of my profession I am often in the company of honourable men who seek justice and to protect against moral turpitude in all its terrible guises. In parallel with the law, there are more unorthodox ways perhaps, to bring about a just resolution.'

'Do you already have someone in mind?'

'I do. I would trust him completely to enter the viper's nest and stop the flow of poison that comes in our direction. Will you trust me to instruct him in what needs to be done?'

'There is no-one's wisdom and judgement on this matter that I would trust more.'

'Then it shall be done. I shall meet with him at the earliest opportunity.'

'Should I know who he is?'

'It would be better for you, and for him, if you do not.'

Ned accepted it.

'In the meantime, you should ask your uncle to advise you immediately if he receives any further communications from Nancy and when you return to Smith's Point, you should behave as normal. Do not

give anything away but be watchful of Nancy, there will be a time, very soon I hope, when she will realise the true intentions of her lover. I will write to you when my instructions have been carried out to let you know the merit of our position.'

The next day Thomas Slattery turned the corner onto Endicott Street, it was early, the street was quiet. Even respectable gentlemen, who did not visit it, knew that Endicott Street kept unusual hours.

It was just past dawn and already the pungent smell from the backlot privies coupled with the acrid smell of lye overwhelmed his nostrils and he had to raise his handkerchief to his nose for some relief.

He knew No. 25 to be a low-end parlour house rented out to working class boarders although the majority of its residents were prostitutes. He did not expect the house to be awake but it was his intention to take them unawares and the early hour would also ensure as few people as possible to see him on this street.

When he reached the door he raised his stick, knocked loudly, and waited. No response.

He knocked again, longer this time, until eventually a man's voice came from behind the door.

'Who knocks at this hour? It is enough to wake the

dead. Come back at noon, we will be happy to receive you then.'

'Sir you would do well to open this door unless you wish trouble to befall this house.'

'Whoever you are I do not answer to threats. Leave my house.'

'I believe there to be an illegal bar on these premises and all manner of other delinquent activities that, at my bidding, some will decide no longer to turn a blind eye to. Open up I say.'

He heard shuffling from behind the door and then the sound of the key turning in the lock and a heavy barrel bolt being released from its socket.

The door was opened to a small crack by a dishevelled man who by Thomas Slattery's estimation was in his mid-thirties. Coarsely shaven, with sky blue and red eyes heavy from sleep, he stank of liquor. He looked out suspiciously and Thomas saw that he had his foot jammed behind the door to ensure no forced entry.

'Who are you? What do you want?'

'I believe you will consider me a welcome friend once I have discussed my business with you. May I come inside? I expect that you would not want to conduct our conversation on the street.'

After some hesitation, reluctantly Silas Browne

opened the door and let him in, closing it quietly behind him.

'Well, state your business sir, I wish to return to my bed.'

'Perhaps we could discuss our business in the parlour so that all the house might not be disturbed.'

'They will have been disturbed well enough already by your knocking. This way.'

He led Thomas to the front parlour where he already knew, despite its impeccable appearance, nothing genteel or of a decent nature ever took place there.

'I will not sit thank you.' Silas had not offered.

'I say again, state your business.'

'Indeed yes, I do not mean to detain you unnecessarily. My business concerns Mrs. Nancy Miller, I have reason to believe you are intimate with the lady, is that true?'

'None of your business. By what right do you enter my house asking me these questions?'

'By right of all that is lawful and decent. I have reason to believe from reliable sources that your relationship with Mrs. Miller is of an inappropriate nature and that she has been ensnared by you by means of lies and false promises.'

'I do not know of whom you speak.'

'Come now, is your memory so short, she was only in this very house the day before yesterday.'

'Do you spy on me sir?'

'It is not difficult to observe a man who has enslaved a married woman of good character through alcohol and drugs bringing her to a helpless point of addiction. Worse perhaps, she believes you to have a true affection for her, she does not see how she is used by you.'

'It is all lies. You have no proof.'

'I can prove it with no trouble sir if you wish me to. You use the lady as your pawn in a game of extortion from which I know you to have already benefitted considerably. Know this, I could and I will, have you thrown out on the street for any number of reasons not least the illegal bar and gambling you run from this house. All your sources of ill-gotten gains will cease and I will ensure you never again secure a property in this city to trade from.

Trust me, my contacts are of considerable influence and the law is on my side. There will be no question of any man coming to your rescue, you shall be out on your own sir with no future prospects.'

'Why should I believe you have such powers? I do not even know your name, reveal yourself.'

'My name is of no consequence to you although the power I have over you is. Be assured, I have eyes *all around this city which will turn a blind eye to the activities of this house if I please it, but those eyes will not be blind to your efforts to corrupt the character of a married woman and destroy the reputation of good men. Do you understand me sir?'*

'You bluff!'

'The risk is yours. I am on the side of all that is good and decent, you are on the side of all that is corrupt and dishonest. The Aldermen of this city are keen to wipe away men of your leanings and restore this city to the highest moral standing. Be assured sir, since you have debauched Mrs. Miller and plied her with alcohol and drugs, she no longer knows her own mind or the words that fall from her lips, so you cannot stand with any confidence on any information she has ever entrusted to you.'

Silas Browne considered that he could easily give her up, he was becoming tired of her anyway, she was too needy. There would be other opportunities, and he had prospered well enough already from his association with her, she was not worth the risk.

'Tell me, what is your decision? Will you desist in your odious attempts to extort money from men of good character and standing? Trust me, you cannot even imagine how far I would be prepared to go to protect decency and integrity, you will surely be the loser in this.'

'I will not succumb to empty threats; however you can be assured that any association I have with the lady will cease, it suits me.'

'Very well. Do I have your word that neither you, or your wife, if that she be, or any associate of yours will ever make contact with the lady again? If she comes to your door you should send her away and do her the kindness of revealing what your true intentions have been towards her so that she might be released from any misguided affection she has for you. Also, you must promise you will make no further contact with her family nor publish any lies relating to them. You should make no mention of my visit, if you do, be assured I will act swiftly to ruin you.'

'You have my word.'

'Then I will take your word to be as firm as any gentleman's. I think we have concluded our business and I will bid you good day. I do not expect that we shall meet again but I will of course retain a watching interest in your activities Mr. Browne. I am sure you understand.'

Silas searched for some final words of defiance, to save face, but it was useless. In sullen silence, he led Thomas Slattery to the door, and he was gone as quickly as he had appeared.

Thomas went directly from Endicott Street to Charles' office to share the news of his visit and his confidence that the matter was closed. Nancy would be spurned by her lover but she would never know their part in it.

CHAPTER 24

Wednesday 7ᵗʰ May 1884

Charles was looking forward to his afternoon with Ned. He had not seen him since the exhibition and was savouring the opportunity to spend time with his friend and celebrate his success. In the lightness of his mood, as blithe spirit overtook him, he knocked *hello* in morse on the door, ...-.. .-.. --- Ned would be oblivious to its meaning but it entertained him to do it anyway.

In his pocket he felt for the small, gift-wrapped box, a belated birthday present for Ned, he was sure he had chosen well. A specially commissioned Gorham silver card case, finely etched on one side with the image of a rowan tree underneath which it read *virtus sapientiae et tutela,* on the other side a simple circular cartouche of delicate leaves bearing Ned's initials.

The door swung open *'Charles, it is so good to see you.'*

'You too my friend.'

'Come up to the parlour. Will you take some lemonade?'

'Thank you, I will.'

They were greeted by the spring sunshine that poured in through the windows lighting every surface it touched with a clear pure light, while the sweet cooling breeze that only May brings, circulated soothingly around the room. It was by far Charles' favourite place at Smith's Point, it had no pretentions, simply everything a soul in need of rest and renewal could want.

'Please sit.' Ned offered Charles the most comfortable chair as always and poured them both a glass of lemonade.

'You look well and in good spirits.'

'I am indeed, the weather has been fine these last two weeks and I have found myself outdoors most of the time. I fear I become more and more like some wild animal that resists the containment of four walls!'

'Well, I see it does you no harm at all. Of course I am bound to ask, is Nancy here, does she know of my visit?'

'She does, but she will not join us. She sits sulking in the studio after our latest disagreement this morning I am afraid. She had no patience to sit for me as promised and that led to an argument,

nothing unusual, regretfully a regular occurrence as you know.'

'She will avoid me, us both, then?'

'Perhaps it is for the best.'

'Can we talk freely?'

'Be assured, she will not hear us.'

In his uncertainty, Charles lowered his voice, just to be sure.

'She must have been most satisfied with the results of the exhibition; I suspect Messrs Williams & Everett already encourage you to produce more work for them to show?'

'Yes, all except three sketches and two watercolours have been sold. There is talk of a further exhibition this winter but as you know I can be no slave to time, I am not sure that I will be able to build an adequate body of new work by then. Perhaps next spring.'

'It is wonderful to see you gaining such admiration for your work. I can see that this place continues to be an inspiration to you. That I cannot see you as often as I would like, because you place yourself out here in the wilds, is a sacrifice I am prepared to make in the interests of great art!'

'Well, I am certainly well-suited to this remote, simple living and that of course has been my standing excuse for never accepting any of your

offers to travel to Europe or visit the grand boulevards of Paris; savour the artistic heady heights of Montmartre.'

'I may have always accepted your rejection of the idea with great reluctance but never without some understanding of your reasons. I simply wished for you to have opportunities to be among your peers, enjoy art's shared language, extend the boundaries of your creativity if you wished to. Ned, the light and the air seem so different there and I have always found it to be a place where the people, art, life itself manifest themselves as something quite intoxicating.'

'I can see that for some there could be much to be gained from it but I cannot believe there to exist a more beautiful changing spectrum of light than here in Manchester. I am confident that the sun favours it every bit as well as Montmartre! No two days here have ever shown themselves the same to me. I believe that what this place offers up will exceed my days and out run my opportunities to capture it all.'

'Victory is yours! I shall forever remain silent on the matter!'

Ah well, it is good to know when you are beaten! To be serious my friend, I do not take for granted your efforts to encourage my painting, but I am content. Remember I had the finest teacher in my mother, she had an extraordinary talent, even though she never received public recognition for her work. She had a way of showing me how to open my eyes without judgement, to trust what I see, even if I do not see things as others do.

'She was a remarkable woman.'

'She was.'

Charles drank his lemonade as he considered whether he should have one more try. *'Perhaps then a trip just for the enjoyment of the travel?'*

'How dull I am Charles! I am sure I will never consider the prize of visiting foreign shores great enough to suffer the inconveniences of long-distance travel and being away from my home. Perhaps I was destined to live the life of a recluse! All I know is that I hope to live out my days here.'

'What about Nancy? Do you think she will want to live out her days here with you.'

'It has always been difficult to navigate the way to what Nancy wants. Since that bad business with Browne, strangely she seems in some ways more settled, although it gives me no pleasure to consider that perhaps she has given up the idea of love.'

'And she still never mentions anything of him?' He kept his voice low.

'No, never, and I am confident that she does not suspect that you or I know anything of it.'

'It is a wonder that her disappointment at being

spurned by her lover has not manifested itself in any way that showed itself to you all these years.'

'I think Nancy too proud to reveal any failures or frailties to me although I know that her anger and disappointment is often directed at me in other guises. Arguments are rarely about the complaint she raises, rather the unspoken issues between us, so there is no satisfactory resolution to be had by either party. What I observed at the time was her quiet fury, her deep rage. The echoes of indignation she felt as the victim of such a cold betrayal resonated long after the event. I believe she continues to feel it. Still, as I say, she is proficient at diverting her ire towards others. Nancy has always been quick to blame all but herself for her fate, and so she does.'

'Blames who?'

'You, my family, all the innocents of course.'

'That must be an enduring burden for you as I know you would seek to protect us all.'

'I have become accustomed to it perhaps but it has been easier since she left.'

'What do you mean, left?'

Ned looked shaken by his own words.

'I do not know why I said that, please excuse me, my mind plays tricks!'

'Has she left you Ned?' Charles asked hesitantly. *'It is such a long time since anyone has seen her.'*

'No, I cannot fathom why I would have said such a thing.'

Charles could see that Ned was confused and the shock of his words was clearly etched on his face.

'Are you feeling quite well Ned?'

Ned's lips moved, as if to speak, but nothing came out.

'Nancy is here is she not?'

'She is.'

'Then it is simple.' Charles stood suddenly, left the parlour and went down the corridor to the studio. Standing outside the door, he knocked and waited. Nothing. He knocked again, still nothing.

'Nancy, it is Charles, may I enter?' No reply came.

With a rising sense of foreboding he turned the handle, pushed open the door and entered the studio. There she was.

In the centre of the room was Ned's easel and approaching it, he found himself standing right in front of a portrait of Nancy. Painted bathed in the light coming in through the window, head turned looking over her shoulder towards the watcher, reproachful eyes questioning the interruption to her solitude. Ned had captured her wild spirit and the confident demeanour and substance of a woman approaching her middle years. Still as beautiful, in fact the passage of time had made her more so, her face having shaped into its full potential.

Although enraptured momentarily by the painting, the cold reality of no living, breathing Nancy shook Charles. Where was she?

He went from the studio to Ned's study, where he also slept, not there. He ran down the stairs and went room to room with no sense of trespassing even when he entered Nancy's bedroom, because he already knew she was not there.

The bed was made and the room neat, everything as he might have expected, that was until his eyes fell on the battered laundry bat leaning against the wall under the window, why was that there? In every sense the scene seemed alive to him as if she had just stepped out but a stale, dense, air filled the room and he knew no body had broken the skin of it for years.

On her bedside table was a photograph of Ned, against which leant a pressed red rose, long since faded but in its time carefully and tenderly placed. A hope for something to be gained, or a reminder of something lost, he did not know which. Now he felt like and intruder, so closing the door gently, he moved on.

Finally, he entered the kitchen where he found

Mary singing quietly to herself while she baked bread. His sudden appearance had caught her unawares and in her flustered state she had dropped the loaf pan she was holding.

'I am so sorry to have startled you Mary.'

Mary quickly retrieved the loaf pan from the floor and dusted the flour from her apron.

'Good day sir, I did not know the master had visitors. I am sorry I have been in the garden and did not hear you knock. She did a strange kind of awkward bob, not quite a curtsy. *'Do you require refreshments?'*

'No, no, nothing for you to do, it is only a short visit and I shall not stay for supper. I wonder, do you know where your mistress is?'

Mary looked stricken by the question. *'My mistress? I do not understand sir.'*

'Might she have gone into town this morning?'

Mary looked uncomfortable as if she were about to break a confidence.

'It is not my place to speculate as to the whereabouts of my mistress, or to discuss the master's private business, where Mrs. Miller has gone is for the master to confirm.'

'He knows I am speaking with you' He lied *'If you do have an idea of where she is, please tell me where I might find her.'*

'I do not know sir.'

'Does she never speak to you of where she is going?'

Mary looked confused. *'She has not been in this house sir these last four years. The master said she had gone away but I do not know where and I would not presume to ask. I do not want to give the master cause to doubt my discretion, that is all I know.'*

'Of course, thank you Mary, I know Mr. Miller values your loyalty most highly. Let us not speak of this again inside or outside this house.'

'Yes sir, of course sir, I understand.'

Mary was relieved that his questions would go no further but felt emboldened by their discussion.

'May I ask, is the master quite well? He does not eat much these days and restful sleep seems to evade him. I would not want to think of him suffering if something ails him.'

'He is quite well I believe, and there is no reason for you to feel any disquiet, he would be most touched by your concern for him.'

Mary blossomed at his words *'He is a good and decent man, one of the finest in my eyes.'*

'He is indeed. I am sorry to have disturbed you Mary, I will let you get on with your work; I hope I have not spoilt the bread through my interruption.' He smiled to put her at her ease and left.

Returning to the parlour, Ned had not moved from his chair, but now sat slumped with his head in his hands.

Charles sat down quietly not wanting to stir his obvious distress. He then began a line of questioning that he hoped would reveal the truth of events to Ned himself.

'Ned, she is not here.'

'I cannot explain it, she is here, but she is not. We argued only this morning.'

'In the studio?'

'Yes, in the studio.'

'Could it have been one of your dreams?'

Ned did not answer.

Charles waited, eyes fixed on Ned's bewildered face, until finally he spoke.

'Charles, I think something to be wrong. I see her and I hear her voice but now, as we consider the implications of my confounding words, I cannot say that she manifests herself in flesh and blood. I do not know what it means. Am I going mad?'

'I have just spoken with Mary. She says that Nancy left this house four years ago.'

'I do not understand. How can she know that so surely to be so, but I do not?'

'I think your mind denies what it knows to be true

and so you have been able to live on day to day in the unreality of her physical presence.'

'Why would I do that?'

'Perhaps you feel some shame in your wife leaving you and it has altered your perspective so you have rejected reality because of it?'

'I do not think so. I believe if Nancy were to leave me for a happier and more fulfilling life elsewhere, I would accept it with some relief, I have always sought her happiness even though I have known all these years that I could not offer it.'

Charles reached for his glass and averting his gaze from Ned asked *'How do you fare with your back pain these days?'*

'Why do you ask?'

Again, Charles waited.

'As you enquire, it is much improved and I do not find myself so debilitated by its effects.'

'What is the cause of the improvement? Do you still use Laudanum to ease your suffering?'

'Laurie...' Ned uttered quietly.

'Who is Laurie?'

Ned waved away the question.

'I do of course still take it.'

'Apart from it's addictive nature which would

ensnare any man, there is growing evidence of its dire side effects, including the night terrors and vivid hallucinations it can bring about.'

'Do you suggest that I have been hallucinating?'

'I only seek a logical reason for all this as I do not consider you to be in any way mad.'

'So, you suggest that I may have been seeing and hearing things that are not there, are not real? that I am...' he cut off abruptly and a look of horror seized and froze his face. Eyes staring as if he were seeing something that Charles could not, colour gone, he suddenly had the hollowed-out look of a cadaver.

'Ned, what is it? What afflicts you so terribly?'

Ned's voice was weak, lower than a whisper, like all air had left his lungs. *'I can see it.'*

'See what? Ned what do you see?'

'I see my hands around Nancy's neck, I see her eyes desperately searching my face, I see her dropping lifeless to the floor. Charles, she died at my hands. I know where she is.'

'Can you be sure? Perhaps your mind plays tricks again.'

'Now I see it, I know it to be real. I can take you to her.'

Ned stood and had to steady himself with the

arm of the chair as he swayed like a blade of grass whipped by the wind. Charles got up too and without speaking followed Ned's lead. They went down the stairs, lifted the door latch, and left the sanctuary of the house. They walked down through the garden in silence until Ned stopped suddenly under the rowan tree. Dropping to his knees, like a marionette, strings cut, he smoothed his hands along the surface of the ground, as if feeling the stretch of cool canvas. '*She is here. This is where she lies.*'

Charles looked at the ground, he wanted to reject Ned's confession, find every reason to believe that it was not so, but as he looked he could see that the earth appeared different where Ned kneeled. Richer in colour, disturbed, giving way to flowers that bloomed nowhere else under the tree. In that moment Charles felt closer than he had ever been to fear and panic.

'*Are you sure Ned?*'

'*I am sure. I killed her. With no one else in the world to love her. I killed her and buried her here.*'

He began to sob uncontrollably.

Instinctively Charles looked back at the house. The kitchen door was closed.

'*Ned we must go back into the house. Come with me I beg you. We must speak.*'

He hooked his hand under Ned's arm and gently lifted him to his feet. *'Let us go into the house my friend.'*

Ned looked at him blindly and followed him like a lamb.

Charles sent Mary home with reassurances that she had done nothing wrong. He asked her to take the next three days off, she would be paid and was not in any trouble. From her demeanour he was satisfied that she had seen and heard nothing and had no tale to tell, her only discomfiture was her concern for her master.

Back in the parlour, neither one spoke for a few minutes until finally Ned's sobs subsided giving way to a trance-like state. Charles continued to wait for some small drop of composure to fall on both of them and then, when time had done its work, he was the first to speak. *'Ned, I know you to be a man who would not harm a fly, let alone commit such a heinous act. There are things to be said and explored so that we might find the answers that can reconcile these clear conflicts of character.'*

Ned nodded but did not look up. He just stared down at his hands spread in his lap, the hands of a murderer.

'Tell me everything of what you remember. Did you argue?'

Ned lifted his head, pupils growing orbs of

black as his eyes began to focus, eventually finding his lost voice.

'We did. She began an argument under the guise of a complaint about Mary saying that she was lazy and insolent, accusations with no merit at all. I knew her anger to be fuelled by the rage she felt at being jilted by Browne, I understood that this would inevitably come in my direction. She said terrible things, wild accusations and bitter insults directed particularly at you Charles. She made her disappointments about married life very clear to me. I begged her to desist but she would not. My reluctance to enter the realms of her unfounded grievances simply elevated her frustration. She spat in my face Charles.'

Ned paused and took a deep breath. *'I promise, I left the room, left her to contend with her own anger.'*

'So, you did not see her again that evening?'

'I did not think so until now. I took Laudanum that evening to calm my nerves and quell the rising pain in my back. I fell into sleep quickly and deeply, entering the terror of my dreams.'

'Tell me about the dream.'

The nightmare came back to Ned vividly now that shock had lifted the lid on his memories.

*'All was silent and the darkness was only lit by a distant lamp. The ground began to shudder and

move violently beneath my feet and so I reached out to grasp a lifeline. My hands tightened around a silken rope, my knuckles white, as I clung on for my life.

Then, my grip released, I felt myself descending into a pit, a black hole. I carried something in my arms, weighed down by it, but unable to see what it was. A canopy of green swayed above me across a sky of burnt umber and gold. My body felt heavy and my feet sank into the earth below.

I looked down at my hands, but they were coloured as another man's, not my own. Dark brown, lined, nails blackened. Tiny red insects crawled on my skin and then fell to the ground around my feet colouring the earth. All the while I could hear Nancy's voice, not cruel and hateful, but loving and gentle – do not worry my love, all will be well, it is not of your doing.

I laid down my burden and felt light again. I no longer sank into the earth but trod lightly following a welcoming warm light that guided my way.

In the morning, I remember I awoke soaked in sweat but with a peaceful feeling. In my restored state of mind, I gave no thought to the earth under my nails nor the mud on my slippers.

It all makes sense to me now, what it all means, poor Nancy. I must give myself up immediately.'

Charles had to think quickly, now that Ned had made his confession, there was only one dreadful destination for him.

'Ned, listen to me, we must consider whether you intended to kill Nancy.'

'Of course I did not.'

'We must also consider then whether you were aware of your actions at the time, if you knew your own mind.'

'I was not. I did not. I would never knowingly seek to cause her harm.'

'These things I know to be true, so I must ask one thing of you. Wait until tomorrow to make your confession to the authorities.'

Ned searched Charles' face trying to understand the meaning of his request. *'Why delay the inevitable? I must face punishment for my crime.'*

'If you took a life, then the law will dictate the price to be paid, but if you value true justice and indeed our friendship, please do this one thing for me. I ask just a day to consider the circumstances of your case.'

'Just one day?'

'Just one day.'

'I have sent Mary away for a few days so you will not be disturbed. I need you to stay here, go nowhere. I shall return here tomorrow by one o'clock at the

very latest, I promise you shall have the release your tormented soul craves. I beg you, please give me your word that you will speak of this to no one until then.'

Ned stared at him; Charles waited.

'Ned? Please.'

'You have my word.'

'Then I shall leave you. We will speak tomorrow and together we will revisit all the details of that terrible night and will ensure that justice takes its course. Until then, you should pray for God's grace and mercy. As it should be for all men, I promise, we will seek justice in God's name.'

As Charles took his leave he had no understanding himself of why he sought to delay the inevitable by another day - they would both be in a place of wretched torment until then - he just knew that he needed more time.

CHAPTER 25

Thurs 8th May 1884

Charles paced the floor in a vain effort to shake off the paralysing fatigue he felt. After leaving Ned yesterday afternoon, he had come directly to his office in Elliot Street and had been at his desk all night trying to resolve the impossible. A life had been taken, the corollary of that night's events was plain, if found guilty of murder Ned would hang. He had to use every ounce of his willpower to put the horror of the image out of his head; he had to think clearly.

So, what was he looking for? What defence was there?

Charles had always sought and valued justice above all else but never before had it had such agonising personal consequences for him as it did now. This night he had reluctantly assumed the mantle of judge and jury '*I do solemnly swear or affirm that I will administer justice without respect to persons, and do equal right to the poor and to the rich…*'

In all his deliberations, he had tried to anonymise Ned, it was the only way he could focus his mind and consider Ned's circumstances without prejudice, as he would do for any other client he represented. '*...and that I will faithfully and impartially discharge and perform all the duties incumbent upon me...*'

In times of greatest pressure and in the throes of the highest profile criminal cases, Charles was known by his peers to be at his calmest and most sagacious, it sharpened his mind and his instincts. He was at his best in the eye of the storm but he had never had to do his job while in such a deep pit of grief, he felt the debilitation of it acutely, the blunting of his thinking. '*...according to the best of my abilities and understanding agreeably to the constitution and laws of the United States...*'

He found himself in completely unfamiliar terrain, washed over with fear and anxiety. Not since Sarah's accident had he felt so out of control of his thoughts or emotions. '*...so help me God.*'

His collar seemed to constrict around his neck and he felt light-headed never taking the relief of a deep breath, holding everything tight inside him, for fear that any moment of relaxation would cause his insides to spill out onto the floor irredeemably. He could feel the fast, steady thud of his heart in his chest and the rush of blood in his ears, every part of his being active, the streams running through his body racing to every extremity seeking a solution.

For the first time in his life, Charles considered whether he could equally serve both God and the law, he faced a crisis of conscience. The two things had always been inextricably bound together for him, never having to separate one limb from another, simply part of the same body. Now he felt the breaking apart of the divine justice that comes by God's grace at odds with the requirement to uphold the laws of man.

He had tried to consider the mind of God, a futile pursuit, but this night he had felt like a refugee in a foreign land seeking a place of safety, a home where the world could make sense again. Would for instance God punish the child who in their innocence and lack of understanding of worldly things ended a life unwittingly? Would there be a crime to be answered for? Would it be judged as a wilful act of malice?

He kept going back to his bible, needing answers, searching for truth.

As he considered the victim, poor Nancy, her beginnings in life may have taught her to be cruel and selfish but she was innocent in death and her life was as sacred as the next persons, she deserved justice no less. Her life could not, must not, weigh any less on the scales of justice than his love for his friend and his belief in his innocence.

Ned's circumstances had led Charles to the case of *Massachusetts vs Tirrell*. A case successfully won by his father's exemplar Rufus Choate. The trial attracted both admiration and criticism for Rufus, he had gained something of a reputation as a courtroom performer, but Charles knew that this in no way diminished his genius and his fundamental understanding of human nature and how to draw out the best and worst of it.

Albert Tirrell was tried for the murder of his mistress Maria Ann Bickford, a woman of some notoriety and widely considered to be of low morals. He was successfully defended by Rufus Choate with the jury finding him not guilty and acquitting him of her murder even though she likely died at his hands.

The case centred around the fact that Tirrell was known to be a chronic sleepwalker with his family members and others coming forward to testify that they had witnessed him in this state on many occasions since childhood and that he never had any memory of these episodes. Charles knew this also to be true for Ned, he had been there when his family had mercilessly teased him about his nocturnal childhood escapades.

Coupled with his somnambulism, he now knew of Ned's dependency and continued regular use of Laudanum, a devilish partner in all that had taken place. Ned could do nothing about his sleepwalking and in managing his pain he had suffered the negative effects and addiction of Laudanum. Charles considered him an accidental player in this tragedy.

By the time the sun had come up and the street had begun to stir, Charles had built his defence, he believed he could save Ned.

He had considered all the facts.

<u>There were no witnesses to the crime</u>.

For four years Ned had no memory of strangling Nancy or burying her body in the garden. His mind had locked away the events of that night, completely hidden from his sight, until yesterday's sudden realisation.

Ned had suffered from frequent chronic sleepwalking since early childhood and long before his use of Laudanum. His family would attest to this.

Ned had regularly medicated for crippling pain caused by a childhood accident. The family physician would attest to his back injury and prescribing Laudanum following the accident.

Ned was considered a man of integrity and

good character by all who knew him. Character witnesses would be easy to secure in number.

There was no history of violence in his marriage and the only verbal or physical abuse had come from Nancy towards her husband although there were no witnesses to support this unless Mary had seen or heard anything.

Ned did not intend to kill Nancy and had never had murderous thoughts towards her. He never spoke ill of her and was not motivated in any way to harm her. There was no evidence of premeditation.

Nancy had been an often-absent wife and had entered into an adulterous relationship with a man of low moral standing. There was evidence of this but he would not want to produce it.

Ned and Nancy had fought on the evening she was murdered but there were no witnesses.

Nancy had no contact with any of her family members. It was a fair assumption therefore that she would not have shared anything of problems in her marriage.

He knew from Ned that Nancy had no real friends, no one to confide in, Ned had told him that even Mrs. Dean had given up writing years ago as her letters continued to go unanswered. Although she kept her life separate from Ned, he was sure there was no one. There was Silas

Browne of course and all that she had disclosed to him about her marriage and her accusations about Ned and Charles' relationship, but Silas Browne would not want to put himself forward as a witness, he had too much to lose. He would continue to lurk in the shadows of the depraved life he chose to live.

Ned was not guilty of Nancy's murder.

Rufus Choate had won the Tirrell case on circumstantial evidence, Charles must do the same, he must.

He checked his watch, if he left now, he could be back in Manchester by noon. Until the crime was reported Charles was an accessory-after-the-fact.

He tidied his desk, put out the lamps and locked the office door behind him, before making his way to the washroom on the next floor where he hoped he could wash away the stain of weariness and despondency that overwhelmed him.

As he stood in front of the mirror now, he saw the image of his father staring back at him, the march of time accelerated in the last few hours, his future face emerging in front of his eyes. He longed for his father at this moment, his calm and steady knowing, his ability to re-order the world and make sense of man's place in it in the face of crisis and adversity. He had a way of taking away suffering, not by ending it, but by reducing it to its rightful place alongside its superior companions of faith, hope, and love.

He ran the faucet and as it gurgled into life, he splashed his face with the cool cloudy water in the vain hope of cleansing and reinvigoration, but it did not come.

As he dried his face his nose began to drip blood splashing heavily at his feet. He tilted his head backwards to stem the crimson flow and as he rested his head against the wall and closed his eyes, longed-for sleep almost claimed him. Forcing himself back from the brink of unconsciousness, he squeezed the bridge of his nose, until finally the blood stopped. He must not spill out.

He reached for the handkerchief in his pocket, his reassurance in case of any further hematic incidents and as he did, his fingers were stung by the hard edges of the forgotten gift box. Celebrating a birthday seemed such a distant and trivial thing now in the face of life or death and his heart sank even further if that were possible.

CHAPTER 26

Thursday 8th May 1884

In his desperation to get back to Ned it had felt like everything was moving in slowed motion and as he waited on the station platform, heart racing, it seemed as if the train would never come. He pointlessly checked his watch repeatedly, as if by looking at it, he could affect its progress in some way. Looking around him, it irked him that no one seemed to be in any hurry, all enjoying the luxury of time. Did they not understand that yesterday the world had been tipped upside down?

Finally, he heard the rhythmic sound of the train's wheels on the tracks and could see its plumes of steam in the distance. As it pulled in and began to slow, his heartbeat settled too matching its comforting pulse, until the hissing brakes brought it to a laboured halt.

For an hour and a half, he endured the painfully slow progress of the train. His carriage was busy but at least the comings and goings of the other passengers distracted him from his increasingly dark thoughts. Although, did the train normally travel so slowly? Was it always so full of pointless noisy chatter?

A dizzying kind of relief almost overwhelmed his balance as he finally stepped down from the train. Carefully avoiding all the moving obstacles in the shape of small children, luggage, and the flapping tails of ladies' dresses, he looked around anxiously for a coach to take him on to Smith's Point, he could walk, but every minute counted in his urgency to get back to Ned. He would pay extra to be the only passenger, he could save a few minutes, encourage the driver to push his horse harder.

A few uncomfortable and bone-rattling minutes later he was outside Ned's door. All sense of time and place had left him. There was only now, nothing that had gone before, only this moment here at his door.

He knocked and called out, not waiting for a reply, he kept calling *'Ned it is Charles, open the door.'*

'Ned, please let me in. Ned!' Nothing.

He peered through the door's small glass viewing pane. Looking into the entrance hall Ned's overcoat and hat hung on their hooks just as they had when he arrived yesterday. Nothing had moved.

Why did he not answer?

Charles had never given any thought to the merits of physical strength, his mind was the engine and the only power source of his body that he regarded, so it was some kind of primal instinct that seized him as he put his shoulder against the door and pushed hard. He threw himself against it but it did not give way.

He called out again but no answer came.

He was becoming desperate and so searched around for something that would help him break in, he did not know what he was looking for. A snow shovel leant against the porch wall and without thinking he grabbed for it and began jabbing its blade between the door and its frame at the same time kicking his foot hard against the bottom of the door. Eventually a small gap opened up and he pushed the blade in fully, pulling the shovel handle backwards and forwards levering the door, until finally the wood splintered and the lock gave way.

'Ned, it is Charles!' Nothing.

The house was silent. He crossed the hall, and as he stood at the bottom of the stairs, his head began to swim and he had to reach for the banister to steady himself. He looked up in fear of what lay above, holding his breath as he climbed the stairs, not exhaling until he reached the parlour and saw Ned sitting in the chair where he had left him last night.

His head was bowed and his hands were clasped in his lap as if in prayer. Everything in his shape and being was reduced, all hope lost, but Charles' worst fear had not been realised, he was alive.

Charles stood in frozen silence looking down on his friend until eventually Ned lifted his head, eyes so full of sorrow, Charles could hardly bear it.

'Ned.'

'You came back.'

'Yes of course, I promised you I would come back.'

Ned nodded silently.

'Have you been sitting here all night?'

'I have nowhere else to go but to be here in this place where I remembered my crime. This chair is my gaol and place of detention and I must remain here until I move to my time of reckoning. I do not deserve to walk, or look at the sky, or take a drink. I no longer have the rights of any creature on this earth.'

Charles picked up the untouched glass of lemonade that was still on the table beside him from the previous night. *'Drink this, we must talk, and you must be able to speak with fluidity.'* Like an obedient child, Ned took the glass from his outstretched hand and drank thirstily, although he showed no signs of recovery. Something more was going to be necessary. '*We shall both need our strength for the difficult conversation we must have and will need sustenance. Wait here, I shall return directly.*'

He went down to the kitchen with no idea of what he was looking for or where to look for it, he had never had to find his way around one, this was unchartered territory for him. Mary had baked bread, he knew that, so he followed his nose and found the freshly baked loaf inside a bread box. There would be cheese too in the larder he thought, yes bread and cheese would suffice, and more lemonade. He carefully carried a haphazardly loaded tray back up the stairs and set it down on the table quietly.

'*Eat my friend, it will serve us both well not to be diminished by our hunger.*'

They sat side by side in silence.

Ned's distress seemed to consume him, struggling to swallow the bread and cheese, grief constricting his throat. All the while he kept his eyes lowered in a vain attempt to hide the tears that formed steady rivulets down his face. The floodgates were open, Charles had to find a way to close them.

He steeled himself for what had to be done, they would both be entering the lion's den, neither would emerge unscathed. He must find a way to bring Ned out of his distraught state, any hope of restoration would depend on him thinking clearly and rationally, all other roads led to torment.

Once Charles was satisfied Ned had eaten enough to give him some strength, he got up and manoeuvred his chair setting it down directly in front of him, their knees almost touching.

'Ned, look at me.'

Ned slowly raised his head, empty eyes finally following, meeting his gaze.

'Do you trust me?'

'Yes.'

'Do you consider me a fair and just man?'

'Yes, of course, yes.'

'Very well. You have made your confession to me, a fair and just man of the law. You will be tried, I will defend you, you will be judged on your actions and pay the price accordingly. Do you understand?'

'I understand. I accept my fate.'

'Good.'

Charles took a deep breath before continuing. *'Here, in this room right now, I need you to imagine that we are in a court of law. You are accused of the murder of your wife Nancy Miller and the disposal of her body. You have entered a plea of Not Guilty.'* Charles continued quickly before Ned could respond.

'The judge, Justice Gray, sits over there to our left' he pointed towards the mahogany bureau near the window that would act as the Bench for the proceedings *'and the jury sit over there to our right'* he pointed now to the rosewood sofa that Ned had inherited from his mother. *'You understand?'*

Ned looked perplexed, *'But I am guilty and this is not a real court.'*

'I ask you again. Will you allow this court to ascertain whether you are guilty of murder? Do you agree to proceed?'

Ned was hesitant but at the same time carried along by Charles' steadfast conviction to continue and so silently nodded his agreement.

'Imagine that we have already heard the case for the prosecution. They were unable to establish any motive or mal intent on your part or any record of ill-treatment of Nancy by you, nor were they able to present any witnesses to the crime. They could not put forward a single person who would speak ill of your character. Therefore, they have nothing to support the assertion that you would have cause to intentionally and knowingly murder Nancy.

In light of the charges that are brought against you, as your defence counsel, I have considered all the facts and the unique circumstances surrounding your case and do not consider you culpable in Nancy's unfortunate death. Therefore we have entered a plea of Not Guilty of murder.

You may be assured that we sit in a court with a fair judge and a jury of twelve decent men who seek to fully play their part to serve justice, who will hear of your character and the extenuating circumstances of that night, who will consider what is right.

In this part of the proceedings, I will ask you questions and you will answer honestly and to the best of your ability under oath.'

He pulled his bible from his pocket and reached across with it to Ned. *'Place your hand on the bible. Repeat after me, I solemnly swear that I will tell the truth, the whole truth, and nothing but the truth. So, help me God.'*

Ned repeated the oath.

'Do you believe you will receive a fair hearing in this court today?'

'I do.'

Ned was beginning to engage with Charles' earnest imitation of a real trial, and as he did, gradually began to emerge from the grief that had gripped him.

'Then we can begin.'

Charles got up out of his chair, immediately

feeling more in control now he was on his feet. Saying nothing, he walked towards where the jury sat, then turned slowly fixing his eyes on Ned, ready to begin.

'During the seven years of your marriage, were you ever violent or physically abusive in any way towards your wife?'

'No, I was not. I am not a violent man and would never raise a hand to any woman including my wife.'

'Would you consider that your wife was of a gentle and delicate nature?'

'No, I would not say so but I believe she had just cause to be fierce and truculent. She had a hard upbringing and carried the scars of that. I do not blame her that the cruelty and neglect she endured as a child made her adversarial and suspicious in all her relationships.'

'Was she ever abusive in any way towards you.'

Ned hesitated.

'Please remember you are under oath.'

Ned reluctantly responded, *'I have already explained that Nancy was disadvantaged by her upbringing, it would have been unfair to expect her to always behave with civility.'* He paused, considering his words carefully. *'It is true she used cruel words towards me and sometimes she would physically push against me in her frustration. She did once spit in my face as I have already explained.'*

'Did you retaliate on those occasions.'

'No, I did not.'

'Did you ever bear any malice towards your wife during your marriage?'

'No, I never did. She had no one else to care for her in this world and I had once hoped that I could make her happy make restorations for her miserable upbringing.'

'Is it correct that you suffer from chronic sleepwalking?'

'Yes, since a child. My family witnessed many such occasions when I was growing up. I know nothing of it at the time, nor remember anything of it afterwards except perhaps fragments of dreams. I take them at their word that it was a regular occurrence.'

'What kinds of things have they experienced you doing while in this state?'

'Sometimes wandering in the garden in my night clothes or on occasions I understand I would slide down the banisters singing. I might be found eating peaches or the like in the larder, that manner of thing.'

'And you remember absolutely nothing of your sleepwalking episodes afterwards?'

'Nothing. My mother always told me she was careful not to wake me for fear it might disturb the balance of my mind. I did sometimes remember the dreams I had but they did not make any sense to me.'

'Do you consider your chronic sleepwalking to be something you have any control over?'

'I do not. It is an invisible demon that visits me at will without invitation.'

'You are a regular user of Laudanum are you not?'

'You know I am, that I take it to alleviate the debilitating back pain I experience following a childhood accident.'

'Are you aware of its addictive nature?'

'I had not considered it.'

'Are you then aware of the risk that it can bring about hallucinations?'

'I had not known that to be so until you enlightened me last night.'

'Do you consider your regular administering of Laudanum to be something you have control over?'

'I do not know how I would live with my pain without it but I see that my taking of it may not always have been while in possession of my own will and that perhaps Laudanum was in possession of me.'

'Would you say that those who know you consider

you a man of good character?'

'I would say yes although am not sure Nancy would think me so.'

'We will come to Nancy later. What do you say is the foundation of your good character and moral standing?'

'My mother was a Godly woman who encouraged all her children to observe God's word and seek His mercy for our transgressions. We were taught at her knee to treat everyone the way we would want to be treated ourselves. To show compassion and kindness even in the face of adversity. To count our blessings.'

'And you have lived your life this way?'

'I believe it to be the only way.'

'And you live according to God's commandments?'

'I do, I have, but have failed. I have sinned terribly.'

'How have you sinned?'

'You know how I have sinned.'

'For the benefit of the court, please state specifically how you have sinned against God's laws.'

'I took Nancy's life.'

'With intent you knowingly murdered your wife?'

'No! not with intent nor with my knowledge.'

'But still you consider that you are to blame for

her death even though your mind was not there in that moment?'

'They were my hands around her neck.'

'Hands, which had you possessed mind to command them, you would have wished to strangle Nancy?'

'No! Never!'

'I have no more questions.'

With every question, Charles had moved Ned a little further from his place of hellish darkness and the crushing weight of his guilt, engaging him with the pursuit of justice he craved.

Now Ned looked up at Charles expectantly, he had made his confession, he had spoken the truth, he did not seek absolution but he needed to know his punishment.

Here in this mock court, although Charles had taken liberties with the course and substance of the proceedings, he had earnestly sought to expose the truth and had longed that Ned should see it too.

Slowly Charles walked towards where Justice Gray was imagined to be seated to begin his summing up.

'Your Honour, gentlemen of the jury, you have heard my client's responses to my questions. Before you, you have a man, who by his own admission,

lives his life according to God's laws. This is a man who knows no other way of living and has never sought to deviate from a life of decency and the highest level of morals.

His was not a happy or fulfilling marriage, but he remained a faithful husband and did not enter into any violence or abuse towards his wife, either verbal or physical. This is despite the abuses that were levelled by Nancy Miller towards my client. He provided a safe and pleasant home and all the comforts commensurate with their social standing for the duration of their married life.

He is a man of unequivocal good character and I am of the opinion that the true test of this character came during times when difficult circumstances in his marriage were unfairly weighted against him. There are a significant number of trustworthy and willing character witnesses to attest to this.

The prosecution has been unable to put forward any evidence from friends or acquaintances of Nancy Miller that attest to them witnessing any mistreatment of her by her husband for the duration of their marriage.

Justice Gray, gentlemen of the jury, you have heard evidence of my client's afflictions. Struck down by debilitating pain since a child and prone to chronic sleepwalking. By his own admission, these things are not in my client's control, he is a victim of their hold over him. He also confirms his relationship with, and dependency on, Laudanum, now widely recognised for its highly addictive nature and hallucinatory effects. I would ask you to consider that, by his somnambulism and drug addiction's powerful control over him, he was himself powerless to direct his own mind or body.

The law and civilised society uphold the sanctity of life. My client believes in the sanctity of life. He bore no malice towards his wife at any time during their marriage, in fact he always sought to protect her, despite the mistreatment she levelled against him.

By believing in justice, my client understands that there must be consequence and punishment for a crime. A woman has died, but was she murdered? I assert that this was not a murder, it was in fact a tragic accident in which Nancy Miller lost her life.

There is no evidence of premeditation, indeed my client was under the influence of powers beyond his control at the time of Nancy Miller's death and he had no recollection of the events of that night until yesterday, when an unexpected mental disturbance of some nature, restored his memory. Four years later.

I also suggest that, in the event my client had ever been witness to any crime against his wife, he would have intervened to stop it; protected her.

So, should we judge my client today on what he did know at the time of Nancy Miller's death or what he did not? I suggest that we can only judge a man on the thoughts and actions he is in control of and of which he is fully aware.

The prosecution provides no witnesses to the crime. Not a single person who could recall the events of that night or testify to my client's actions.

Justice Gray and gentlemen of the jury, whatever your judgement today in this tragic case, my client will live with the guilt of his wife's death for the rest of his life even though it is evidenced that he never knowingly or consciously had a hand in it. The terrible events of that night will be his lifelong sentence.

My client seeks only a fair hearing and stands ready to accept the ruling of this court.'

Charles had stayed on his feet throughout his summing up. He had paced the floor between the imaginary judge and jury and at important points in his delivery, where he sought his client's silent acknowledgement, had stood directly in front of Ned's chair. He was magnificent, the passion and conviction of his delivery as if his own life depended on it, in many ways it did.

He sat down next to Ned, exhausted. He must not spill out.

'Ned I believe we would win in court.' He

let his words settle. *'Whatever the case for the prosecution, there is only circumstantial evidence and no reasonable man would rule against you. You are innocent of murder. It was a terrible accident. What do you say?'*

'I believe it could be so.'

'I want you to consider something else. In the end, we must all answer to God and ultimately no man has the power to absolve another from his crimes nor decide the appropriate punishment, not even the courts. When you stand before God I believe He will judge you to be innocent.

So, while I am sworn to uphold the laws of man, I cannot separate myself from the perfect justice found in God. And as I consider the merits of every case, observe the laws of this great country, this higher justice will always sit at the core of my deliberations.

When you made your confession to me last night, I became an accessory-after-the-fact, bound by the law to report Nancy's death...'

Ned interjected before Charles could finish *'We must waste no time then in...'*

Charles spoke over Ned *'Please wait and hear all I have to say Ned. Last night in my office I spent hours studying books of the law and you should know, there is an existing case where a somnambulist, a sleepwalker, was cleared of murder, so there is a legal precedence which I believe will ensure you are found not guilty.*

The word of the law has always been my guide, my master, but last night it did not satisfy my intellect or my soul. There is no suggestion of impiety on my part towards our justice system - you should be clear that we would rightfully win in court - but it is the word of God that brings true satisfaction. God's grace transcends all that man has designed and you are innocent Ned, that is why I suggest to you now, we do not go to court.'

'Not go to court? I cannot be released from my crime so easily and I will not allow you to take risks of such magnitude.'

'I risk nothing that I prize when I know it to be right. I can do nothing better than to follow the truth. I do not say this as someone who seeks to protect a friend but as a man who seeks to live under God's higher authority. It is my belief that God will never throw any man away.'

'But how would I live with it? To live such a life of deceit is unimaginable.'

'You will grieve for the loss of Nancy's life, and the Lord knows there is not another soul who will mourn her passing, but do not grieve over your part in it, it was not of your doing. I say it again, you are innocent.

If you agree it, the matter can be settled here in

this room, with no need for you or your family to experience the discomfiture and public humiliation of a trial. Will you agree it Ned? That we never speak of it again to another living soul and that we leave Nancy to rest in peace?'

'Poor Nancy, all alone in the cold earth.'

'It is indeed a tragedy that she has lost her life but there is nothing to be gained now in you losing yours too.'

'Will you agree to let the matter rest here and now?'

'But I must pay...'

'You will pay with the memory of your actions on that night and every day you will have to live with the accidental part you played in her death.'

'Will you let it rest?'

Staring down at the floor, Ned hesitated before answering *'Yes.'*

Charles took a deep breath and exhaled slowly releasing all the anxiety he had endured for the last hour. Straightening in his chair, as he lifted his sagging shoulders, he revealed a white shirt cuff that was colouring red as the blood soaked through his jacket sleeve.

'Charles you are bleeding.'

His nose was dripping profusely, a dramatic

finale, as all the pressure finally burst. Taking out his handkerchief and pressing it under his nose, he tipped his head back and closed his eyes savouring the relief of the blackness. *'You should continue your life as normal Ned, create beautiful art, pray for Nancy's soul, nothing more is required of you. Remember, speak to no one about this, you are an innocent, no murder has been committed in this house.'*

'What about you? Can you continue day to day with the burden of our secret?'

'God knows it all Ned, He will be my judge and the one to whom I will always answer, I will continue to live under His grace and mercy.'

'It was a bad day, the day you first met me, I have brought you nothing but trouble. You could never have expected that you would be called on to be my saviour and protector on so many occasions.'

'Know this, I am grateful for our friendship every day Ned.'

CHAPTER 27

Friday 9th May 1884

It had been a second sleepless night for Charles as the magnitude of the last two days' events had pushed out to the furthest edges of his brain consuming his every waking thought. His conscience was clear but he was still disturbed at a deep level that he could not reach and there was to be no respite from the cruel *flying horse carousel* of all that had happened endlessly circling in his head. It exhausted him but try as he might he could not get off.

He knew a court would find Ned innocent of murder, but the trial of it, he knew that Ned would not have been able to endure it. He had already suffered to the limits of his ability, he could take no more, it would break him.

Yesterday after the trial he had stayed a while with Ned to try and lift his spirits and restore some equanimity. They had talked, albeit in a laboured and awkward way, about other things; his paintings, his family, until little by little Ned had come back to the land of the living.

If Ned had feigned a semblance of normality he had done it convincingly and eventually Charles had left with a promise from him that he would visit Beacon Street on Saturday. Tomorrow. Charles thought time with Sarah and his parents would be just the tonic he needed, people who knew nothing of what had happened, people who just liked and cared for Ned for the gentle and decent man he was.

Charles had neglected his own affairs over the last two days and would need to spend a long day at his office to make some gains on the preparations for his next case, even though he had woken in a debilitating state of exhaustion, he must apply himself. A complex and violent murder case, the defendant, a tragic victim himself of circumstances that had played ill against him.

Albert Cobb was a hard-working family man who had never troubled the law, but his ice wagon had been seen outside the house of the wealthy heiress at the wrong time for him, and the right time for the murderer inside.

A slew of over enthusiastic witnesses put Albert at the scene of the crime and in their wild imaginings he became a menacing, brutal figure, far away from the quiet, shy man Charles had come to know him to be. In the absence of facts and the real murderer, the ice tongs in his hand became the murder weapon, their sharp pointed jaws, the cause of the victim's fatal lacerations. Charles could prove that they had never gripped the victim's flesh, did not match the stripes on her neck, that they had only ever bitten the slippery 25lb blocks of ice Albert delivered across the city.

He would not be paid for defending Albert Cobb but he would willingly pay the price with his time and expertise to save an innocent man's life. The ironic parallelism of his cruel circumstances and those of Ned, was not lost on him, he knew this poor soul deserved justice as much as Ned.

Now, as he drew back the curtains and looked out onto the street, despite the continuing disquiet he felt inside, everything of the outside world looked as it should. As if nothing had happened. As if his world had not shaken. From here he could see people going about their everyday business seemingly without difficulty, but unable to see their secrets, the hardships and disappointments of their lives.

He set about his daily morning routine of carefully laying out his clothes - muted colours today - all the time with a feeling that he was being watched. Ludicrous he thought as he looked over his shoulder to check, no-one there of course. He felt it again and as his eyes travelled the room they settled on Ned's painting of the rowan tree.

It had the power to move him as much today as when Ned had first given it to him and he had purposely hung it directly facing his bed so that it was the first thing he saw every morning when he woke.

As he approached the painting again now, he marvelled at how the picture so vibrant and clear faded into swirls of watery lines blurring into each other when he drew near to it. Like the men and women on the street, it was an image that only the distant eye could appreciate, up close it fell into pieces, did not make sense. It had always elevated his spirits before but today its colours seemed to tell a different story and it was sorrowful in its hues. Nancy lay beneath it and now that was all he could think of when he looked at it.

At breakfast, his subdued demeanour did not go unnoticed.

'Are you well Charles?' His mother asked.

'Yes quite well mother thank you. I am sorry if I seem distracted I am working on a difficult case that is causing me some consternation. All will be well as always. No need for you to worry.'

She heard his words but she saw what only a mother sees. He was pale, he looked drawn, his eyes hollow and grey. Something was amiss.

'Perhaps you should take your rest tomorrow and

not join us at the theatre. We would be sorry not to have you with us but you must take care not to cause yourself exhaustion.'

'Your life would not be any the poorer for missing it' John Broadbent offered mischievously.

'John, what do you mean? It is by an exciting new playwright; everyone raves about him.' Elizabeth countered.

'Perhaps, but if I never see another play where they make a drama out of the pouring of a cup of tea or find deep meaning in the putting on of one's boots, it will be too soon. I find real life has enough drama to fulfil my appetite for it!' He winked at Charles and Sarah.

Elizabeth tutted but she knew he was right and smiled to herself without letting him see.

'I have invited Ned to visit with us tomorrow. I hope that is not inconvenient in any way?'

'Not at all, we will be so delighted to see him. It is such a long time since he has visited with us and we have so much news to catch up on. Might he like to join us at the theatre tomorrow evening?' She glanced in John's direction, a signal to say nothing more about the play.

'He intends just to visit for the day. He will join us for lunch and then perhaps a walk in the park. I am sure he will also want to spend some time with his

favourite protégé and look at some of her work.' He gave Sarah a knowing smile.

'We shall all look forward to it immensely.' John Broadbent nodded his approval in his wife's direction. *'How does he do?'*

'He is well.'

'Might he bring Nancy? As you know, I have long wanted to meet the elusive Mrs. Miller.'

'She will not be accompanying him.' The words caught in Charles' throat.

Elizabeth Broadbent knew not to enquire any further. There was sadness and despair in the unspoken words between them and she grieved again for Ned's unhappy marriage.

Charles carried his uneasy feeling to the office and back home with him that evening. The house was asleep by the time he returned, but despite his exhaustion, he was too much awake to retire for the night.

He went straight to his study. Usually, his place of sanctuary and tranquillity, where he could expand his mind with all manner of things that interested him, tonight it felt small and claustrophobic. He sat down heavily in his armchair and tipped his head back staring at the ceiling. It was a relief to look at something blank for a while.

Still a rested mind eluded him.

He stood slowly feeling the age in his bones and his muscles, gravity had a greater pull on him these days, all the lightness of a youthful body gone. In all his forty-five years, he had never considered his mortality, his approach to the grave, until now.

A beam of light lit the room, there was a full moon, all creatures would be feeling restless tonight he thought. He went to the window and looked out, there was not a soul on the street now, only a stray dog sniffing its way along the park railings looking for any scraps it could find to fill its empty belly.

He had always loved the view from this window. Its position gave him a clear line of sight up and down the hill and across the street to the common where the moon lit the branches of the Elm trees with glowing silver. These rows of majestic old gentlemen who had stood unmoved for a hundred years, quietly observing the frenzied progress of this city, steadied him again with their disregard for all the trifling pursuits of man.

The soft chime of the mantle clock told him it was midnight. He should go to bed but still he felt the strange frisson of energy coursing through his tired body that kept him from his rest. He could read to help him relax but could he absorb even one more word today?

In desperation, he sat at his desk, ready for what?

He took a sheet of paper from the drawer, dipped his pen in the ink and began to write.

Who am I?

I am Charles Broadbent of Beacon Street, Boston, Mass.

I was born to John Broadbent and Elizabeth Broadbent (nee Jones) on 2nd January 1839.

God has blessed me with a loving family who have supported and encouraged me in all my life's endeavours. I have a cherished sister, Sarah, who I dearly love.

He stopped and smiled at the thought of her. He was fifteen when she was born, so precious, so wanted. She was the longed-for antidote to all the many times of confinement when his mother had emerged with her arms empty.

I have good friends, the very best of them is Ned, and I enjoy the company of many close acquaintances.

I have been successful in my career and achieved respect and admiration among my peers as I have sought to uphold the law in this great country.

I am interested and take pleasure in a great many things. Art, literature, world history and politics and all things relating to the human condition; that which separates man from beast.

I enjoy good physical health and consider myself to be of a hearty disposition.

I expect to continue expanding my mind and grow in my knowledge and skills although I think it may now be too late to learn the piano to any level of proficiency.

I live a privileged and comfortable life able to go wherever I please, purchase all the things that bring comfort to man, travel the world if I wish.

In all this I believe I have missed something profound.

His hand hovered over the paper, as if the moment the ink touched it, he would have to face the truth.

I never considered my heart, what it is to be Charles Broadbent, just this earthly man.

Perhaps these are the laments of a man of middle years whose ambitions no longer shine so brightly and so he finds himself looking back over his shoulder rather than setting his gaze full ahead.

But these middle years are perhaps when a man sees things most clearly and for what they truly are.

I conclude that while I affect the meaning of

my day to day and contribute to it, it is what I freely receive from others, what I <u>cannot</u> affect or command, which has the greatest value to me.

Today I feel alone. How can a man be lonely with so many who care for him in this world? Still, it is true, I feel alone, I must consider the source of it.

I am not unhappy with solitude indeed I actively seek it for study and expansion of my mind, time for spiritual reflection, for rest and relaxation.

I have no lack of opportunities to socialise, my diary could be filled three times over with invitations to luncheons and suppers, the theatre, opera, or any other manner of enjoyable pursuits although I have never been invited to go ice-skating.

I have the love of my family, I have the respect and admiration of my friends and colleagues, God has abundantly blessed me in so many ways, I am a fortunate man by all accounts.

<u>So, what do I lack?</u> He underlined the question.

He sat back in his chair, he had reached the crux of the matter, he had gathered together the bountiful blessings of his life. What was missing?

For as much as he was deeply troubled tonight, he considered whether he had ever felt true contentment and peace. He had, it had come to him on a sunny afternoon, sitting on a boulder looking out to sea, Ned beside him whistling while he painted.

Someone to call my own in this life.

There it was, his answer.

Now weariness replaced the tiredness he had felt, he tore up what he had written, it was out of him and he had no more use for it.

He could sleep now.

CHAPTER 28

Thursday 8th May 1884

When Charles had left him this afternoon Ned had wanted to go with him, afraid to be alone with his thoughts, instead he had sent him away with reassurances that he was fine and would visit him at Beacon Street on Saturday.

The rest of the day had passed in a kind of oblivion, the dense fog relentlessly swirling in his head chasing away any remnants of clear thinking or understanding he had about what had happened. He felt light-headed, untethered from his surroundings, like he was floating away from every solid anchored thing, with only the excruciating pain gnawing at his back and the weight of his guilt reminding him that he was fixed to the ground. He tried to cast off his despair, send it away, but every time the wolf crept back hungrier, teeth sharper than before.

Time seemed to slip away without measure and at twilight he found himself standing on the balcony watching the light fade over the trees and the last strings of silver disappear from the surface of the sea as he had done thousands of times before. Tonight, the day at its closing glory reflected nothing of the ugliness he had wrought on it, how could beauty remain untouched, unaltered by its death at his hands?

Later that night 'Laurie' went to his room with him and as he sat on the edge of his bed he poured his nemesis into a glass, quarter full, then half full, burnt umber turning to burnt sienna by the glow of the lamplight. He lay back on his pillow, closed his eyes and drank the bitterness slowly as a warm feeling washed over his body.

Sleep did not come, but he lay awake listening to the distant sound of the sea like soft breathing and a gentle breeze blew into his room shifting the curtains soothing him. Then one by one his mind gave face to all those who had loved him in this life.

More than apparitions to a longing soul, in turn, they appeared to him as real as if they were sitting at the end of his bed. Murmurings of conversations reached his ears sometimes words rising out of the cacophony, '*We must take care of him. He is too tender-hearted for this world. It is not his fault.*' His mother, his sisters, his aunts, Charles, Uncle William even Frank gathered around him as if blocking the path of anything that sought to harm him. Behind them all, a shadowy face from a photograph, Walter.

The man who could have been a father to him, took his place silently at the back, small and insignificant.

At the first lifting of the darkness, the sound of a chickadee came in through the open window. Insistent and enthusiastic it sang loudly filling the room with its presence *chickadee-dee-dee-dee, chickadee-dee-dee-dee*. Ned felt the bird's call was meant for him *time-to-get-up*, *time-to-get-up* so grudgingly he pulled on his robe and went to the window.

There in the pale morning light sat the chickadee in the uppermost branches of the rowan tree, its black cap and bib fluffed up, more and more excitable.

The little bird persisted, on and on, until finally Ned answered its clarion call.

He went to his studio, and as he opened the door, there was Nancy just as he had left her. Lines soft and mellow, warmer, lovelier than he had ever seen her, his Nancy. He touched the cold canvas briefly with his fingertips tracing a lock of her hair as it fell over her shoulder like a sparkling waterfall. He searched her face for judgement but there was none. He craved punishment, some measure of retribution to set his guilt against but she smiled steadily at him, eyes without accusation.

Then following the increasingly persistent call from outside, he opened the doors onto the balcony, pulling his robe tighter around him against the chill air.

Standing now within striking distance of the bird, it was fearless, not cowed in any way by his close proximity, seeming to sing even louder now that it had its audience, *chickadee-dee-dee-dee, chickadee-dee-dee-dee.*

'What do you try to tell me?'

'*Come-to-me-Ned, come-to-me-Ned*' came the answer.

He would go. He went down the stairs, lifted the latch and stepped out into the spring-sweet air. He had no shoes on his feet but the grass was long and soft and kingcups leant him their golden heads as cushions underfoot. As he stood under the rowan, he looked up taking in the comforting overshadowing of its branches.

The bird had stopped singing and had hopped down to a branch just above his head. As it did, a single white feather fell and brushed his face, stirring the echo of something long passed. Then the bird dropped to the ground, its tiny beak pulling at something in the earth, something that glinted. Ned knelt down to where the bird was jumping and circling excitedly and scraping back the soil he saw a flash of green. Then uncovering more, a flash of red, of blue, of gold. As he dug his fingers into the soil with the bird watching on from safe distance, something sharp stabbed him, then up came the four-leaf clover brooch.

He turned it over in his hand, the pin red with his blood, then carefully replaced it in the ground covering it over with soil. It should stay with her, she had little else.

He remained on his knees, her body beneath him.

'I am sorry Nancy, I failed you, I failed all your hopes of love. You deserved more from your life than this early grave with no one to mourn you. God forgive me for what I did to you.'

The bird started up its lusty campaign once again. *Chickadee-dee-dee-dee, go-to-the-sea, chickadee-dee-dee-dee, go-to the sea.*

He looked to his right, towards the sea, stood and began to walk. First over the soft yielding grass laced with miterwort and foamflower, then over dry stony earth where wild columbine took its chances against the whipping winds. Finally, through the cedar canopy and over cold sea-washed rocks to the edge, sea beyond, waiting.

There was no sound now except the hushed rhythmic breaking of the waves on the shore and the strange melancholy song that was carried on the wind from Singing Beach. He savoured its cool breath on his skin and smelt the salt in the air before he stepped forward sinking into the icy water as the world fell away and sleep held on to him. Lungs drenched, heart rushing, down and down he went until everything was black.

A hand reached out from the darkness, a face appeared, Uncle William was there.

Ned grasped for his hand *'save me father.'*

CHAPTER 29

Saturday 10th May 1884

Ten o'clock.

Charles was back at his study window and looking down the hill hoping to see Ned come into view but the street was deserted and a mist hung thick and heavy almost like a cloud had dropped from the sky, the haze shortening his sight and ghosting all the street's familiar landmarks. He could normally see down the street to a distance of five lampposts but today he could see none, so he opened the window and leant out, in vain hope of a clearer view.

Finally, a figure emerged out of the mist, but it was not him. Nor was the next or the next. The weather had probably hindered his journey he thought. He closed the window and looked around his study for something to fill the time and quell the onset of the rising anxiety he felt.

He would try to distract himself with a book and as his eyes scanned the shelves, they came to rest on Thoreau's *Walden.* He had read it before, but now it held more attraction, the idea of casting off all life's material trappings and living simply in the woods, he felt he would be more open to its principals on its second reading. Living deliberately, open to the beauty of nature, free to think and discover life's finer fruits; surely a prize worth having for any man.

Making himself comfortable in his armchair, he stared blankly at the book in his lap, absent-mindedly running his index finger along the line of dust that had settled on the top edges of its brown cloth cover from years of slumbering on the shelf.

Eventually he opened it, but despite his commitment to give it his full attention, his eyes flicked to the mantle clock at least a dozen times before it eventually chimed eleven o'clock.

He would begin again, but by the time the clock chimed midday, he had re-read the first page over and over without any comprehension as the words flowed past him without stopping.

He would not be coming.

He closed the book, tipped back his head and shut his eyes, as he cast his mind to the painting of the rowan tree and the inscription on the back.

May we never mourn tomorrow what we celebrate so joyfully today. While we are

friends the best is always yet to come.
He wept for the second time in his life.

CHAPTER 30

Sunday 10th May 1885

He found he greatly enjoyed the new sensation of sun-warmed sand between his toes and had spent the last hour happily scooping up one foot and then the other from the beach, fine sand running freely through his toes like an hourglass, with no requirement to measure time at all.

He was still to his bones a Harvard man and would be content to be back at his desk tomorrow morning, but the last year had taught him that there was so much more to Charles Broadbent than his legal career. He had spent his whole life seeking truth and justice but it was only when events forced him to enter his own imagined cabin in the woods that the greatest truth had sprung to life for him.

Here, with his trousers rolled to his ankles, jacket discarded and waistcoat half unbuttoned he took on something of a Mark Twain character although contrary to their ragamuffin attire, his scruffily worn clothes were expensively made and his straw hat was a fine Bollman. With his top collar button unfastened, he could breathe and move more easily and freely, although he knew it added to his look of dishevelment.

In all this, he was not blind to the attention he was attracting from those passing by and without any discomfiture, he considered their reaction to him.

In his deliberately carefree style of presentation, children clearly saw him as one of them. They smiled at him conspiratorially, and had they not been restrained by a tightly held hand, he was sure would have enthusiastically joined him in his happy pastime. Or then perhaps it was just more that opposite poles attract - he was old and they were young.

If he was a magnet to the infants, he was not so to their parents.

The men gave him disparaging but sympathetic looks, he had lost his mind perhaps, some kind of idiot. By the look of him, he could certainly not be a gentleman, still, there was a contradiction in his appearance which they could not reconcile. As Charles himself now became the voyeur, he caught the glimmer of something deeper in their eyes, envy perhaps, all trapped in their buttoned-up lives.

The women were more openly curious like they might want to come and sit with him and talk about all manner of things. Instead, they hurried their children by and with every *'good day'* and tip of his hat, their hurrying a little faster. He did however observe that each one took a friendly backward look over their shoulder as if to say, it would not be proper to stay and talk with you, but I would like to.

At last, there was a lull in the stream of spectators that flowed by so he reached for his bag and took out a small box opening it to reveal a palette of untouched paints. He set it down beside him and then took out a sketchbook. He ran an unfamiliar hand over its stiff linen-faced cover and then opened it to reveal the first virgin creamy-white leaf ready for his artistry, or lack of it. He was as *at sea* now as he had been all those years ago when he stood behind a stranger in Cotton's and asked for help.

No need for panic, what had Sarah told him? He took out his scribbled notes.

Wet the paper all over with a brush. She had demonstrated it for him and it looked easy enough so he took out a little bottle of water and wetted his brush.

Start at the top of the paper with the sky - Cobalt Blue perhaps - and work the watery blue with your brush from left to right to left down the paper watering it down further as you go. He was doing it.

A sky of sorts was emerging on the page.

She had also taught him a trick to bring clouds to the composition. *Take a small ball of cloth and dab away some of the watery blue.* It worked; clouds appeared on the paper although he thought them more Altostratus than the Cumulus he was aiming for.

Now for the sand - *mix Cadmium Yellow and a small amount of Prussian Blue and Alizarin Crimson and paint a straight line across the width of the paper two thirds of the way down.* He did it, but it looked too bold, the hard line creating a harsh separation on the paper. Still, he committed to stick to her instructions regardless. *Add more water to the brush blending out the line drawing the paint down the paper to the bottom – left to right to left.*

It was like something magical; his painting was beginning to resemble the scene in front of him at least in outline shape and hues. He continued, seagulls in the sky, boats on the horizon, until finally he had a painting. He was pleased with it and more than a little surprised. He added his initials to the bottom right-hand corner of the page and set it to one side on a rock to dry.

He would never paint a masterpiece but as he contemplated his naive efforts he understood that there was perhaps a greater joy in the doing than there was in the achieving. Another realisation that had come to him late in life.

As he sat on his boulder, eyes fixed ahead, he found himself humming a tune to himself as the words drifted through his mind. *We shall know each other better when the mists have rolled away… We shall know, as we are known, nevermore to walk alone…Face to face with those that love us, we shall know as we are known… When the shadows have departed and the mists have rolled away…*

'Charles Broadbent!'

He turned to face the voice coming from behind him and there were Sarah and Frank, both agog, both laughing.

'My darling brother you look like an urchin!'

Charles joined them in their laughter as he looked down at his crumpled clothes and bare feet in the sand. *'I take no offence in that, I have enjoyed the lightness of my attire and if there be some likeness between me and an urchin, so be it.'*

'We should make haste if we wish to catch the four o'clock train. Shall Sarah and I go ahead and you can catch us up? Your progress will be quicker than ours.'

'Yes, she is very heavy to push is she not?'

'No, she is not heavy at all.' Frank blushed.

Sarah turned and looked up at Frank *'Ignore him*

my love, my brother teases you and you are too sweet by far to counter his jesting.'

'She is right Frank, I am sure you will be as old and grey as I, before you become accustomed to the Broadbent humour.'

'We shall go ahead then?'

'Yes, I will gather my things, put on my shoes, and make myself altogether more presentable so that you are not embarrassed to be seen with me!'

Charles watched smiling as the newlyweds began their slow, happy progress along the path towards the station.

He picked up his painting now dried by the sun and slipped it into his bag. Then having emptied the sand from his shoes and buttoned-up, he collected up the rest of his belongings.

Feeling as if he was standing side by side with his friend once again he cast a final look at the sea. As they shared the view together he understood that there is this life and there is what is beyond, but with no line between them, unless you choose to draw it.

'Slow down, you get too far ahead of this old man!' he shouted after Frank and Sarah as he ran to catch them up.

Printed in Dunstable, United Kingdom